IMAGO

Roselle Angwin

Indigo Dreams Publishing

First Edition: Imago
First published in Great Britain in 2011 by:
Indigo Dreams Publishing Ltd
132 Hinckley Road
Stoney Stanton
Leics
LE9 4LN

www.indigodreams.co.uk

ISBN 978-1-907401-38-1

British Library Cataloguing in Publication Data. A CIP record for this book can be obtained from the British Library.

Designed and typeset in Minion Pro by Indigo Dreams.

Papers used by Indigo Dreams are recyclable products made from wood grown in sustainable forests following the guidance of the Forest Stewardship Council.

Printed and bound in Great Britain by Imprint Academic, Exeter

Imago

Author's notes and acknowledgements

This book has had a long and turbulent journey to its final home with IDP. Written in the early 1990s, it did the round of the mainstream publishers. Many liked it; some didn't; some found it 'too esoteric'. It very nearly found a home with one of our foremost publishers, but in the end was rejected as being too 'minority interest'. My wonderful former agent, Wendy Suffield, did a great job persisting in believing in it and in sending it out. Then she left the agency, and the director had to cut his list.

A few years after I first started submitting this ms, initially to my dismay, Tracy Chevalier's *The Virgin Blue* and Kate Mosse's *Labyrinth* appeared, both of which cover similar territory, metaphorically and geographically, to *Imago*. I felt stymied by this fact, and lost heart. Later, *The Da Vinci Code*, very different in content and style, appeared. What this meant, to my advantage, was that the market opened out a little to more esoteric subject matters.

My then poetry publisher took it on. It was due to come out in 2008 —and then the publisher disappeared and the publishing house was dissolved.

Then Ronnie Goodyer of IDP approached me. What was particularly encouraging was that Ronnie had selected my first poetry manuscript for the publisher above. I owe him and his partner Dawn huge thanks.

I want to acknowledge bluechrome for the cover image. Every effort has been made to trace the copyright holder, to no avail.

And I also want to acknowledge Jamie McMillan for first taking me to the Pyrenees, without whom this whole journey might never have happened.

Though to some extent I have drawn on my own, sometimes strange, experiences in the Pyrenees in the late 1970s, the characters in this book are entirely fictitious. But Montségur is a real place, and in the book I have been as faithful as possible to its sad and bloody history. The book is dedicated to all who challenge orthodoxy.

Roselle Angwin, Devon, 2011.

IMAGO

'Imago: the final and fully-developed stage of an insect after all metamorphoses, e.g. a butterfly' OED

'All things are changing; nothing dies. The spirit wanders, comes now here, now there, and occupies whatever form it pleases. . .' Ovid, *Metamorphoses*

Breaking
Devon

ONE

It didn't start as a love story. It started with an ending.

In the chasm between waking and sleeping, life and death, she relives it over and over, unable to pull herself free.

There's the still May evening, fat-bellied moon sliding inauspiciously across Pluto's trajectory, and in the distance the murmur of the Torridge; or maybe it's the light wind rising in the birches. An east wind, its skirts full of unease and conflict, billowing up from nowhere suddenly, setting the horses in the neighbouring field skittering, the hares leaping through tight bronze fiddleheads of bracken.

The air suddenly green with fear, then pricking with hate, ready to combust.

Anger. Her words, each one poison-tipped, aimed at the heart. Greg's eyes, glittering under the moon, pale as frogspawn. His fingers yanking at the sleeves of her silk summer dress, tearing.

The car accelerating out of the drive in second gear, spitting gravel, away from the little white town, away from the party, roaring up the hill back towards Exeter.

The dress gaping like a wound and Annie's hip aching from half stumbling half being pushed into the car, banged against the jamb. His cheek swelling and a sour odour coming off him. Her hand stinging. She can't believe this is happening, this conflict; can't believe it. Once there was love. Once she loved him; they loved each other. How long ago?

There's the briefest comfort of horse sweat through the open window, then the saltmud tang of estuary; then only diesel and burning rubber. The engine shrieking.

Truck lights around a right hand bend and Greg swerving.

In its moment of unfolding the present becomes the past and, as history, is always fiction. So later she questions, over and over, did she imagine it? What is real? Because here, in this present moment, terribly, terrifyingly, Greg seems to throw the car to the right, straight at the offside corner of the lorry's bonnet.

The instant before the impact stretching on and on, dreadful, soundless, tunnel-dark, empty, eternal.

The moment exploding around them.

She thinks she hears his neck snap, a sound like distant gunshot, chilling; then his face fading away as she slides beneath dark waters; but his mouth pursuing her, open, in shock, in agony, in triumph even.

The car spinning.

Noise; and then only the silence of blackness.

In the hospital bed her broken body convulses and she cries out; and again, as she will later in the camper van in her lover's arms; then alone on a frozen March mountainside, suspended between centuries; and as she will, again and again, in the lonely ebb of l'Estang des Sangliers, where the square stone house fills up night after night with voices, trapping her in its unending darkness like one of the haunted boggy bottomless pools high on the Dartmoor of her childhood, in which she fears she may drown.

TWO

She visits other places in her pain.

There's a rocky scrubby mountainside, crisscrossed on its snowy flanks with tracks of hare and wolf and wild boar; sometimes the clawed spoor of brown bear.

There's a low stone building, amongst small fields of rye and barley, hardly bigger than its attached goose-pen. In the dark smoky interior one wall is taken up with wooden hooks and rough shelving carrying bundles of all the herbs of the mountains: centaury, absinthe, thyme, oregano, rosemary, wild marigold, juniper, agrimony, jostling with pig bladders and clay jars of oils and unguents, cloth bundles of root and bark.

There's a tall stone building, candlelit in the citadel's midnight.

There are hands, soothing hands in the dark blue night; laying-on near the heart, on the body's subtle pulses, on the temples. Her hands; sometimes others'.

There's a lavender field, and summer sun, and a lover's arms, and a murmur that might be wind, or the sea, or traffic noise; the scent of pine and juniper; blue mountains. She dreams white horses and black foals.

There's the fire that swallows them all. Flames. She dreams flames. She doesn't know if it's the past or the future or if it's someone else's life.

When she opens her eyes for the first time, the sunlight striping the white ceiling through the hospital blinds both puzzles and dazzles her. Her field of vision is limited by the fact that she cannot move her neck. Then she becomes aware that there is a face close to hers, a face that she recognizes. She stares at the face. Somewhere the other side of the clouds stuffing her brain a name for the face hovers, just out of reach.

Her friend Rosa stretches out a hand, and gently strokes back a strand of Annie's hair.

The red fabric of Rosa's sleeve leaves shock-waves on Annie's field of vision. Annie can see that her friend's dark eyes are swimming but is unable to respond.

'Welcome back, stranger. I'm enormously glad to see you. We thought we'd lost you. It's been months.' Her voice shakes. 'You–' She starts a sentence then stops. 'You know how black and shiny your hair still is, even though you've been so ill? Well, nearly—it's—it's—uncanny, somehow. Strange, I mean. I mean—'

Annie drifts. It costs too much to concentrate. She has no sense of where she is, no recollection of why she is there. Dimly she feels that there is something pushing at the edge of her mind for entry; a perception of overwhelming pain. In her peripheral vision are tubes, wires, apparatus; the form lying on the bed, which she realises after a delay must be hers, is encased in a huge framework. She has an impulse to put out a hand and touch the structure, but nothing happens, nothing connects anywhere. Annie closes her eyes again and gives in to the grey clouds.

Rosa comes in most days. She asks no questions, and for the most part simply sits quietly holding Annie's limp hand. Sometimes she'll come in just for a few minutes on her way home from shopping or picking up children, or she might bring a book and share Annie's silence and solitude for an hour. Her presence soothes and strengthens Annie enormously, especially as fragments of memory start to impose themselves.

Unasked questions are finally beginning to form in her head, and a fear, a dread that lingers, accompanying waking consciousness but as yet without a shape or a name. This, combined with the continual physical pain, conspires to make staying awake unbearable after a certain length of time. Rosa's affectionate presence and her small snippets of information from the world outside, of faculty news, of friends and colleagues, of Rosa's family, all make, for a little while each day, an alternative to sleep, a place of refuge for Annie. Briefly she can almost forget the insistent clanging intrusion of the enormous thing which she knows has happened but of which as yet she has remembered no details, except the perception of flames; flames and unbelievable pain.

Rosa never refers to what's happened other than oblique allusions to events from 'before your accident', and Annie cannot bring herself to ask. In the weeks following the accident she is more concerned about surviving the continual ache in her body from moment-to-moment, identifying where the pain is locating itself so that she knows when it has passed. Getting through each day without whimpering, suffering the indignities of regular monitoring, bedpans and bedbaths and drug-administration, the changing of sheets and tubes and drips and the minute steps forward in movement feel like major achievements in themselves.

Annie's returning memory is selective. After a while she has fewer problems following parts of Rosa's stories and news, beginning to recognise the names of colleagues and friends. She knows that she herself worked at the University where, Rosa has told her, her post is held for her still. Her close friends and family, all of whom visit as often as she can bear it, serve to anchor her where otherwise she might find herself alarmingly adrift. But in almost all of them she's conscious of a kind of worried guardedness, as if they are either deliberately withholding something from her, or resisting asking something of her. Her mother's eyes particularly hold a kind of troubled unhappiness.

Her memory totally fails her concerning the small elderly woman who comes in several times near the start of her convalescence, though somehow she connects her with storms, and a place that isn't England. Annie, during her stronger more lucid moments, is aware that there is something familiar about her, and is bewildered that the old lady does nothing more than sit and rock and cry, grasping Annie's hand. She comes to think of her—once she has started to recover enough for her mental processes to begin to judder into some sort of order—as The Frog. Her slightly mottled, loose, creased skin draped over fine bird-like bones fascinates Annie, whose visual faculty has become, if anything, sharper, if only in contrast to her other abilities.

As she is not sure who the elderly woman is, and therefore quite who or what she is crying for, Annie retains a certain detachment from the woman's pain. Nonetheless she misses her when she stops visiting. It is many weeks before Annie's memory, with a shock, places the old lady as Greg's mother.

It falls to her father finally to bring up the subject of Greg, several weeks into her recuperation. As soon as her father comes in that day, Annie is aware from something about his bearing and the expression on his face—a mixture of unease and determination—that he has something important to say. Though a kind, supportive man, like many of his male contemporaries he is not comfortable with the world of emotion, which he sees as a peculiarly feminine weakness.

Her father sits down, folding his angular frame rather stiffly into the economical hospital bedside chair to Annie's left, between Annie and the window. Annie can't now read his face as it's against the light, but knows that hers would be all too clearly visible if, as she suspects, something awful is to be called up. There's a slight pause in which she can almost hear her father shepherding his thoughts into the right shape for his injured daughter's ears.

Annie breathes *in one two three pause out one two three pause* to try and relax a sudden tension which shoots through her damaged neck and ribcage in spasms of pain. She looks at the ceiling and, waiting for her father to speak, tries to calm herself by picturing the flowers which would by now be out in her garden. In a vase on the windowsill are huge floppy giant sprays of carmine and white roses from her parents' home, extravagant and voluptuous against the neat white bland impersonality of the room, and Annie searches for their scent against the sterile hospital air.

Her father clears his throat and puts his hand up to readjust his glasses, then awkwardly leans over to pat her arm. Perhaps he has a sudden concern that his action might have hurt Annie, for he lifts his hand abruptly and removes his glasses, passing his hand across his eyes.

'Sorry, my dear, didn't think. How's the pain today?' Then, uncharacteristically, without waiting for an answer he rushes on. 'Your mother is concerned that you might not know about Greg. You do know, don't you my dear, that Greg died in the accident?' He peers at her myopically, unhappily.

Even against the light Annie can see the anguish in his face. Greg?—Greg. Her husband Greg. Greg whom she had loved, Greg whom she had hated. Greg whom she could not leave, and who had tried to kill them both.

Greg's mouth. A blistering impact.

Everything stops abruptly; even the flickering of tree-filtered sunlight across the walls and ceiling seems to freeze. A perception of enormous grief, a tidal wave. She can't catch her breath, or open her mouth to speak; and in any case no words are there for her. Something stirs and heaves in her head, and an avalanche slides across her mind, blacking out the patterns on her ceiling.

stands the hibiscus on the floor beneath the window. 'Would you like the blinds drawn? It's a stunner of a day outside.'

Annie blinks and nods, unsure what to say.

Alex draws up the blinds and is back at Annie's bedside in two strides of his long legs. He bends and lightly kisses her forehead, then hands her the avocado and sweeps the books off the chair onto the floor. 'I've come to bring you up to date with 13th century French romance!' He grins, self-mocking. 'Betty Chadwick's course is continuing in September—I don't know whether you'll be out by then?—looks unlikely, from all the apparatus—but I thought you might like me to fill you in on the last few sessions. I've brought some books, and also I taped a couple of seminars; they didn't mind when I told them it was for you. Why are hospital chairs always so bloody uncomfortable?'

Annie's clutching the avocado still. His words tumble over her. She can't speak, even if he'd been leaving a space for her to do so.

Alex looks at the avocado in her hand. 'Didn't think. Guess you can't do much with it like that, can you? Sorry. Shall I find you a plate and spoon? Or shall I ask them to feed it to you for supper?'

Annie's breathless with emotion at Alex's arrival, his comfortable manner, his casual thoughtfulness. She's especially grateful that he didn't gasp, or compose his face into steadied carefulness on seeing her and the residue of her injuries, as most first-time visitors do.

'Supper would be lovely,' she manages. 'Thank you.'

'Hey, careful now—that was almost a smile!'

She'd met Alex the year before. He was doing a year's poetry residency in the English department, so they had coincided several times within the faculty calendar, and also at departmental social events. As Alex's own poetry tended towards the modern, experimental and anarchic, Annie had been surprised when he had signed up, as she had, for a series of lectures and seminars on mediaeval France. Annie's interest had been purely literary; she was wanting to learn more about the rise of the Romance as a literary genre, and its roots in the Courts of Love and troubadour verse, with a view to broadening her own lecturing facility.

Alex's interest, it had turned out, was more historical, political and philosophical. Though the troubadour cult interested him, he was more interested in the emergence and persecution of minority groups, especially with regard to religious persecution. His own BA thesis in Comparative Religion, fifteen years before, he'd told Annie, had centred on the political and social underpinnings and impacts of the eternal conflict between heresy and orthodoxy, and as a political activist he was motivated by minority issues and human rights.

Annie had always thought of him as a twentieth-century visionary. He was fascinated by ideas, ideals and others' visions, and the lengths they might go to defend them. His natural world was that of campaigns and causes; his passion expressed itself through his words and music, through the possibility of positive change, righting wrongs. His fierce interest of the moment lay in the Dominican persecution of the adherents of the Cathar faith in the south of France during the twelfth and thirteenth centuries.

He and Annie had found a meeting point, over the duration of Betty Chadwick's course, in a shared and growing interest in the body of Grail stories that arose at this time, and of what they might express beneath the Christian overlay.

Alex calls in at the hospital once a fortnight or so after that first visit, sometimes more often. Their friendship is easy, casual, warm. Alex's visits become increasingly important in the long slow weeks that follow, as she teaches her body once more to obey the still all-too-laboured instructions of her brain. The process of learning to think again and of physical retraining is arduous, and the returning flood of memories and the accompanying feelings utterly exhausting. Much of the time Annie succumbs to cycles of hopelessness and depression, followed by numbness.

Throughout this time Alex's inexhaustible cheerfulness and enthusiasm buoys her up. He does much of the talking and seems to gauge accurately just how much intellectual input Annie can deal with at any one time.

He talks a lot about work, and literature, sometimes about a musical project, and also about his children; rarely about either his home life or his wife, Kate. Annie had met Kate a couple of times. She was pretty, quiet and rather timid-seeming, and, it seemed to Annie who was guiltily aware that she was being faintly patronising, probably a wonderful mother and devoted wife.

He doesn't ask her about the accident; like most of her visitors, he probably doesn't know how to broach the subject of Greg's death. Like everyone else, he knows nothing about Greg's occasional infidelities and his later and frequent drinking bouts and the abuse that increasingly went with them. Alex probably assumes, along with everybody else, Annie thinks, that she is totally grief-stricken and probably desperate to avoid thinking or talking about it.

They are only partially right. She is indeed grief-stricken, and finds thinking about what happened almost unbearable. But quite clearly, alongside her grief, is a corroding mixture of guilt and rage. Greg's death was not a 'clean' death; the creeping horror of her sense that the crash was a final act of violence directed against both himself and her has left his anger hanging, unresolved and accusing, wherever she turns. The natural guilt involved in her confusion about their turbulent relationship, and especially the final row, has left Annie with a burdened sense that she could have done more to prevent it. In addition to that, she's left with the equally natural but illogical guilt that she has survived and Greg hasn't. Then there's the black rage.

Annie and Greg had no children. It was unclear which of them had 'failed'—for failure it seemed to Annie. The first time Alex speaks of his children on a hospital visit she listens a little sadly, as well as with vicarious pleasure, to the obvious joy he finds in them. Before, earlier in her marriage and when she was still very much enjoying her work, Annie had been aware only of a slight wistfulness when other people spoke of their children; no big deal. Now, with the present and immediate past full of pain, and the future a long way away and totally uncertain—for the hospital has still not committed itself to a guarantee that Annie will walk unaided again—a sharp sense of desolation at her childlessness occasionally visits her. When Alex has gone that first day, she adds the particular emptiness of the would-be parent to the list of torments that fill her lonelier hours; and for the first time in many years cries herself to sleep.

FOUR

It is a wild, grey late November day. Already at four o'clock the elderly sodium lights in the grounds are on, and the nurse has come in to close Annie's curtains and bring her a cup of tea. Annie accepts the tea, but asks for the curtains to be left open. After so many months bedridden she's beginning to despair of participating in the outside world, and the storm-blown clouds and dancing leafless branches outside her window are a welcome contrast to the routine monotony of hospital life. Annie, propped up against her pillows watching the jackdaws tumbling down the wind like acrobats, is thinking about going home.

'Well, if you carry on like this, you'll be home for Christmas,' the young houseman had said that morning, straightening up from flexing her knee. 'Good news, surely?' he'd added, seeing the shock on her face, before leaving her to the nurse.

She has been warned that her right leg might need to be re-set in the Spring; the multiple fractures have not healed as cleanly as hoped. Because of the complications of her various other injuries, including a fractured neck, damaged spinal column and broken ribs, the doctors have not wanted to put her body through the trauma of further operations until she's regained a lot more strength. Her doctor has told her that the only reason she's alive today is because the first person to stop at the accident knew enough about First Aid not to attempt to move her. He had stayed, supporting her neck, until the ambulance arrived.

When she thinks about her future she is filled with a kind of numb horror. The idea of managing the practical details of her life as a semi-invalid for a while yet is overwhelming. Added to that is the trauma of going back to their house for the first time since the accident on her own, still ill, at Christmas with Greg dead. In addition she doesn't yet feel she has a future of any sort worth contemplating.

Then there was that other shock, after lunch. The young nurse, Alana, whose company Annie enjoys the most, had just brought her water and painkillers, and Annie braced herself to ask the question.

'Alana, I've never quite understood—what about my burns? Nobody's ever said anything about them. Did they mostly heal when I was unconscious? Surely I wasn't in a coma for that long?'

Alana stared at her. 'What burns, Annie? You weren't burnt. Fancy wishing burns on yourself as well! Weren't the fractures enough?' She moved round the bed and supporting Annie's head competently plumped up the pillows with one hand. 'What you need, love, is a really good night's sleep. It's all these drugs confusing you—painkillers, sleeping pills, whatnot— there now, we'll soon have you straight. I'll just put the lamp on—getting dark so quickly now. Home for Christmas, did Dr Mortimer say?'

Annie opened her mouth to protest about the fire, the flames, and then remembered the car crash. The car hadn't caught fire, they'd said. ('You were lucky.' *Lucky?*) Annie cannot speak.

As day turns to evening and the northern hemisphere moves onwards towards the shortest day, Annie feels completely overwhelmed by confusion, desolation and anxiety, as if her physical near-paralysis has laid claim to the rest of her, too. When Alex knocks and puts his head around the door, she bursts into tears.

Alex comes over and sits on the bed beside her, his arm around her shoulders, and for the first time Annie tells someone the whole story as far as she can remember, including Greg's drinking and their final row. Alex listens without a word, simply stroking her arm as she slows or catches a sob, his kind tawny eyes filled with concern and warmth.

Afterwards she leans back against Alex's arm, drained and voiceless, but hugely relieved to have acknowledged the pain and the rage and the guilt and the grief and have it heard and accepted.

Both are silent for some minutes, as darkness presses closer to the windows. Part of Annie's mind registers that Alex must be able to feel her shaking. Suddenly she's conscious of the blue circles beneath her eyes and her unbrushed hair. Alex's hand moves, as if to stroke her face, and then drops again. Alana puts her head around the door, and almost instantaneously withdraws again.

'I should have known,' Annie says. And then again: 'I should have known—' quietly now, sadly.

Alex is silent for a minute. Annie sees the unasked questions in his eyes, flitting across his expressive face. He holds her eyes, only inches away.

'You mean about the—about Greg's—you mean about the crash?'

Annie looks away, and nods.

The silence seems to swell.

'Why?' he asks in the end. 'Why should you have known?'

Annie draws a long uneven breath. 'Because I usually do. Know these things, I mean. It's . . .' She doesn't finish the sentence; her eyes avoid his.

The room becomes utterly still. For long minutes Annie looks out of the window at the darkening world, aware of Alex's hand, inches from hers, on the hospital sheet.

'So that's it,' she says eventually in a quiet small voice which sounds both alien and childish to her, totally lacking in her old pre-accident confidence and self-containment. 'I was so scared of telling anyone about it.' Her voice shakes; she swallows and tries to force a matter-of-fact tone. 'What finished me off, I think, was the idea of going home for Christmas to an empty house. I can't face having to think, or remember. But I'm desperate to get out of here; it's been like being in prison, or limbo. At the same time, I'm petrified. When I look towards a future, all I see is blankness. And I can't look to the past. Does that make any sense?'

Alex nods, his head resting lightly against hers.

'Of course I want to go back. But it's so—safe here. You know? All that matters is the next tiny step. Sitting up for longer each day, or learning how to shuffle to the loo with that frame. A bit more movement in my wrist, or one less dose of painkillers. Someone else to take care of cleaning, buying and cooking food, making decisions on drugs and drips. If I can't get out of bed, I can ring for help; a nurse will even get rid of visitors who stay too long.' She puts out her hand to touch Alex's arm. 'I don't mean you. Never you. But—you know; all I have to do is stay alive.'

Alex doesn't say anything for a long time.

Annie, exhausted by the telling and overwhelmed by an uneasy mix of exhilaration that she'd told the story and survived, and bleakness at the memories stirred up, wonders if he has dropped asleep, and is considering how she might gently extricate herself so that she herself can sleep when he stirs. He holds her for a long moment, then stands up.

'Annie, I'm so glad you told me. I don't know what to say that won't sound trite; I hadn't any idea about—what happened.' He looks at her for a moment, his mobile face criss-crossed with different emotions. Turning, he crosses over to the window and watches the birds being tossed down the dusky autumn sky. Again he stands silent, his hands in his pockets.

Annie looks at his slender figure, his long legs and unruly hair. His presence has the un-self-conscious grace and contained energy of a prairie animal, perhaps a horse. Even when quiet and still, she thinks, he seems so very alive. Annie wonders wearily when it was that she lost her own vitality, became so neat and sedate.

A phrase of Jack Kerouac's from her student days suddenly detaches itself from a far-off part of her brain: 'The only people for me are the mad ones, the ones who are mad to live, mad to talk . . . the ones who never yawn or say a commonplace thing but burn, burn, burn like fabulous yellow Roman candles.'

On cue, Alex speaks. 'Halfway between Bonfire Night— which of course is really Samhain, the old Celtic Fire Festival — and the winter solstice. When the world goes into darkness like this it's the pits, isn't it?'

Annie stares. The hairs on the back of her neck prickle. *Fabulous yellow Roman candles*, she thinks. The phrase repeats itself over and over. Then *Flames*. Her mouth is dry. *Did I speak out loud?*

Alex turns his head. 'Annie? You OK? What's up?'

When she doesn't respond, he asks again. 'Annie?'

Eventually she makes her lips respond. 'I'm OK,' she says. Her eyes are so heavy. *I need to sleep.*

Annie closes her eyes. For a long time there's silence.

Alex's voice, when it comes, makes her jump. His back is still towards her, and the grey dusk is turning to night around his silhouette. There's a faint patter against the windows, of windblown leaves or rain.

'I hate to do this to you now of all times, but I have to go. I'm late. Please just remember I'm your friend; I'm here if you need me, if there's anything I can do.'

Alex stoops and picks up his battered old rucksack and slings it over one shoulder. He turns and looks at her a moment, blows her a kiss, and is gone. Annie slides carefully down under the sheets and closes her eyes again.

* * * * *

Trying out my newly-free right wrist, just out of plaster and weak. Writing. Haven't written in my journal since—before.

Claire's arrived, thank God. For once in my life I really need someone to stand between me and the world for a while, to help me out of this bloody year, to help bring me back from the dead, from the land of the dead. It'll be OK as long as I can remember not to look back. Now I understand about Lot's wife: the paralysis of regret, the inability to cut ties. I've spent so much of my life looking over my shoulder, held by my past or trapped by my fears. Petrification.

Stupid. Stupid. I could kick myself. I've frightened him off. Alex. What made me tell him what I did?—Three weeks now since he came in. I feel such an idiot.

There's something else, too. At the time it didn't bother me much. I've felt so weird in so many different ways since the accident. Afterwards I felt frightened, though. I remembered later that I had similar experiences several times as an adolescent, and then they stopped. It's only thinking about it now that I remember the same thing happening a couple of times in the early part of my marriage. The last time must be over ten years ago, though.

It starts out as a physical thing, a faint feeling of nausea. Then I feel as if I'm falling sideways, almost like falling through a crack. In the past, sometimes, I remember now, I would have a sort of flash of blackness, but blinding, and it would feel as if suddenly there was no ground beneath my feet, rather like on the Rotor at the fair, but without the sound. Then it is as if the world grates and slides on itself; the image that comes to mind every time I think about this is a rift valley forming, great tectonic plates sliding out of junction; and then it's as if time is no longer seamless but overlapping, looping back on itself.

I had been looking out of the window; and suddenly I felt myself slithering between worlds. I can't describe it any other way. For a moment it was as if the hospital walls dissolved and I was someone else, somewhere else, in a different country, in a flickering landscape, now dark, now light; and I couldn't tell if it was the past or the future pulling me. I felt weightless, transparent, carried like a leaf on a river. There were many of us. Then there was an explosion or crash, and I was burning. I remember screaming. The next thing I remember is the nurse's face floating above me, white with alarm. Her hand was on the buzzer by my bed. I had a great hollowing pit in my solar plexus, and there were feet drumming down the corridor towards me. I was sweating, and then vomiting and vomiting.

* * * * *

The day before Annie leaves hospital, Alex comes in. Annie is dozing, and feels shock drain her face and her limbs at his voice, to be replaced instantly by a hot surge both of pleasure and of remembered embarrassment. Alex, too, seems agitated.

'Annie, I'm sorry I've not been in before; there've been some problems at home and it's been difficult for me to visit. I've been wondering how you've been, though; the nurse tells me you're going home tomorrow. Wonderful! She says you've made huge progress. You must be so relieved.'

Alex balances on the bottom of the bed but doesn't take his rucksack off his shoulder. He pushes his hair back and his generous, laughing eyes search for Annie's; she notices a look in them she hasn't seen before—slightly anxious, slightly abstracted. She doesn't know what to say, and feels her heart thumping and her body stiffen with awkwardness. She is suddenly aware that she's well enough to be dressed and up, and conscious, again, of her unwashed hair and uncared-for face. To cover her confusion and discomfort she finds herself, unusually, gabbling.

'I suppose I am relieved; yes, of course I am. I'm—well, I'm a bit nervous too; I haven't seen the real world except through the window for over half a year. I'm really looking forward to simple things like sitting in my garden or putting on my music, and going out to buy a Sunday paper. It'll be great to have all my books around me again. Claire, my sister, is staying with me for a month or so to help out. It's going to be a while, though, before I can go back to work. I'm going to go through my notes—and the ones you made for me—on Betty Chadwick's course over Christmas, just to try and kickstart my brain again. Of course you've finished your residency now, haven't you? What will you do?'

Even as her social self asks the right questions and gives the right responses, inside Annie is screaming silently at the uncrossable distance between them. The real questions— *what now? Will I see you again? Did I frighten you when I told you about Greg?*—turn over and over, unvoiced. They make a mockery of the superficialities Annie and Alex exchange, banalities that serve simultaneously to both maintain and nullify their tenuous bond.

Alex doesn't mention returning to the faculty, or Betty Chadwick's course. He doesn't say he'll see Annie again, though he does of course say he hopes Christmas won't be too bad, and that Annie's strength soon returns. He doesn't ask her plans for the future, and when he stands up to go in his characteristic swift motion after their ten-minute conversation he makes no move to touch her. He throws her his lightning smile and swings out of the door just as Claire comes in.

'Who was that *sexy* guy?' she enquires. As Annie, reeling with despair, tries to find a coherent response, the bland innocuous room reverberates with all the unspoken questions, the unapproachable answers. Once again, the afternoon is rushing towards darkness. It seems to Annie suddenly as if all the lost words have become a host of tiny birds, beating themselves against the windowpane and blocking out the light.

The day Annie goes home, as Claire is carrying her bags down to the car, a nurse brings in a hand-delivered envelope. It has Annie's name on the front in a fluid, fast script.

The painting on the front of the card is Rosetti's 'Proserpine', all flowing dark hair and wintry silver-blues, subdued colours except for the scarlet pomegranate flesh. Proserpine/Persephone stares off to one side with her navy eyes focussed on something out of sight. The picture jolts Annie; something in the girl's eyes hooks a response in her. The story, if she had known it, remains submerged, apart from a vague memory of an abduction into a world of darkness.

The card is unsigned. Inside is a quote in the same loose and beautiful writing: 'There is a dark wood, and there is a figure standing in the depths of that wood. The figure has its hand outstretched. And at first you turn in fear and walk away. But there will come a time when you will have to enter that wood and approach the figure, for he or she is your Other Self, all that you might be. Your own true knowing.

'And you will take each other by the hand and hug, and suddenly you will notice that the wood is not dark at all, but

THREE

Annie has just been wheeled back from physio one day and is lying on her bed, experimentally tensing and relaxing the muscles in different parts of her body. Much of her is still encased in plaster or bandages, and her neck is in a collar. Physiotherapy consists mainly of some breathing exercises and a few minutes' sitting, lightly stretching any part of her body that can bear the mobility.

There's a tap on her door, and a huge hibiscus plant appears, accompanied by an armful of books and an avocado clutched in a familiar long-fingered hand. Beneath it all is a pair of old jeans and some serious walking boots. Above a crimson flower Alex grins his wide, teasing grin, and Annie fleetingly notices a few more wrinkles around his eyes than she remembers. He's younger than Annie, but his face looks much more inhabited, lived-in; rumpled even. He raises his eyebrows at her, eyes dark with concern, pleasure and his usual mix of liveliness and teasing humour. Annie smiles back, carefully, because of the stitches, delighted and surprised to see him, a little shy. His hair, shoulder-length and wildly curly, has lightened with the sun to a red-gold, and there's a sprinkling of grey hairs at the temples that she doesn't recall seeing before.

'Hey, lady, just look at you lying there with nothing to do! Even while we talk your poor departmental Head is tearing her hair out about you. You know you're indispensable? Yep. Apparently it's impossible to find any kind of Annie-substitute to strike fire into the hearts of all those fresh-faced eager young undergraduates. Must be easier ways to get a sabbatical?'

Alex looks around for somewhere to deposit his armful, and carefully piles the books and avocado onto the chair while he glowing and dappled and vibrant with life. And you will have entered the Dance, become your own true self. And the wood will be golden with laughter.'

FIVE

'For Christ's sake, Kate! I've had it up to here with your suspicion and your possessiveness! For fifteen fucking years I've had to account for every bloody movement—I'm only amazed you don't follow me into the bog! I'm not accountable to you; I'm not accountable to anyone. I've been for a fucking *walk*, OK? Sometimes I just need to get out, give myself a break, breathe some air, listen to a bird or two, just THINK without having somebody listening-in to the sounds in my head even!'

Alex can't believe he's just said what he has. He can't believe how easily he succumbs to temper at the moment, and yelling at Kate like this is unforgivable. He looks at the slight androgynous figure of Kate in her Levis and chunky bright jumper; notices the shock and hurt in her eyes and instantly collapses inside with guilt and pity. 'I'm sorry, Kate,' he mutters. 'Sorry. I know I'm a shit sometimes.' He closes his eyes and groans, thumps his fists on the table, lowers his head. Sam's small face appears around the door, thumb in mouth. Alex hears whispering; Laurel, no doubt reassuring her younger brother that the world isn't about to fall apart. Alex gets up and picks up the boy, kisses the top of his head and carries him back upstairs to bed.

When he comes back down Kate's standing at the sink, back to him, washing up. From time to time there's a small sniff. Alex feels a sudden rush of intense irritation. He wants to throw something, anything, smash the kitchen. Sometimes it's hard not to hate himself.

He thrusts his hands into his pockets and goes to stand at the window, looking out at the sky. To the north, over the hill above the houses the sky's lowering, purple. Perhaps it'll snow, he thinks. I can take the kids tobogganing, try and make up for some of my moodiness recently. I'd feel better if I could get down to some real work, get that piece finished and set to music. Perhaps Pete would come round tomorrow and help me transcribe the string part. Christ, I wish Kate would stop bloody snivelling. I don't know how much longer I can stand this, stand any of it. Would I have stayed with her if it hadn't been for that pregnancy and miscarriage all those years ago?

Pointless asking himself this.

A huge rush of guilt and anger.

He breathes on the windowpane and rubs a clear patch with his sleeve. He stops himself from shouting at Kate to quit sniffing; it isn't her fault that he doesn't love her. It's just that he feels so suffocated. He's tried so hard to do the right thing by her, he stayed with her through her rough patch after the lost pregnancy, he's given her the two kids she wanted and he shares the caring for them. He gave up his dreams of travelling; he gave up studying for his second degree. Mostly they get by financially, with his residencies and workshops and readings, as well as the odd gig with local bands and what he sees as his 'real' work, the creative solitary writing and composition, which is, to his dismay, not flowing at the moment. He loves the kids passionately, desperately; he and Kate are often reasonably comfortable together, still occasionally joke and laugh. He's resisted temptation each time it's presented itself, so far.

And still he can't get it right. He supposes she must sense deep down that he doesn't love her as she loves him. It just isn't there for him. If he's brutally honest with himself she neither stimulates him intellectually, nor excites him sexually. They don't 'meet'. He doesn't feel any real sense of *belonging*. Should that matter? The truth is, it does.

He turns and looks at her back and feels almost paralysed with guilt and an exasperated kind of pity. How can she be stimulating when she puts so much of herself into the kids, into being the perfect wife and mother? He groans, and out of habit and contrition bends down to collect together Sam's Lego. 'Sorry,' he says, bleakly. 'Sorry. Not your fault.' Any minute now, he thinks. Any minute.

Yes.

'I sometimes think you don't really love me, Alex.' Oh Christ.

With perfect timing, Laurel comes in the door. He hugs her, mostly out of genuine affection and remorse; partly, he knows, out of gratitude. Saved from himself again. Laurel sits down at the table and glances at her mother's rigid back. She looks accusingly at Alex, who grimaces and shrugs slightly, acknowledging that he's being a shit and that there's nothing he feels he can do about it. Laurel bends her blonde plaits to her homework in a resigned grown-up sort of way. Alex looks at her ten-year-old head and his heart turns over. He goes and sits beside her.

'What are you doing, sweetheart? Need any help?'

The tension in the air hasn't really abated. Bodge, the collie, hasn't emerged from under the table where he'd crept when Alex shouted. Now he pushes his head against Alex's knee, and Alex puts his hand down. Bodge licks it and whines faintly. Kate sighs.

'Can you help me with my project, Dad? It's on woodlands, and I need to draw different kinds of trees and describe them.'

Just outside Exeter, in Ide, Annie lies sleepless, stiff and aching in her bed, watching the moonlight, trying not to think. Across the moon passes a now-familiar flood of faces, silhouettes of crags and towers, shapes and symbols she both does and doesn't recognise. The stuff of her nights.

Despite the February cold and the unheated room her face and her hands are burning. She moves to push the covers down but has the absurd and fleeting sense that her wrists are thonged behind her back. Her mind struggles with twin realities: the fact that this is a physical impossibility, here in her bed in Ide, lying on her back, and the intruding sensations of raw soreness and bloodless hands. In terror of being engulfed she once again, as most nights, flicks on the bedside lamp and struggles to sit upright, sweat beginning to bud on her forehead.

Across the river on the northern outskirts of the city with the light off and the same moon stretching white fingers into the corners of the room, because of guilt, because he can't stand his mental picture of her pale unhappy face and her snuggling attempts to get close to him, Alex makes love to Kate. He is, as always, gentle and considerate if not entirely honest or passionate. Their lovemaking is, as always, smooth, practised and flowing as a Vaughan Williams pastoral but with no great crescendos; worse, no intimacy. He knows this. With the ease of nearly half a lifetime together, he knows what Kate needs, and at least, thank God, his body can usually respond, even if part of his heart is absent. He knows that his main motivation is pity tinged with remorse, not love; and wonders if that's wrong. His meditation teacher's voice repeats a phrase in his mind. What does 'right action' mean in this situation? *Christ knows*, he thinks.

He watches her face, wan in the moonlight, eyes closed, as she moans and he slips inside her. He closes his own eyes, knowing that any moment now she will open hers and gaze searchingly, almost pleadingly, into his for the reassurance she is looking for. Even with his eyes closed her gaze will be almost tangible. He feels, sometimes, as if she is trying to pull his soul out through his eyes; as if she's sucking him dry.

Now, he knows, she'll sleep, physically comforted if not entirely emotionally reassured.

Afterwards, Kate clings to him, strokes his face.

'I love you, Alex . . .' This is his cue. He hugs her, grunts in what he hopes is a reciprocating, warm, sleepy way and feigns the slow deep breaths of someone on the verge of dropping asleep. He can almost hear Kate plucking up her courage to ask him again if he loves her. Oh God, please Kate, please just go to sleep . . . and miraculously, she doesn't ask.

Alex lies and watches the moon move around, take its fingers out of the room, and listens to the owls calling to each other across the valley. He waits for dawn and wonders, as so many times before, if finally this might be the last time; if he can find the courage and the callousness tomorrow to bring himself to tell her that he no longer loves her, that their time together is at an end. And what about the children? whispers the punishing voice inside him. Could you really do that to them?

For the rest of the night, Alex wrestles with his own personal spectres and a free-floating sense of failure. Failure in his work, for his composing and writing alone are not enough to pay the bills. Failure in his marriage and his inability to make Kate happy. Failure to live up to the promise of those early years. And failure in his spiritual life, too, for his lack of integrity and honesty, his lack of courage in his inability to make a commitment either to stay wholeheartedly in his marriage, or to get out. And, bitterest of all, the failure to live his life as he wants to, in an honest, joyful, creative way with integrity and without the kind of compromise that keeps him locked within four small terraced walls, chained by someone else's needs.

Alex doesn't tell Kate that he no longer loves her. Neither does he ask Pete to come over and help with his music. It hasn't snowed, so there's to be no tobogganing. Unable to stand being inside any longer, he tells Kate that he's going to the university library to do some work. He strides out of the door in his motorbike leathers, wrapping his scarf around his neck as he goes.

The cold wind stings his cheeks and whips tears into his eyes, and he gulps down the February air almost thankfully. Alex doesn't really know why he's going up to the university, except that at the back of his mind he feels that it might stir his brain up, get the words or music flowing again. It's true that it will offer him the quiet that he can't find at home.

He suppresses before he even formulates it the thought that he also connects the university with Annie.

Five or six hours later he has, to his delight and amazement, written the first draft of the vocal score to the embryonic composition, *Lento*, that is his current project. For months the disparate threads in his head have been churning, and tangling, and now suddenly, out of the blue, they've come together. It feels like an enormous achievement. Alex's black mood disperses, and as he swing out of the library, jubilant, as if on cue a flock of white doves fly up in front of him, brilliant against the pewter clouds. Alex reads this as a sign of something or other auspicious, and decides to go and have a pint before going home.

Striding down Gandy Street he stops dead; emerging from the Arts Centre and heading towards the Museum on crutches is Annie, accompanied by the same person who entered Annie's hospital room as he left, the last time. For a moment Alex stands frozen, completely immobilised by conflicting impulses. The first is to carry on, fling his arms around Annie and tell her how much he's missed seeing her. He's shocked at how his heart races. The second, virtually simultaneously, is to slip down the nearby alley and cross Queen Street with as much speed and willpower as he can muster. He absolutely does not need further complications in his life; and besides, until he has resolved at least in his own mind what needs to be done about his marriage he has no business letting another woman into his heart. Annie has already unknowingly stepped further in than is safe or comfortable, given his current situation.

Annie disappears round the corner without seeing him. Alex hesitates for a second, then turns down the alleyway. He pushes her out of his mind and goes to buy some blank tapes.

Instead of going into a pub in town, Alex does a detour through the industrial estate to go to the Double Locks. He needs to be by water; and besides, their beer's good. He throws the bike up the short ramp to the slatted wooden bridge over the canal and rattles across far too fast, the vibrations shaking his body. He needs something, though he doesn't know what; probably to push the bike to its absolute limits up the M5 to Bristol and back or something equally stupid. The kind of thing he used to do as a lovesick or angst-ridden James Dean-emulating teenager. He takes his pint outside and sits by the canal, forcing himself to read back over the work he had did in the library. He knows it's a triumph, but it's lost a little of its edge in the last hour.

After a while, restless, he wanders back around to the front of the pub to join the small cluster of dedicated bikers comparing the merits of the diversity of classic bikes that are as usual drawn up outside the Locks. One of them offers his tobacco pouch; Alex accepts, and rolls himself a cigarette. It's been a long time since he's hung out with the boys, smoking, slouching, forgetting briefly that he's a married man, focussing thankfully on the comparative charms of the Harley versus the Bonneville versus the Norton or the Honda Goldwing.

Dusk falls. Alex, uncharacteristically, is partway through a third pint and a second roll-up.

'Coming for a burn, mate? There's some shit-hot bikes here tonight.'

For the second time that day, Alex is torn between two possibilities: freedom versus responsibilities. He takes the third option—another pint, on his own, outside; just the gathering dusk and a ghost-white swan floating like a cloud on the motionless February water.

SIX

When she wakes at dawn from her usual sporadic and unrestful doze Annie knows there are eyes in the garden, many eyes, eyes she loves. And voices. A familiar tongue, not English, not French, either, but similar to the latter. A strange deep peace seems to wash in with the greenish scent of damp foliage and moist earth from the outer world through her open window, and momentarily inside and outside blur, as day and dark are blurred. The garden is alive around her, and the walls are gone and she swims in the unnamed landscape, both contained and released by the power of the natural world to reorder something of the inner world, fragments falling together perfectly, each into its own place. The imaginal world and the world of the senses come together, bringing that peculiar tranquillity that alights in moments when one fits the landscape like a second skin and there are no boundaries.

When she wakes the second time that morning, this time from deep sleep, sunlight is pouring over the sill and under the curtains like molten honey. For a second she is disorientated, and then the objects and furniture in the room reassemble themselves into the contours and waymarkers that delineate for Annie the landscape that signifies 'home', in the way that things, through long association, do. Today the whole room, with its apricot and gold tapestries that she'd woven years before, in the days when she still thought she could make it as a painter and textile artist, glows like a sunflower field; so different from the cool blue room, now the guest room, that had once been the bedroom shared with Greg.

For a moment she lies there, trying to remember what it is that is happening today. It is something that she has actually been looking forward to . . . ah. The first day of Betty

Chadwick's new course. A big step back into the land of the living.

She swings her legs over the edge of the bed and, using her arms as props, levers herself upright. Mornings are still difficult; she is invariably stiff and aching, with limited mobility in her neck as yet. Out of plaster, now, she still needs to go back at the end of May for her right leg to be re-set. She moves rather stiff-legged—like a heron, she thinks wryly—to the window and pulls back the calico curtains that Claire had made for her at New Year.

As she waits for the kettle to boil, Annie opens the back door to let in the scent of the wet garden. April always reminds her of a court jester, peevish, sullen and sunny by turns, lightning fast and startlingly unpredictable in its changes of mood and tempo. One minute caressing, one minute insulting. Cartwheeling storm-clouds over new gold and green growth in the garden. She loves the promise of April generally; this year, it manages to raise a faint glimmer of optimism in her, where nothing else yet has. She has become good at going through the motions, learning to function again, but nothing has seemed to really touch her.

Today the new honeysuckle and clematis growth romping over the top of the wall seem like a promise. Annie leans against the doorframe and breathes in the sharp air and watches the bluetits savaging the cherry buds as they do every year. She realises for the first time that actually she cares about spring coming, that she cares about the patches of watery sunlight dappling the ground and touching the first bluebells to a luminescence under the apple-trees, that she cares, at last, about living.

She needs to write to her sister and tell her that all the love and care that she put into nursing her over Christmas and New

Year was not in vain. If it hadn't been for Claire's endlessly patient, endlessly strong faith in her—and in some kind of divine grace—she might not be here to stand in the almost-tangible waves of growth from the stirring garden. Annie leaves the door open and takes a cup of tea back to bed, and allows herself to care about what clothes she is going to put on to celebrate emerging from the darkness, emerging from winter back into the world.

Annie, carefully lowering herself into one of the hard lecture room chairs, glances around her. One or two familiar faces catch her eyes and smile in welcome, and she smiles back, touched; but her eyes move on involuntarily rather faster than she intends; than she knows is polite. Twice round the room and she is sure he isn't there. Her disappointment is almost physical; she has been so sure of Alex's presence that she has conjured up a three-dimensional picture of him, black and white Palestine scarf thrown round his neck, tilting his chair back, arms folded, long legs stretched out beneath the chair in front of his, hair glinting copper like the sun. She can almost count the pens in his pocket, see the twined gold and silver ring that he wears on his wedding finger, feel the texture of the worn patch on the shoulder of his jacket where his rucksack is habitually slung. She reprimands herself. What is she thinking; he is a married man. How can she allow herself this daydream?

She herself has only just arrived in time, and she props her leg up on the empty chair in front of her and takes out her pen and clipboard as Betty Chadwick starts to speak. Annie pushes the image of Alex away and hopes grimly that she can remember how to switch her brain on.

'So to pick up where we left off last term, with the arrival of the Romance on the mediaeval literary scene.'

Annie watches Betty glance around at the faces in the lecture-room with a twinge of amusement. How well she remembers that feeling—the need as lecturer on the first day of a new term to reassure oneself that they all look more-or-less as if they remember what they are here for.

Betty continues: 'So the Romance. You have to understand what a huge innovation the Romances represented. This was a totally new genre. Up until this point, the types of stories that circulated tended to be warriors' epics; bloody and often gruesome tales that celebrated triumphs of warfare, revenge, successful raids and campaigns, male loyalty. Any relationships portrayed were the bonds of liege to lord, knight to knight. Marriages were almost always strictly strategic, expedient. Family connections and feudal structures were rigid. It wasn't that they left out romance; romantic love actually didn't exist as a cultural construct—if I can speak of it like that.'

Betty pauses for effect, and repeats herself; 'Romantic love did not exist before the Middle Ages. It was an invention of the troubadours and the Courts of Love.'

Annie stops making notes and stares at Betty.

'So we're talking about a major revolution, the repercussions of which have shaped our own attitudes. For the first time, women came into their own as worthy of more mention than mere chattels. However, they also became symbols of something greater and less personal, of which more later, when we come to the Grail legends.

'Meanwhile, let's look at this revolution a moment. Someone said—' Betty bends her sandy-white head to the page, cropped hair bristling with efficiency and enthusiasm for her subject— 'ah yes, C S Lewis said that compared to the huge social and cultural changes that occurred during this epoch—and we're now talking 12th century—the Renaissance was a mere surface ripple.' Betty looks up at the students over the top of her glasses, a caricature of an academic. She pushes them further up her nose with a freckled hand, and Annie feels a surge of warmth for her. The minute gestures of humanness seem especially touching when your main company for many weeks has been the rain, the radio and the inside of your own head. Somewhere deep inside Annie thinks she feels the very first twinges of what might be a thaw beginning to occur. For now, recovering from her initial disappointment at Alex's absence, she firmly focuses her mind on Betty and the troubadours.

'A great flowering began. Remember that the troubadours themselves—good morning and welcome, Mr O'Connell, better late than never—were bringing the seeds . . .' and Annie hears no more. Alex! Alex is here. She feels the blood drain from her face and her heart pounds. She struggles with herself, but her body resists her conscience. Slowly, surreptitiously, and somewhat painfully, she tries to twist her head enough to see where he is. A couple of rows back and to her left his tall figure is sliding down into a chair and lowering his rucksack, turning his head. Catching sight of her in the same moment, she can see from several yards away the light leap into his eyes and the lines around them deepen in his wonderful smile. This throws her into more confusion. Fleetingly she wonders whether he can hear her shallow breathing. She can feel his presence from her own chair. She's forgotten how much she likes his face.

Annie forces her head back to Betty Chadwick.

Half an hour later Betty Chadwick snaps her glasses case open and Annie stirs. Skimming down her notes she realises that she has only taken down about two sentences on the troubadours. Damn. And Alex won't have taped it, either.

'I should tell you,' Betty is saying, 'of a conference that's happening in the South of France this summer, near Carcassone. For those of you who might wish to take this further, the core subject matter will be the Cathars—we'll look at their history over the next few weeks—and their possible connections with the Grail material. It will be a broad-spectrum conference in that it is a gathering of experts working in several different fields; historical, naturally, and linguistic and literary, but there will also be an eminent psychologist there whose special interest is in the paranormal and reincarnation, and various authorities on the religious or spiritual aspects of the period we are talking of. I have details for anyone wanting to follow this up.'

Annie only half takes in what Betty was saying. Most of her mind is wondering whether she can simply slip away, so that Alex will not guess how pleased she was to see him. She forces herself to wait until Betty has finished, then pushes herself up, forcing her mind on to what Betty was saying. A conference. France. This summer. Maybe what she needs? She manoeuvres herself towards the front—then Alex is there, before her, standing in her way. He is looking directly at her with his broad easy grin.

'Alex—' she starts to say, and Alex speaks at exactly the same moment.

'Annie, my darling, how great to see you!'

They both laugh, and Alex grabs her hands. 'Coffee, did you say?'

'No—'

'I need one. I don't believe you don't. Lead me there.'

He drops his arm easily around her shoulders, and scrutinises her with his lively eyes. 'You feel like a little bird. Well, not that you're that little—short, I mean—but I can feel your shoulder-bones, sweetheart. I'm nervous they might snap if I were to give you a hug. Are you eating?'

'Eating? Oh yes,' she replies, thinking she might cry if she isn't careful. 'Mostly.'

'You're looking just as beautiful as always, lady; I didn't mean to suggest you weren't. Just a little fragile. How have you been? I've thought of you a lot, and wondered how it was when you came out of hospital.'

The moment stretches between them. A thousand questions run through Annie's mind, starting with the possibility of deflecting what he has said so as to keep the conversation impersonal and therefore undangerous. Then she wants to ask him how he is, how his work is going and, of course, what has kept him away for so long. She wonders if there is any way of asking that without seeming accusing; and without straying into territory that cannot bear safe fruit.

She wants to know, too, about that card he sent and the quote it contained, but can't imagine how to open that conversation. She says nothing, but his eyes stay on her face: warm, encouraging, slightly enigmatic. She wonders if the depth of her confusion is visible. As she looks at him his face changes. He holds her eyes. She can feel a smile beginning in her own.

'I'm doing OK,' Annie replies eventually. 'It's been a long winter but it's beginning to feel as it it's nearly over. I'm thinking I might aim towards coming back here, lecturing I mean, in September. How are you? What have you been doing?' She drops her eyes and moves towards the exit.

Alex adjusts his stride to Annie's, opens the swing door for her. She is glad she has worn a long skirt; she's acutely conscious that her leg is still rather a misshapen scarred mess. Not that Alex would mind; nor that she should mind him minding.

'I've been quite busy, I guess; I've had this musical project I've been working on. For ages it was stuck at the embryonic stage, but the last month or so it's started to come again, thank God. I feel so bloody frustrated when that happens; it's like psychic constipation; you can feel all this creative ferment but nothing's happening. I wonder when I'm in one of those patches whether it'll ever flow again, whether the Muse has just upped and winged it somewhere else.' He smiles, as if to himself. 'But tell me about you. You're walking! When I last saw you you thought your leg might need re-setting; what happened about that?'

They make their way fairly slowly down the corridor towards the canteen, chatting easily. Alex acknowledges almost as many people as Annie does, despite his much briefer connection with the university. He is always warm in his greetings, Annie noticed; she is also secretly pleased to note that he accords to none of them the open pleasure and attentiveness he seems to give to her, even when the person is young, female and gorgeous.

In the canteen, Alex steers her to a seat by the window and lopes up to the counter to collect two cappuccinos. Long minutes later he comes back with a tray full of assorted dainties: Greek salad, a wrap, some olives, a chunk of baguette stuffed with cheese and coleslaw. He takes his jacket off and slides into the bench opposite her.

'I'm vegetarian. I wasn't sure if you were or not, so I didn't take the chance. The wrap is mushroom, cheese and sweetcorn in a thick sauce apparently; I asked them to heat it up. Here, shall we simply share it all?'

He breaks the baguette in two and hands Annie a piece. Suddenly, she's ravenously hungry. Is her appetite coming back, finally? She's also very tired, now; it has felt like an extraordinarily full morning. Alex grins at her over a mouthful of baguette, licking mayonnaise off his fingers, and she suddenly feels light-hearted. Once, she remembers, life had been fun. She has that to look forward to: re-discovering fun without Greg's disapproval. Just her own inhibiting fears to overcome. She cuts the wrap in two.

'Isn't it strange,' she says on impulse, 'how your own fears, once you've identified them, are so much smaller and more easily tackled than you think they're going to be?'

'Mmmm?' Alex raises his eyebrows questioningly.

'But somebody else's fears always seem much larger and more restricting?'

Alex stops chewing and looks at her for a moment, consideringly.

'Well, yes,' he replies. 'Something you have some degree of control over always feels much less threatening of course than something you haven't. You only feel out of control when you can't see the limits of something. The extent of it I mean.'

'How do you mean?'

'I think I mean that if you can't map it, it rules you—if you allow it to. I'm not sure you can ever really see the extent of anyone else's fears, not really. Can you? One, I mean. I guess you have the choice over whether you let it affect you, though.' He stops to take another mouthful. 'But. You can just step back and let it happen, can't you, let it wash over you. Without reacting I mean. Without it affecting your freedom to be who you are. Maybe.' He stops, and something like wariness, or misery, seems to sit on his face for a moment. 'Bloody simple in theory. Nothing to it. And anyway, what's personal happiness against war, starvation, poverty, torture?' Alex sighs. There's silence for a minute.

'But what on earth made you think about that, anyway?'

Annie stirs her coffee, keeping her eyes on the spoon.

'I'm not really sure. I think I was thinking about coming back out into the world, and how it feels to be facing it alone, starting over.' She pauses.

'Mmmm. That's a bit tough. Sounds tough I mean. Tell me more?'

'I was terrified; but now I've taken the first step, I no longer feel so completely overwhelmed by my fear. It's as if turning round and facing the fear has diminished it, its hold on you, even though it might not go away.' Annie glances quickly at Alex's face, in a sudden flash of renewed terror at having made herself so visible.

'Mmm yes,' responds Alex through a mouthful. 'I think by looking it in the face you somehow map it out, maybe get a feel of its size and territory. And real courage is about doing something *despite* the fear, isn't it? We think that brave people don't feel fear, but actually they're just better at not letting it stop them than other people. Don't you think?' He waits for her eyes. She nods. Alex continues. 'Besides, it's much more exhausting and destructive spending your life running away from fear—living in fear of fear itself—than actually turning around and facing it. Facing it actually gives you more energy, makes you stronger. Wholer. Somehow.' He paused to take another mouthful, and they both sat in silence for a moment. Annie considered his words.

'Here endeth the first polemic . . .' Alex glances over at Annie, who smiles. 'That's what so many of our fairy-tales are about, aren't they? Things like Beauty and the Beast,' he continues. 'I've been reading them to Sam. He loves the bit where she hugs the Beast.'

Annie takes a sip of coffee and reflects on what Alex is saying. She can feel his eyes on her face. She swallows. 'I was wondering about what exactly it was that has kept me from really living, over the last few years; whether it was Greg's fears or my own; or whether it was my fears of Greg's reactions.'

There's a long pause. Alex watches Annie's face and doesn't say anything.

'I've not taken any real risks for such a long time now. The biggest risk I take these days is parking for ten minutes without buying a ticket. It's been a long time since there's been any edge in my life. You get more and more closed down, your circumference becomes smaller and smaller. Eventually you can't even see over the wall—' she pauses '—the wall you've built between yourself and the rest of the world.'

She stops, suddenly listening to her own voice and feeling a little silly, and very exposed and vulnerable. *This* is a risk, she thinks. Can I do it? What's the cost? And what's the cost if I don't? This man understands. This man is so easy to talk to. She looks up.

Alex looks into her face and gently stretches a hand over the table. 'You nearly died, lady, and lost your husband, and here you are talking about no "edge" in your life!'

Annie looks at the hand, the ring, the long fingers. Before she can reach out her own hand she becomes aware, out of the corner of her eye, of a paunch looming at the edge of their table, a paunch sitting on a shiny Spanish tooled leather belt strapped over a buffalo-head buckle. Oh no.

'Mind if I join you, Annie my dear?'

Without waiting for an answer Dr Schwarzkopf— Blackhead, as he is known to his students—drops his bulk onto the bench beside Annie. Annie raises her eyes in dismay to Alex's face. Alex has withdrawn his hand and widens his eyes in amusement and mock horror at Annie. Blackhead, with a cursory nod in Alex's direction, has his hand in his pocket and withdraws a large off-white handkerchief and a crumpled packet of photos. The latter has 'SAFARI 92' neatly printed across the envelope in large red letters. Dr Schwarzkopf pushes the photos towards Annie and flaps his handkerchief and raises it to his nose, drawing breath. Annie casts a surreptitious and despairing glance at Alex, and stiffens for the expected trumpeting bellow, and Alex rises swiftly and smoothly to his feet, sweeping the rest of their lunch on its paper plates off the table with one hand as he reaches for his rucksack and jacket with the other.

'Delighted to meet you, Mr Whoever-you-are, but this lady has an appointment with the doctor in ten minutes' time, and I'm the taxi. Now if you'll excuse us, I'll need to give her a hand out.'

He carefully pushes the paper plates, folded over their contents, into a carrier bag he extracts from the front pocket of his rucksack then into the rucksack and slings it over his shoulder, before striding round to Annie's side of the table smiling expectantly and firmly at Dr Schwarzkopf. With the same expression he glances at Annie and raises an eyebrow, extending her a hand. Dr Schwarzkopf glowers and grudgingly stands up, grunting. Alex smiles charmingly at him and bows to Annie.

'Your motorbike is waiting, madam.'

As the doors swing to behind them he grins a little guiltily at Annie. 'Sorry about that. Bit presumptuous of me, I suppose, wasn't it? I just felt we hadn't finished our conversation, and I wanted you to myself. Can we go and find a patch of lawn somewhere for a little while? Is that all right by you?'

Annie, overcome by a confusing mixture of tenderness and amused indignation, can only nod.

SEVEN

It is a May morning gentle as apple-blossom.

Annie is sitting on the steps down from the back door with her knees apart and her stiff leg stretched out in front of her. Her old stone-coloured jeans are already smudged with a scattering of dark peaty soil. She is, for once, tranquil, mindlessly repotting all her geraniums and pelargoniums, a job she loves. The minute she plunges her fingers into earth her brain switches off, and she is now totally immersed in what she is doing.

Rosa looks over at the peaceful figure from where she is kneeling weeding Annie's herb-garden, then stands up and dusts off her hands. She leans over the coffee-pot on the little wooden garden table and tops up her own cup with lukewarm coffee, then starts towards Annie.

Annie comes out of her reverie and smiles towards her friend. 'You look like a flame, or a firefly—that red skirt and all your hair,' she says, holding out her cup. Annie feels more relaxed and comfortable with her than with anyone else. Their friendship extends beyond Greg, beyond all the significant events of adulthood and even of adolescence. The two of them grew up together; unlike most of their friends, they both come from the Westcountry and had attended the same primary school. Rosa's the only person with whom Annie feels she can be totally uncompromisingly herself, even when that means sitting in silence and doing her own thing for an hour—not that that happened often, as she herself is, she knows, a voluble extravert whose natural world is that of communication.

As Rosa swings towards Annie, skirt swirling, with the coffee-pot Annie smiles gratefully, and puts her hand out to touch Rosa's arm in affection.

Rosa comes and sits beside her on the steps. Annie pushes her hair out of the way with her wrist, then cradles the cup that Rosa has refilled in both peaty hands. They sit shoulder to shoulder looking out at the garden, talking of this and that. The phone rings and Rosa stands and goes to answer it.

'It's the hospital, Annie. Can you come and get it?'

Annie returns to the garden thoughtful. 'They've offered me a bed at the end of the month for my leg to be re-set.'

'That's brilliant, love. It's earlier than you thought, isn't it? How d'you feel about it?'

'I don't know, really. Going back in, even for a few days, will be odd, but this feels like the final phase now. Until my leg's been done I don't really feel I can close the door, move on past the last year.'

Rosa takes a gamble.

'Annie,' she says, then hesitates. She takes a deep breath. 'You hadn't been happy for a long time before the accident, had you? I used to see the look on your face, sometimes, when you didn't think anyone was looking. It was hard not to ask you; perhaps I was wrong to wait for you to volunteer information. I just didn't want to pry, but you know how much I love you. What exactly was it with you and Greg?'

Annie instantly looks down and plunges her hands back into the bag of compost.

Rosa too looks away. She plucks a blade of grass from between the slate facing of the steps and twirls it. Annie struggles with herself. She's not told anyone about Greg's violence. Rosa knows about the rows, she knows about the drink, but this is something else again. Of course she trusts Rosa. Why can't she speak of it? If not to Rosa, then to whom?

Annie sits on, motionless, unspeaking.

Rosa suddenly gets up and stands in front of Annie. 'Look, Annie, for God's sake. Can you imagine how upsetting it makes me feel, how angry, when you shut down like that? I'm your *friend;* I *care* about you. I hate it when you blank me like this. It's an insult to our friendship.' She bangs her mug down. 'Wake up, wake up, for God's sake, before it's too late and we all leave you alone to shrivel up on your dry rock.' She glares. 'I hate having to pussyfoot around you while you quietly and firmly close doors in my face.' She stares at Annie, and Annie glances at her and then down again.

Rosa gets up and strides across to the other side of garden. Almost immediately she's back. Annie glances up. Her stiffened shoulders drop slightly, and instantly Rosa sits back down beside her. She touches Annie's arm lightly. 'Look, I love you. Sorry if that hurt. I didn't mean to wound you; just—I just feel so frustrated that you won't let me in, won't let me help. That's all.'

Annie stirs. 'It's just—I'm—I'm not sure it was an accident, Rosa. I'm—I think—oh God, Rosa—' she bites her lip; tries to hold in a sob. 'Greg killed himself. You see. He tried to kill me, too . . . I think.' Her breath quavers as she speaks. She brushes minute specks of soil off her jeans. 'He'd been drinking, and we'd had another row, you see. I feel like I'm going mad thinking about it.' She's weeping now, soundlessly.

There's a long pause. Annie has her hands to her eyes.

'But—but—oh God, Annie. Oh God. What—why? I mean do you know —?'

'He hated me, Rosa. At least, towards the end. Nothing I did was right,' Annie continues in a thin tight matter-of-fact voice. 'We just seemed to fight all the time; you know that. And you know sex had been—difficult. He thought I was unfeeling; the more viciously he blamed me for what was wrong in our marriage the more I just—couldn't stand him touching me, and the more he attacked me. At first it was just verbal, and then as he started drinking more he started to hit me too. I began—it got—I began to dread him coming home.'

'Oh God—I had no idea…'

Annie is shaking. 'I know. No one did. He could be so lovely, so caring, so engaging. He was so kind when I met him; so funny…'

'Oh God, Annie. I don't know what to say –'

Annie draws a huge shuddering breath. 'And he killed the lorry driver too.'

'But the inquest report said it was an accident blackspot, Annie. It could have simply been just that. And there weren't any witnesses, were there?'

'I saw him turn the wheel towards the lorry, Rosa. It's the last thing I remember—'

'Oh Annie. Have you let this out? You know I'd have shouted, screamed, thrown things—it's so therapeutic. You have to. It's part of grief—'

'Shut up,' says Annie. 'Please. Not now, Rosa. I think I need to be alone a minute.' She drops her head on her knees, and her whole body crumples. Then she is crying and crying and crying; weeping in great racking sobs as she has never done before. Tears pour through her hands onto her knees, and her whole body is shuddering.

Rosa hugs the bent shoulders, then gets up and tiptoes away.

Half an hour later Rosa brings tea over to where Annie is stretched out like a ragdoll in the garden chair.

'What you need, love, is a breath of sea air. There's nothing like the ocean to soothe your mind, put it all in perspective. You can shout it all into the wind, have the sea carry it away.'

Annie sips her tea and looks at Rosa out of swollen eyes. The idea of 'shouting it all into the wind' fills her with horror.

'I know you'll hate the idea. But the sea has the ability to dissolve anything put its way, you know . . . it really does . . .'

Annie puts her mug down on the arm of the wooden chair. Closing her eyes, she tips her head back against the high slats. She can't be bothered to go and find a cushion, but she's so thin now the chair hurts her. 'If I had the energy to go anywhere, then the sea would be nice. If I could just be spirited there.' She can feel the sun dappling her face through the apple blossom.

'Annie, I'm going to take you to Budleigh. No arguing, OK? You don't need to do anything, not even talk. You can just sit there. What about we finish our tea and you grab a sweater?'

Other than a couple of people walking their dogs and a scatter of gulls, the beach is virtually empty.

Rosa stoops to the smooth rounded pebbles. 'Look, Annie, each of these is a little artwork!'

'Oh Rosa, you're so positive. It would take more than a miniature artwork, or even a hundred of them, to inspire me right at this moment. All I can raise an interest in right now—and even that word is too active, demanding—is unconsciousness, oblivion. I don't care what shape it takes.'

However, she follows Rosa down the steep pebbled shelf towards the edge of the water, where Rosa bends to slip off her espadrilles. She twists the edge of her long red skirt into a coil and tucks it into her belt.

Annie concentrates on managing her limping leg and staying upright. She catches up with Rosa who is admiring the waves creeping over her toes, draping her feet with frills of brilliant green and carmine weed. 'Look at this pebble, Annie,' she says undaunted; 'the crescent of gold here and all those russet and mauve splashes on the dove-grey. Put it into your pocket; you need a talisman. There's something about beach pebbles that reminds me of babies, somehow; their moistness, the purity of their features. Do you see what I mean?'

'Mmmm-hmm', responds Annie non-commitally, looking off towards the horizon.

Rosa carries on wandering.

Annie turns back inland from the sea and sits down. After a moment she takes her moccasins off and stirs the pebbles with her feet. Several of them wear a delicate filigree tracery of peat-brown, jewel-red or emerald seaweed, feathery fronds plastered and dried onto the contours of the stones. Nowhere are there any corners or sharp edges on the beach; a continual complex flow of curves and waves. Even if you couldn't see the sea, you could tell it was a seascape, Annie thinks; no sharp edges around the sea. Especially on this coast; the red sandstone cliffs in the distance bordering the bay are clean sweeping shapes, defined without being angular, hollowed and scooped and rounded by millennia of water, winds, weather. There is a full-bodied femininity to them, devoid of the jutting serrations that a slate or granite landscape would offer. Rosa is a sandstone person, soft, warm-coloured, yielding, easily abraded. She thinks that she herself might be granite; enduring, hard-edged, radioactive in the fissures. Annie lies back and hunches her body against the pebbles until they have yielded to her contours. She can't get her body to relax. She closes her eyes.

Annie's ears are full of the mesmeric, sensual shush of the tide, the rise and fall, rise and fall, rise and fall. Against the hypnotic lull are set other sounds; the light percussion of pebble on pebble, the haunting cries of seagulls. In the distance is the occasional liquid melody of a small flock of oystercatchers. From somewhere out in the bay the faint pulsing drone of a motorboat reverberates around the cove; all of these noises woven as minor incidental threads, symphonic embroidery; and she and Rosa of no greater or lesser moment than the seabirds or the motor-boat. Mere specks on the edge of this bay, this very small section of the sea, like ticks, mites, on the ear of an elephant.

Already the sea is beginning to work her magic.

Annie is unfolding, little by little.

—*The ocean is a circle, thinks Annie, drifting somewhere between waking and dream,—a vast unbroken circle. Like that description of God—'a circle whose circumference is nowhere and whose centre is everywhere'. Or is it the other way round? An unbroken circle, arms stretched wide, holding all our separate little islands, gathering us together. Or maybe we're really so many breaking waves. In our concern about how and where we break we forget where we come from, what joins us. We think our wave is the ocean, our sentence the whole story.*

— *We are where the sea and the shore meet, she thinks*—neither one thing nor the other, but both. Some half remembered lines float through her head: 'Now wet, now dry, now fecund, now barren, now tossed, now caressed, standing or swimming.'

— *Swimming or drowning. We learn to swim or we drown. She can fill your blood or she can devour you, swallow you whole, spit out your bones.*

— *Am I going to choose to swim?*

When Rosa wanders back barely an hour later Annie emerges from a light doze.

'My God!' says Rosa. 'You're smiling! And you look like a mermaid there, sprawled on the pebbles, hair streaming over them. You see? Wasn't I right?'

EIGHT

Last night I woke up with your face, Greg. I put my hands up to my face, and they were your hands, and I touched your face. I was looking out into the dense blackness of night through your eyes. I screamed, and screamed and your voice echoed back at me through the chambers of my skull. I wanted to tear my eyes—your eyes—out of their sockets, rip off this alien so-familiar skin. I didn't sleep again. Where are you now, Greg?

Once we loved each other, Greg. Do you remember that first summer in the house? We had planted the trees, fruit-trees, our gesture of faith in the future, though then we still lived in the present. 'Our record' that summer was Eric Clapton's 'Ocean Boulevard'; do you remember the evenings when you would come to me and lean your lead against mine, and whisper: 'Won't you please read my signs / be a gipsy / tell me what I hope to find /deep within me . . . Read the stars for me Annie, read the stars for us.' I could tell you the movements of the planets and interpret their language.

And I would hesitate, because I knew you were only half serious; you were a scientist, you couldn't allow yourself to believe something that appeared to have no rational basis. And you would take my face between your hands and look me in the eyes, and say 'Go on, Annie, tell me how good it all is, how lucky we are.' You called me your 'energy cartographer'— teasingly, because you didn't use the word 'energy' the way I did. My way of course was half-baked. But it fascinated you. And you called me your gipsy.

And I would take out my ephemeris, and my chart of the summer sky, and show you where the planets spun in their orbits, explain to you the invisible webs they wove, the aspects they were making to each other, the angles that spelt harmony or dissonance. I would remind you as always that astrology is a sacred art whose maxim is 'as above, so below', and I would tell you what you wanted to hear. I would tell you you were articulate, charming, charmed; that you had a great future if you chose to specialise. I told you you were sexy as hell; I told you how lucky we were. We seemed to be, after all, so compatible intellectually, physically, politically. In those days we never stopped talking, sharing ideas and dreams. Besides, we loved each other, and we didn't need the stars to tell us that. You'd have your fingers in my hair, as if scared that you'd lose me to the heavens—perhaps just bloody possessive, that Scorpio moon. And you'd watch me with that half-smile, indulgent, tender, that drove me wild with fury—you loved that. I told you to lay off the alcohol; that addictions would be your downfall. That was a joke—in those days you hardly drank. And your cue, because you would murmur that you only had one addiction, and press your lips to mine and your body against me, and tell me how much I turned you on when I was being serious; and especially when I was looking cross. And after a brief struggle—that was part of the deal—I'd forgive you for patronising me, and overlook the significance of your difficult aspects to Neptune in Libra.

   I never told you that your Mars and Pluto were inauspiciously square both my Venus and my Mars, and that if I thought about it the violence symbolised by such an aspect scared me. I never told you that I knew we'd have no children together, either. I am not a fortune-teller—I try not to read the future. Though sometimes it speaks to me whether I invite it or not. But the stars; the stars map out present energy patterns in the cosmos, suggest tendencies, that's all.   Symbols. Why shouldn't we too experience those? As above so below. Hermes Trismegistus.

I am also a coward. I saw what I wanted to see. I told you—us—what we wanted to hear.

But one day you pushed me. You had taken in more than I'd assumed; when I thought you were indulging me perhaps you were actually listening. One Saturday you asked me what the next year looked like for you. You were twenty-nine; time for some big life-changes. Should you go for that consultancy? Should we take a year off, travel? I was washing up the breakfast dishes. I laughed and looked at you.

'I'm not a fortune-teller, Greg,' I put my dripping hands round your neck, kissed you. 'What do you want to do?'

You looked down at me, serious. 'You're my court astrologer, sweetheart. I want to know what I should do. Get out the charts, would you?'

I know I hesitated. I didn't want responsibility for your future thrust into my hands. Besides I'd been looking forward all week to our promised walk on the moor. But you insisted.

So I got out your chart. And what I saw was your father's imminent death; and as I saw it, so I realised that I knew all along. I must have blanched; I didn't know what to say to you. You stared at me. 'What is it, Annie?' I covered up, dissembled, looked at the rest of the chart, tried to find something to say. And you insisted and insisted. You were good at tenacity, persistence. You knew I was not telling you the whole truth. You looked at me straight, concerned. You reminded me of the total honesty we'd promised each other in the early days; that dishonesty wasn't just about lying, but also about not saying what was true.

Things are different for me now; I'm older now, I don't just have black and white vision as I did then. Sometimes the truth benefits from being filtered through compassion, from being refracted a little. You need to gauge your audience. Then again, who are we to decide what someone can or can't take? What arrogance. So now I try and walk the middle way.

Then, that day, you insisted, and I told you. I told you as gently as I could, but bluntly. How else can you do it?

He died. He did die. That's when everything changed. Five small words fractured our world, great purpling cracks. I was no longer the gipsy. Suddenly I was the witch. You held me responsible for your father's death. Oh, not rationally, of course, But in the chaotic, messy tempestuous places of the heart you believed it was my fault. As if I should speak and the heavens obey me! You started to look at me with fear, with dread, with loathing. I had forgotten; for after a while we patched up the cracks, plastered back our ceilings. But I think something went then, slipped away from us. Did either of us really want the truth? The Truth? Any truth? The whole naked uncompromised flat-wide-open truth, unsugared? 'Humankind cannot bear too much reality.' Suddenly we had become real, and there was nowhere to hide.

You never called me gipsy again. I never read the stars again, for you or for me. I didn't see your death in the heavens. I didn't look. You can't blame me for that, though God knows I blame myself enough. But that evening, Greg, that last dreadful evening, I knew. I smelt it. Blame it on the wind, the phase of the moon, call it intuition, call it paranoia.

I loved you once, Greg, more than I have hated you since. I am trapped by both. So I lie here and look at the clouds, look at the trees, look at a world happening outside my window. A world in which I cannot find my place any more. I don't know who I am, what I want, how to live. I no longer read the stars.

* * * * *

Outside Annie's front door, a motorbike draws up. Alex leaves it idling and remains sitting, propping the bike with long legs. He takes off his helmet and runs his fingers through his hair, hesitating. The house looks closed, impenetrable. It might as well be a fairytale castle in an impenetrable forest, shut tight upon a princess locked in the past, petrified, like Lot's wife. A hundred-year-old barrier of invisible brambles, and me without a machete, he thinks to himself. What's with all this fairytale stuff I keep remembering, he chides himself; you can take symbolism too far.

He smiles at the faint but clear note of a cuckoo—summer approaching fast, with all its warmth and ripeness. Things could shift, turn, in summer. In the distance he hears a stream, faint note against the distant motorway, legacy of twentieth-century living. The motorways have become our wasteland, he thinks. Time to pick up my campaigning reins again.

He looks at the house and tries to imagine Annie's life within it. Set back on the edge of Ide it's surrounded on three sides by a walled garden. He knows from having ridden past it before stopping that there is a small arched gateway leading into the garden from the side. The views at the back have to be wonderful, though the front presents an unreadable facade. It is old; nothing quite level or symmetrical. From the architecture it might at one time have been a toll-house, or a lodge for a now-extinct estate. The wall extends along each side of the front of the house; an ancient pear-tree swings branches out into the street, and climbing amongst them is the fresh green growth of a creeper, uncurling young leaves. It isn't a huge house, but surely too big for Annie on her own. He wondered if she's lonely; or if her general desolation over the last year has become amorphous, undifferentiated.

Still he hesitates. He hasn't intended to come out, but he knew after this morning's lecture that he probably would. Betty

Chadwick's course is, he knows, Annie's lifeline, her connection with the outside world. He knows she has caring friends and family, because she has spoken of them; but he doesn't like to think of the possibility of her being on her own on a sunny May day. Despite her surface coolness he is well aware how vulnerable she is. And he's a little concerned that she didn't show up today.

Without thinking, he revs the motor, as if the bike might make the decision for him. Then abruptly, for the second time, he turns away from Annie's proximity; and starts the short ride back into town.

From her bedroom Annie vaguely registers the sound of a motorbike lingering, revving and pulling away. She opens the window wider to hear the stream better over the noise of the traffic, then climbs back into bed. Against the welling backdrop of her bleakness, she hardly even notices the cuckoo calling summer.

NINE

Alex and Annie sit side by side in the lecture-hall. Through the open windows drift the sounds and smells of summer; distant voices, a strain of music, the gentle dull thwack of tennis-balls on racquets, the hum of a lawnmower and the accompanying green scent of freshly-cut grass. From against the one closed window, next to Alex, comes the tiny dry rustle of butterfly wings, rising minutely in volume and speed as the butterfly finds itself further imprisoned by the edges of a cobweb.

Alex quietly gets up and cups the fritillary in his hand, gently thrusting it out the window. Annie, finding it hard enough to concentrate with Alex's distracting presence beside her even when he is still, turns her head to look at his tawny hair curling over the collar of his old brushed-cotton shirt. A sunbeam licks his hair to flame, and Annie, not for the first time, wouldn't be surprised to see Alex emitting sparks. She forces her head and her mind back to the lecture.

This is Betty's last lecture of the summer term, and Annie is losing her thread. She shifts in her chair, resettling her leg, in plaster for the second time, and hot and itchy as well as aching. She longs to scratch it, plunge it plasterless into a cooling, rushing moorland stream. She frowns as a spasm of pain shoots down her calf.

Betty has been talking about the Grail legends and their continuing importance to the twentieth-century psyche. She has just come to the end of telling the story of Perceval.

'The quest for the Grail is a continuing quest; it is never truly over. I am an historian, not a philosopher, as you all know; but the meaning behind these stories fascinates me. I am told that the quest for the Grail is about the journey to consciousness, to wholeness, of the human being; or, dare I say, the human soul.'

Suddenly it seems to Annie that these words are for her alone. She's jolted awake.

'Self-realisation, as the psychologists would call it, or God-realisation if you are religious. It is not an event, but a process. The Grail is not an object to be found, but an understanding, an insight, patiently waiting, as the novelist Lindsay Clarke says, for our attention. There are locations in this world—and the mountain of Montségur, near Carcassone, of which I spoke last week, is one of them—where the spirit of the Grail seems to pulse almost tangibly in the landscape; along with all the pain and bloodshed and confusion associated with any quest for meaning.

'But the Grail castle is not an external place, either. The Grail is part of us, resides in each of us; only we can set it free, so that it may then in its turn liberate us, set us free like the waters which revitalise the Wasteland.

'There are, someone said, three paths to the Grail: the way of the Mind, the path taken by the knight Bors; the way of the pure Spirit, which was the one for Galahad, and then the third path, the Path of the Heart. My contacts in the fields of psychology and spirituality tell me that it is the path of the heart which is the one most needed in our society today. This is the path taken by Perceval. This has also been described as the Middle Way; the path through. Perceval does not set himself apart from society and relationships. Perceval takes the long, hard challenging journey towards self-realisation through the path of love, of relationship, with all its pain and pitfalls. So I leave you with this: take the Path With Heart. Or, in the words of that great man Joseph Campbell: *Follow your bliss.*'

Betty Chadwick coughs in a slightly embarrassed way and shuffles her papers. There is a resounding silence in the room, as the students simultaneously adjust their ears to the unaccustomed metaphysics from the reliably pragmatic Betty Chadwick, PhD, and take in and contemplate what she has said.

Annie is pinned to her chair. There is a choice to be made, and she knows it. The path she has always taken—safe and reliable. Or a new path, unknown, unsafe and with a completely unpredictable destination. One, sterile. The other creative—her creative work, her painting and weaving, at last?—and with no guarantees.

The way out is the way through . . . Perceval does not set himself apart from society and relationships . . . the path with heart. How do you even start to follow the path with heart? And something in her chimes suddenly with joy. Something seems to flutter, to unfold, the way things do when you suddenly stumble upon something important to you that you didn't even know was lost, but without which, you now realise, survival seems impossible.

Here is an answer, before she's even formulated the question. She feels Alex's eyes upon her, and for a long minute resists them. Then rather shyly she turns her face and looks at him. The world seems to hold its breath for a moment; blood rushes in her head and she feels the prickling of pressure behind her eyes. She can see a vein pulsing at Alex's temple, something veiled in his eyes. Then, so quickly she wonders if she's imagined the previous expression, his face resumes its usual open honesty that always makes Annie feel slightly uncomfortable, almost fraudulent. It is so naked somehow; so painfully direct it feels to her almost challenging. His eyes flare at her and there is a long moment in which question and answer, question and answer, fly unvoiced between them.

Annie feels something lift away from her in a huge sighing release.

Then the room erupts in applause and appreciation, and Betty Chadwick takes off her glasses and rubs her eyes.

'I should remind you,' Betty continues, 'that there are just one or two places left on next month's conference on the Cathars and the Grail in the Languedoc in the South of France. See me now if you're interested.' She bends to gather together her books and papers.

Annie's heart starts to thump painfully. 'Yes, NOW!' the universe seems to be shouting. 'Aren't you tired of this provisional living, this always holding back, this hollowness? Take a breath, jump!'

She stands, and hobbles up to the front of the room. There's a small press of students fingering the literature uncertainly.

She doesn't allow herself to think. She takes the clipboard and signs her name with the attached ballpoint with decisiveness, belied by her shaking hands. Betty notices, and puts a hand on her arm, and smiles into her face with an unusually personal warmth; she's not an unemotional woman, but as a rule keeps her lecturer's distance between herself and the students, bringing a brisk impersonality into her seminars and lectures. Annie smiles a little wanly at her, and then drops her eyes, feeling vulnerable.

There. It is done. No turning back. It is much more than just signing up for a conference, she suddenly knows. It is as if time has been sharpened to a point, as if the whole of her life has been concentrated and focussed on this one moment, as if everything has been designed to bring her to this brink. The landscape the other side of this moment is unimaginable, and yet irresistibly compelling. The room around her freezes for the briefest moment into a tableau, and then there is a bustle as time resumes and the room resolves into its usual human pulsing, like the minute hiatus between the diastole and systole of the chambers of the human heart.

Quietly, from behind her, Alex takes the clipboard and pen and signs his name in his bold flowing script underneath hers.

* * * * *

Annie is leaning forward over her coffee. A wing of hair swings over her eye. She pushes it back.

'Sandalwood,' Alex says.

'Hmmm? What?'

'You smell of.' He closes his eyes. 'Do you ever think how blissful it would be to give up consciousness indefinitely?'

Annie looks up. He still has his eyes closed.

Silence sits between them. Then Annie opens the subject gently, almost gingerly.

'What Betty was saying about taking the path with heart, following your bliss . . . I'm not entirely sure about it . . .is it merely self-indulgent? Selfish? What if, for instance, following your heart means hurting someone close to you, if your blisses don't coincide?'

For an instant Alex keeps his eyes closed. When he opens them, she sees the wary look again.

'My God, lady, that's a big question. I don't know either. I haven't resolved that one. I—sorry, Annie, I was going to be flippant.' He pauses. 'What's in my head, though, is *carpe diem*. Better to live one day as a tiger than a thousand years as a sheep.'

For a while neither speaks or moves. Alex stares at his hands. 'I'm not sure why I said that. All I know is that it makes sense, it *feels right*,' he continues. 'I don't mean do what you like and fuck the rest.' He looks up at her. 'I mean if you're not following your bliss then I suppose life can only be a hollow sham, an empty compromise. And I suppose too the people around you are suffering then as well from your lack of heart, and probably your suppressed resentment into the bargain. You're responsible for your own happiness. I mean we are each. Maybe we owe it to each other as much as to ourselves to sort out where it lies.' He pauses, reflecting.

'What I'm never sure about is how far you are responsible for other people, and their feelings. It's obviously not enough just to look out for yourself; but are you responsible for someone else's hurt at your actions? I never seem to be able to get this clear in my head.'

'Mmmm. Dunno. I think my feeling is that you are responsible *to*, rather than *for*, in relation to other people.'

'What d'you mean?'

'I mean you have to take responsibility in the way you act towards them; you are responsible for your behaviour, but not their feelings, your actions, but not their reactions. Otherwise aren't you playing at omnipotence, disempowering them?— that's how it seems to me, anyway.'

'Playing God, you mean?'

'Yeah, I suppose.'

'I hadn't thought of it like that. That makes it sound like supreme arrogance, assuming control over someone else's life. But if you detach yourself that seems so cold, so uncaring.'

'But it's not black and white, like that, really, ever, is it? It can't be uncaring to want the best for someone else, to *want* them to have the freedom to be in charge of their own lives, can it? I think we have to be really clear about our motivations.' He sighs and scrapes his chair back abruptly. 'It frightens me how often we call dependency love.' He's silent for a moment, looking away from Annie.

'What do you mean?'

'I mean that taking too much responsibility for someone else's wellbeing is unhealthy, dangerous even, for both people. Don't you think?'

'But love's *about* caring for someone! Caring that they're OK, that they're happy.'

'I don't think I mean that. I mean *you*—*I*—aren't in control of someone else's happiness. We might want it for them, but it's their right and responsibility to find it. Dependency and power games are miles away from real caring, real love, aren't they?—but we all seem to confuse the two so much of the time. Well, I do, anyway.'

'But that sounds like what you just said it wasn't: that we do what we like and damn the consequences. Regardless of other people's feelings?'

'No, no, not at all. I just think that caring for somebody's got something to do with supporting them while they look for their own answers, not thrusting yours upon them. That's what we're here for, isn't it? Working out stuff?—There are people who would say we come back time after time—I mean successive incarnations—until we get it right. Until we know some of the answers and things start to fall into place and we stop fucking up all the time.'

'Buddhism, you mean? Karma?'

'Yeah; but in the Christian church too. Betty's stuff. Gnostics. Cathars. They all believe that we're here to work out soul stuff; and we come back until we do. It's as if we live out a particular story that our soul creates through a number of different lives, different bodies that we wear.'

'Mmm? Tell me more?'

'Karma. Karma's a funny one, I think. Lots of people—I mean, it's easy to misunderstand it. It's not like a great cosmic chequeing account, earning credits or debits as some people seem to think. It's about knowing about cause and effect, and taking responsibility for the consequences of your own words and actions. You know: what happens tomorrow is because of thoughts, words, deeds of ours today.' He glances up at her.

'It also doesn't mean turning away because others' problems have nothing to do with you. Us, I mean. It means allowing people to work it out for themselves, but supporting them in their enquiry . . . So you travel alongside them. And maybe not for the first time, either; perhaps you draw to you, or incarnate with, certain people—maybe the same ones—time after time till you learn to listen right.' His eyes find hers. 'Am I talking bullshit?'

Annie shakes her head.

Alex looks down at his hands a moment. 'The least we can do is listen. And then—to get back to what we were talking about—walk alongside them, with honesty and integrity. Assuming you're behaving with the best intentions and with as much awareness as you can you've surely done all that's possible. Haven't you? If you're acting with care and compassion, what Buddhism calls metta, loving-kindness, then I don't see that you can go too far wrong.'

'God. I'm not sure . . . Well, I don't suppose that means that you won't ever hurt anyone again; but you're saying that if your intention is right, is compassionate, and you're not being brutishly insensitive towards them, then they have to take responsibility for their own hurt, even if you trigger it?—That seems very convenient. Too convenient.'

Alex thinks. 'Yes. I think I am saying that. But I know what you mean. I don't think it's ever quite that clearcut, of course; it's not an absolute truth. And you put sex into the equation, passion, marriage, and all this neat conceptualisation goes out the window.' There's a pause. 'Theories are fine, aren't they? But then rationalisation just bottoms out. But still; isn't it only when we begin to realise that we can choose how to react to any circumstance that we start to feel in control of our own lives, to feel free? Surely we would or should want that for someone we love? Call me an idealist, but isn't it only insecurity and fear and hubris that hold us back?'

Annie gazes at him. Alex takes a mouthful of coffee and runs his hands through his hair. He scratches his chin. From behind Annie in the kitchen someone drops a tray of crockery, and curses.

'Going back to where we started—I wonder if, when you know in your heart what the right thing is, that you just have to trust that ultimately it's the right thing for the people around you, too, even if it doesn't look like it at the time?' He laughs and goes on: 'Or maybe you're right; maybe that's a cop-out, just another fucking New Age justification for doing exactly what you want to do, no matter how many other people it screws up. I wish I bloody knew.'

He leans back and crosses his arms and sighs. The tension between them elongates, and for a moment the afternoon air fizzes, seems filled with static. Annie thinks of the fritillary, almost catches its colour on the air, the sound of wings. Then it's as if something snaps. Alex looks tired suddenly, flat.

Annie smiles uncertainly at him. She sees signs of stress around his eyes that she hasn't noticed before. He looks a little rumpled, too; his worn check shirt, in the mossy greens with thin contrasts of yellows and blues which suit his colouring so well, is missing the top button; she can see twists of copper chest hair and a slender leather thong against his collar-bones. The ends of his curls are caught under his collar; Annie fights an urge to stretch out her fingers and gently release them.

The noises from the room around them start to intrude again; the spell is broken. Alex seems subdued; Annie registers on his mobile face a fast-changing tide of emotions.

'Bloody hell, lady, don't know how we got there. Too much.'

'Alex I—it meant a lot to me that we could talk like we just did. Real talk, I mean, instead of just polite chatter . . .'

Alex suddenly leans forward, making Annie jump. With an urgency that takes her aback he seizes both her hands. 'Annie, my darling, it's time we talked properly.' He seems to be forcing his usual voice; the light-hearted casual affection that is his habitual tone with her chimes oddly with the intensity that she senses behind his words. 'There are other things that need to be said. I'll give you a call, OK?'

And then he is up and gone, swinging out through the canteen, weaving in and out of tables and chairs with the suppleness and speed of a water-animal, or a puma.

The glass doors at the end of the café bang shut, and Annie sits on alone with a cold cup of coffee gripped in her now-shaking hands, and her heart racing.

TEN

Alex doesn't call.

Instead something unspeakably awful happens. Annie receives a letter addressed to Mrs Hamilton—which in itself gives her a shock, for she has never taken Greg's name, always using her own name, Greenwood. The letter is typewritten; an old-fashioned typeface with a worn ribbon. The 'o's are clogged and solid. The letter is smudged and a little grubby, as if it's been sitting around a while. The postmark is Bedford, which means nothing to Annie.

'Mrs Hamilton.

You won't know me. There is something you should know. A year ago I had a baby. The father was your husband, Dr Greg Hamilton. He of course died just before my son was born.

I was a patient of his at the time. I am sure you realise the implications of this.

I know a lot about you and your marriage, and I know that I gave him what you didn't or couldn't—or wouldn't.

I have all his letters.

I need money. He had promised to provide for us—in fact we had talked of a future together. I need to hear from you within a month. Please write to C A Phillips at the above address.'

The address is Poste Restante, Bedford.

Annie reads the letter three times. Somehow she cannot make sense of what is being said. Her head is reeling and the words do not impress themselves on her brain. Her stomach is reacting, though; it feels scooped hollow suddenly. She feels her knees weaken; her unplastered leg seems to give way. She crumples, and something splits and separates in her; she sees her body sliding to lie stretched, bloodless, immobile on the slab of the kitchen floor. Her hands are trembling like an old person's, and the room is rearranging itself in front of her eyes. Her mouth is dry and she can hear a rhythmic rasping sound. Greg's face rears up before her, laughing, sneering, ugly with hatred as it was on that last evening, and she covers her eyes. She feels nauseous and her head is pulsing as if she has banged it. She realises she is sobbing loudly, a coarse racking tearing sound in her throat, like ripping canvas.

She gradually becomes aware that underneath her shock is a huge anger, bubbling like molten lead in the pit of her stomach and leaching slowly into her limbs. She listens to the rage, the white-hot rage, and her head starts to clear of everything else. She picks herself up off the floor – a small part of her brain is slightly embarrassed at her own melodramatic reaction, however private.

With the anger comes a slow tide of realisation. Of course. Of course. That would make sense of everything. The strange coupling that bound Greg and her, Annie, together indissolubly, that had seemed so like true recognition, love, soul-matching in the early days, and obsession later; Greg, with his strong sense of commitment, of loyalty, his stubbornness, his inability to give in and acknowledge failure, acknowledge when he'd got to the end of something, could never have left her, Annie. Better to take her down with him when he could see no other way out.

Annie's chilled. White rage. Terror. Fire and ice.

She reaches for the phone and dials Directory Enquiries. The familiar smooth plastic in her hand is somehow soothing;

the everyday action serving as a signpost, delineating the boundaries of reality, normality. Her heart is pumping so hard her whole body is shaking with it, and her voice is dry as she asks for the number of a C A Phillips. The operator asks for an address, and responds that since there isn't one it may take him a moment to go through the list. The line goes dead, and then half a minute later a recorded voice tells her in polite and stilted tones that sorry, no number is available. Annie, fired by her fury, rings again and asks for the number of the main Post Office in Bedford. Here she is told that yes, it is quite possible that there is a C A Phillips receiving mail at this address Poste Restante, but that they can tell her nothing else at all about it. Thwarted, Annie crumples inside again.

Half an hour later, when most of her tears have dried up, Annie tries to ring Rosa. There is no answer. She cannot call Alex. Who else can she speak to? What must be done?

She has never felt so alone.

She feels like Sisyphus—all year pushing an inhumanly huge boulder all the way up this stony, thorny, desolate mountainside, only to have it roll all the way back to the bottom, taking her with it. She cannot believe that only two or three days ago she was smiling, laughing, emerging from her forest, talking with Alex, planting seeds for a new way of living.

* * * * *

Annie is curled up on her side, numbly, with her plastered leg jutting awkwardly, in front of the fire, which, somehow, she has managed with an autonomous mechanical part of herself to light. It is June; there is no need for a fire. It is still daylight outside—a gentle warm evening. The curtains are closed.

But Annie has felt something inside her go out. Right now, she wouldn't care if the fire consumed her.

She has her head on her hand, in which is still clasped the letter. Dimly, at the edge of her mind, insistent as an unwelcome visitor waving from across the road, a remembered image is intruding, a story she heard once about the Aboriginal custom of bone-pointing. The bone is pointed and the ill-wished victim is disempowered, soul-stolen. Their will is hooked out of them, like a winkle on a pin; and there is no life without the will to live. Choiceless, they slide inexorably and hopelessly towards death, a gradual and increasing decline in their health and wellbeing the only manifestation of great inner devastation. Annie thinks that it must be like dissolving from the inside, and shudders. She feels bone-pointed.

Beside Annie is the phone. She has wailed, incoherently and terribly, at Rosa. Rosa, as Annie learns later, is in the middle of a crisis of her own with one of the children, has listened with increasing anxiety and dread to the sobs. Annie sounds as if she has finally cracked; Rosa feels helpless and horrified, she tells her. Only last week she had finally allowed herself to believe that Annie was at last out of the worst, through the wasteland. She had even started almost to shine, as she hadn't for years. Rosa had seen the beginnings of a new person cautiously emerging from the ashes; a whole new person. And now here is Annie inarticulate with grief and rage, and Rosa cannot leave the house; *sans* husband and car, temporarily, she is trapped. Annie will not leave her house; and besides the buses to and from Ide are rare enough in the daytime, let alone the evening. Annie has no car, since the accident write-off, and until her leg is out of plaster she couldn't in any case drive.

On the other side of the city Alex is sitting in a Friends of the Earth meeting. He has—for tonight at least—gritted his teeth and blanked out his turmoil, guilt and despair, and is fighting, too, against the tiny spark of exhilaration and freedom that has been trying to ignite his heart since he started to recognise and acknowledge that he cannot carry on as he has been. Not, that is, unless he is prepared to face soul-death.

This month's campaign is the plight of the last handful of European brown bears secluded—or trapped—in a tiny pocket of the French Pyrenees. They are threatened now by extinction in the name of 'progress'; by the driving of a huge multi-lane highway through their wild mountainous habitat, a high-speed tunnel connection between France and Spain. A small group of international activists is out there now fighting the Somport Tunnel, and in his imagination Alex is in campaigning mode, angry and passionate, out there with them.

He is self-aware enough to know that his identification with these marginalised bears springs partly from his own sense of being squeezed, his own fear of extinction. Maybe not in the literal sense, but suffocating still for all that it is an abstract and largely self-imposed state.

In less than a fortnight he will be on his way to the Pyrenees on a different quest. The synchronicity of this does not escape him. He knows he has reached a passage in his life where events and possibilities converge, a point where his past actions, thoughts and desires have collided and merged, the whole defining and deciding his present, and throwing this into sharp focus.

He feels he is on the brink of something huge, and that he is being offered choices and chances that may not come again. 'Two paths diverged in a wood . . .'

Alex has known for a long time that there are two ways to live—one safe, unchallenging and relatively risk-free; and largely joyless. One continuously risky, requiring an openness of heart and a willingness to live on the edge, be insecure and vulnerable; a way that guarantees nothing, where all waters are uncharted and all sands are shifting. A way that holds out no promises of success, or sanity, or even survival; and that holds out, too, simultaneously, the promise of everything, to he who dares. Alex is by nature a warrior, and for too long now he has lived the life of a sheep. No-one looking at the outside of his life would ever judge him to be anything other than a tiger, albeit a friendly one; but Alex alone knows what it feels like inside his skin, and when it really matters.

And then there is Kate, who haunts him wherever he turns, accusing, reproachful, tearful. And there are the children. This is where he arrives, every time. There is no road out of this forest.

Alex brings his attention back to the here and now, to this stuffy upstairs room in a backstreet pub, where to the drifts of beer and cigarette smoke rising through the floorboards they are all discussing the publicity campaign for the bears to which they are committing themselves.

ELEVEN

Rosa stands in her kitchen. Annie, who has found herself incapable of doing even the most trivial of tasks and hasn't eaten or slept for the best part of two days, is sitting where Rosa has almost physically deposited her half-an-hour earlier after collecting her by car from the hospital.

Annie has just had the plaster taken off for the second and final time. Ordinarily it would have been cause for major celebration; after all, it is now over a year that she has been in and out of hospital, plastered and unplastered. This time, as the plaster came off and the still fragile swollen and stitched leg was bandaged, Annie barely noticed, apart from a momentary surprise at the fact that she could still remember how to bend her knee.

Rosa's kitchen is a glorious glowing mess. Handfuls of shells and feathers and stones jostle with pottery mugs and jars and wooden bowls and implements on every available surface. Hung from every possible nail or hook or protrusion are huge ragged bunches of drying herbs or flowers. Books are piled haphazardly wherever there is a flat surface empty enough to take them. On the buttercup-yellow walls is a random collection of postcards, photographs, quotes and children's splodgy paintings in primary colours. A cork notice board, tilted at a rakish angle that Annie would have felt obliged to straighten had she felt more *compos mentis*, overflows with wedges and layers of notes, cuttings, leaflets, papers. Annie always feels a strange mix of things in Rosa's house; part of her loves the exuberance and chaos and warmth and mess—in it she could be whoever she wants to be; the house, like Rosa, was totally accepting of any state of being. And part of her feels completely overwhelmed and threatened by the total lack of even a gesture towards tidiness, order.

The Rayburn, turned down low because of the summer, is still the main source for cooking and hot water, and Annie is hunched in a chair beside it. On her knee is an undersized tortoiseshell cat, one of an indeterminate number of animals that share the house with the family. The cat is balanced somewhat irresolutely, as if unsure about Annie's reliability. Troika, the huge mongrel, pushes his nose into Annie's rather limp hand and then bounces round the kitchen. His tail knocks over some empty bottles standing near the back door en route, as they had been for weeks, for the bottle-bank, and Rosa bellows at him to get the hell out, which he does.

Even Annie's usual sense of exhaustion at the chaos and fever-pitch noise and action levels of Rosa's house is absent tonight. The heaving atmosphere holds her firmly in its grip, so that there is little space for brooding. Rosa has music on in the background, and from next door come thumps and waves of shrieks and bellows and high-pitched laughter as the twins and younger Dan invent some new and extremely boisterous game.

Rosa, whose normal *modus vivendi* is one of perpetual motion like a bright exotic butterfly, is poised briefly at the outsize freestanding heavy duty chopping board that abuts the work-surface. She is deftly cutting up red, orange, yellow vegetables, all the colours of summer to accompany the dips she has made. She smiles as she slices peppers and carrots and arranges them on wooden plates with tortilla chips and cubed cheese. 'Hey, Annie, you should try wearing these colours instead of those cool ones you always wear. Lift your spirits.'

Rosa clears a space on the huge kitchen table and puts down the vegetables, then fetches the dips she's already prepared—salsa, mustard and pimento, hummus and yoghurt with garlic and herbs—out of the fridge. Annie sees the love and concern in her eyes, but cannot at the moment respond.

From the next room Dan yells and then bursts into wails. Rosa wipes her hands on her jeans and rushes out of the room. Annie carries on stroking the cat rhythmically, mechanically, oblivious to its uncertain purring.

The meal is conducted in a flurry of noise and activity. Sometimes Annie is drawn out by the presence of the children; tonight, she remains untouched and abstracted, despite the efforts of Rosa and the quieter Marcus, until Dan climbs onto her knee after supper to tell her about his new socks and pants, and about how Troika has chewed his trainers.

'And do you know, Auntie Annie, Simon says I can have a go on his c'puter if he can have one of my baby gerbils! And Daddy's going to take me on a steam train on Sat'day! Have you ever been on a steam train?'

Annie holds Dan tight and breathes in the fresh smell of clean child's hair. Rosa gets up to sort out the twins for bed. Annie hugs Dan, and Marcus stands to wash the dishes.

A big, gentle man, Marcus has the kind of presence that Annie ordinarily finds soothing, and that is the perfect foil for Rosa's livewire nature. A physicist, Annie finds him fascinating on the occasions when she manages to engage him in conversations about his work, and he constantly surprises her with his offbeat rather satirical humour. Nonetheless, she still feels after all these years that she doesn't know him well, and tonight her reserves of politeness completely fail her. Her heart sinks when Rosa disappears upstairs with Dan. There is an uncomfortable silence while Annie wonders how to follow Rosa upstairs without it being obvious to Marcus that she is escaping from her discomfort at being left alone with him.

With his back to her at the sink, Marcus astonishes her by saying: 'Annie, Rosa told me about your trouble. I hope you don't mind. You must be feeling terrible about it.'

There's a long pause while Annie digests this. She has almost never heard Marcus make a personal remark of this nature to anyone. That he adores both Rosa and his children is obvious, he is an affectionate man, but he doesn't easily participate in emotional conversations.

And is he referring to the recent letter, or Annie's sense that the 'accident' was actually deliberate? Deciding that he must mean the letter, she feels both touched, and slightly embarrassed, and takes refuge in trivialising banality.

'You mean the letter? Well yes, everything's a bit much at the moment. But I was depressed, anyway; one more thing shouldn't make that much difference.' She pauses and then adds: 'I've been aware recently that I've missed out on children myself; I guess that's made it a bit more painful.' How funny, she thinks. I didn't realise that's what really hurts until I said it.

Marcus dries his hands and turns round to look at Annie. He grunts reflectively and bends to the drinks cupboard. He waves his hand towards it in an enquiring sort of way and pours himself a whisky.

'Scotch, Annie?'

She nods. 'Please.'

Marcus mixes it strong and adds ice. 'It's not my business, Annie, and perhaps I shouldn't stick my nose in, but don't give in to this woman. Call her bluff. Don't let yourself be blackmailed.'

'But if what she says is true—and since she knows my name and address and about Greg's death and everything I think it must be—I can't see what else I can do but respond. Even with Greg dead it could cause a lot of damage to the practice and his colleagues, and I couldn't bear the papers to catch it. It's all been—oh, such a shock, devastating really, coming so much later. I can't think how to handle it at all.' Her face tightens; talking about it brings her close to the edge and she can't bear to break down in front of Marcus.

Marcus comes over and pats her shoulder.

'Greg might have been a shit, Annie, and if—IF—he did this to you he must have been. But he wasn't an indiscreet shit. I don't believe she has any letters; and I wouldn't mind betting she has no proof at all that he had any intention of setting up house with her. She may not even have a child; or not his, anyway. I think she's trying it on. Hold firm.'

Annie bends her head to her drink and fights back tears. She swallows. Her mind has churned this round and round for days; now one thing seeming right, now another. Each time, all she is left with is the incontrovertible fact—presumably—that another woman has Greg's baby, and she has never known.

That the woman might never have had a baby at all, or that if she did, it may not have been Greg's, has not occurred to her. (And if that were the case, what motivation—other than drink and aggression, of course, which might be enough of an explanation—was there for his seeming final act of vengeance?—But this was too much to think about all at once.)

She lets this new possibility sink in. Around the huge bulk of this latest crisis she suddenly sees a tiny distant flicker of light; an outline, the merest candle-flame of hope. What if Marcus were right? She straightens her back.

'Hey, almost the old Annie! A touch of your old fighting spirit there?'

'Hey, you two,' says Rosa, coming in, 'what's happened? It doesn't feel like a morgue in here any more—Annie, you look almost cheerful!'—and she beams in gratitude and love at Marcus and goes over and hugs Annie.

The Annie that Rosa drives back to Ide at eleven that evening is still quiet, untalkative, but something has changed, relaxed.

As she turns to hug Rosa goodnight before opening the car door, she smiles into her eyes and says: 'I don't know how I would have survived the last year without you. You and Marcus, too; and the children. Thanks, Rosa.' She touches her head briefly to her friend's and gets out. As Annie shuts her front door she barely registers the sound of a motorbike pulling up.

TWELVE

Annie opens the door to the knock. For what seems like an eternity Alex and she stare at each other under the white light of the ancient street lamp. Neither can find a voice.

Annie sees a drawn face and agitated eyes under wild tangled curls, the colour stolen out of them by the pale light.

Alex's mouth is dry and his fists clenched, his heart hammering. *I shouldn't have come*—his mind is jabbering, freewheeling, *what the fuck am I doing here? And now it's too late to turn back; I've declared myself by being here. Fantasy turns into reality in the blink of an eye and everything's changed between one breath and the next. Even if I leave now we can never go back to the way we were. The only way out is through.* He swallows and thrusts his free hand through his hair.

The familiar mannerism tugs at Annie, and she feels her initial stunned shock at Alex's arrival turn into something else. She is suddenly aware that she has been expecting him; that here, her present and her future collide with an impact like that of speeding planets. Her heart is thumping wildly, and she is unable to move or speak.

She notices that their hands are shaking, and her lips tremble. She presses them together.

And then in an instant they are in each other's arms, and Alex's dropped helmet rolls across the floor and bangs against the hall chest and his mouth is on hers and his hands in her loosened hair.

Later Annie does not remember how and when it happened, at what point the unspoken question and response flew between them, the tacit acknowledgement and agreement. But she is in his arms and there is a stabbing pain in her heart and then a warmth spreading through her chest like something unfolding, and a beat in her pelvis that eclipses and displaces everything else, even the insistent critical voice in her brain that says she should stop, forbid, immediately and forever, this crazy wild dance that she can feel in her blood. Alex is kissing her neck urgently, hotly, and she can feel him hard against her lower belly through her skirt. All resistance seeps out of her and once again her knees threaten to give way. Alex catches her and lifts her with his arms behind her knees, smiles down at her a brief moment in some irony, and strides down through the dim hallway, hesitates, and then pushes open the sitting room door with his back and elbow. He stumbles briefly and lowers her heavily and carefully onto the sofa. Annie feels herself put her arms up to reach for his neck, and brings his face towards hers. She can hear Alex's agitated breath in tandem with her own. Then the phone rings and the moment is frozen as their lips stop an inch away from each other's, and the displaced feelings—guilt, caution, vulnerability, apprehension—make their size felt. The flood of them intrudes into the space made by the joy of unpremeditated connection with another human being whose nature and impulses and desires, for however brief a moment, fit exactly with one's own.

Annie, shocked out of her rare moment of abandonment of self by the phone's intrusion, lets it ring several times in the hopes that it will stop. As it shrills on, she's unable to stop herself reaching over for it.

'Annie? Are you OK?'

Rosa. Annie draws a breath, shakily. She finds her voice, and is aggrieved to hear it come out as a rather trembling squeak.

'Absolutely fine, Rosa. fine. Why?'

She glances at Alex's head, resting lightly next to hers on the arm of the sofa. He makes a face at her and puts a hand up to stroke her cheek and she closes her eyes. *Very fine.*

'I just had a feeling. I think a guy on a bike pulled up at your door as I left and I just wanted to check you were all right.'

Annie smiles to herself and the heat flares again as Alex strokes a fingertip down her breast under her shirt. She catches her breath. She doesn't know whether to thank Rosa or scream at her. Instead she just tells her that she'll ring in the morning, and that she feels much better after her evening with them all. She puts the phone down.

Despite herself, the imagined scene at Rosa's intrudes on their intimacy. She can see Rosa at her end wrinkling her nose at the dead receiver and frowning at Marcus.

'She sounds strange. I think something's afoot. I don't know whether to be worried or not. Do you think I should be?'

Marcus grins his slow grin at her. 'You're just nosy as hell, Rosa. Why shouldn't she have a lover? That's the most likely explanation. Did she sound as if she was being held at gunpoint or anything?'

Rosa will think about Marcus' words. She has to admit that Annie didn't sound as if she were in trouble. But she did sound a little breathless. Marcus is probably right. He usually is about such things. It just hasn't occurred to Rosa as a possibility, and Annie hasn't mentioned anyone. But then, she probably wouldn't. Rosa will decide, Annie thinks, that if she wants to sleep tonight, a slight huffiness at her friend's reticence—not to say downright secrecy—about a possible love affair is a better bet than probably needless worry and anxiety about her wellbeing.

And here in Ide, the moment is broken, and Annie stands to open a bottle of wine. It's late, but she has a feeling that this might be a long night, and she needs to do something to cover her agitation and confusion and to give herself time to digest what is happening.

Alex watches her back rather distractedly and pushes out of his mind his last dreadful scene with Kate. Never again. He has done it now. This is it: the beginning of his new life, with all its uncertainties and all its possibilities. 'Do you know,' he says on impulse to Annie's back, 'I guess I didn't really doubt that I'd be welcome here—' he laughs at himself a little sheepishly '—but I need to tell you how—' he pauses—'just how amazing it is, to be here with you. Just—the joy. The enormity of it—'

It is four o'clock in the morning. Annie and Alex are half-propped against Annie's pillows, legs interlaced and heads touching. Through the curtains is the gentle bubble of the stream, and occasionally the voice of an owl. The candle, burnt to a stub, flickers tenuously in the breeze from the open window. Alex has his hand on Annie's thigh.

'What happened with you tonight is a completely new experience. I don't know how to speak about it.'

For Annie, too, this is more than just a turning-point, a celebration; it feels like a rebirth. Five short hours, and now no maps, no stars to steer by and no histories to learn from.

And they have talked, and talked, and talked. Annie has talked of Greg, and her despair and loneliness, and the recent shock from Bedford, and she has cried, and laughed, and it feels to her as if she has exhausted the whole spectrum of her emotions and exorcised a year's worth of largely unvoiced pain and grief in a few hours.

Alex has talked to her for the first time of Kate and his marriage, of the pain and guilt he feels, of his certainty that he cannot go back except to collect his belongings, of his anguish about the children, and of the increasing strength of his feelings for Annie. He tells her of his regrets about lost years, lost political convictions, lost opportunities; about the lost love of his teenage years who left him so numbed and careless about his future that Kate's need of him sucked him in. He speaks of the horror he has hardly admitted to himself at so many years trapped by her feelings, her dependency on him.

Annie knows that he must be having to close his mind to what he'll guess Kate must be feeling, alone in her bed in the thin-walled terrace, no doubt sleepless and brimming over with desolation and anguish.

Annie, too, closes her mind to what she knows must be called adultery; holds her thoughts tightly shut against the knowledge that Alex has a wife, who right now is probably hurting badly. She cannot begin to think of it in moral terms. Not now, not tonight. There will be plenty of time for guilt and self-judgement, self-reproach, no doubt, in the harsh light of day, when they will need to deal with the consequences and implications of what has happened tonight. For now, for once, she will just flow, be wholeheartedly here in this precious moment. She feels intoxicated, transformed; somehow all the pain of the last twelve months has had the sole purpose of bringing her to this point.

The candle gutters one last time and goes out, and Alex leans over and finds Annie's mouth once more in the dark, and together they cast themselves onto the mindless ocean that swells between them, connecting them, caressing. Later, they will doze, entangled, a light and joyful if intermittent sleep from which each will surface momentarily and only half-conscious, delighted and amazed by the continued presence of the other. Let the morning come, with its questions and accusations and need for decisions and confrontations; if that be the price for this night, so be it.

Initiation
France

'Mortals have on their faces
An invisible mask which
Matters more to them than their lives . . .
But the eternal Gods
Rub their faces in sweat and tears
And change them into what they are'
René Nelli

THIRTEEN

Alex pulls the VW over, leans across to kiss Annie's eyelid, waits till the road in his rear-view mirror is clear, and reverses at speed, turning off at the junction they had just overshot.

'Are you up for a little picnic, lady? I thought a bottle of fizz and some exotic delicacies . . . and a siesta, perhaps?'

Annie smiles and puts her hand on his knee, and gives herself over to sheer sensuality. Ahead of them now the distant mountains back of the Mediterranean are washed with a purple-blue haze; acre after acre of lavender against the softening gold-and-rose of the sky. The air is scented so strongly she almost feels that, were she a different and less inhibited kind of person, she could roll in it; lavender, salt and an indefinable tang which might just have been foreign soil; slightly resinous, hot and intoxicating, inviting. After the candyfloss pink flamingos, after the astonishingly bright seascape bordered by ochre grasses and little lagoons, after the foam-white Camargue mares with their sooty and charcoal foals, Annie finally starts to believe that she is here, and allows herself to relax into pleasure; for once to slide momentarily into an expanding present. She feels herself pull off both her Englishness and her past, as she might step out of a set of constricting city clothes.

* * * * *

Alex wriggles his arm gently free from under Annie's neck and flexes his fingers, cramped from being bent motionless against the hard, scratchy lower stems of a lavender bush. For ten minutes he has lain with Annie's dozing form pressed against his, struggling with two contrary impulses. The first is quite simply a desire to carry on lying there with Annie's breath on his cheek forever, into oblivion. The second is the near-unbearable mental itching, common to anyone who uses words to make their way in the world, caused by a wild ferment of images-becoming-language demanding immediate expression on paper.

Alex has lived with the demands of the inspirational impulse long enough to know that until he has opened the channels for the words to flow, satisfied the muse, he will not be able to relax. Besides, there is the same fever-hot excitement burning through him as he had felt that day in the library—the verge of something precious. He can feel himself holding his breath. Peak moments nearly always tore him apart like this—to experience the moment to the full by merely being with it?—or to capture it on paper before its magic evaporated, took the sheen off ordinary things which had been transmuted momentarily into extraordinary happenings by this intensity, this otherworldliness?

Stumbling, he half-creeps, half-runs over the baked, stony, umber earth to the van to fetch his notebook, praying that Annie will sleep on for a while on the blanket he'd spread for them. The beauty of the landscape, the completeness he feels in that moment and the creative fire burning through him have left him light-headed, almost intoxicated. Lowering himself slowly, noiselessly, back onto the blanket he glances at Annie and opening the notebook, lets the words flow, without direction, without thought, without concern about their literary value. Simply to write is enough—a record, if he should ever need its warmth, of a perfect moment.

* * * * *

I had the dream again last night; I woke sweating. Not sure if I screamed out loud or not; I felt the scream sour and cutting against my tongue but Alex was still asleep. Terror; like looking into a vast black hole in the centre of the earth, falling and falling. Then the impact. In my dream I was burning; I could feel my flesh crackling and blistering. Greg was there. No, he wasn't; Greg's eyes were there. They were iceblue, expressionless and transparent. And I could see his mouth; his mouth was open, like after the accident, and he was spewing bile. After that everything went black; flickering and sliding like an old monochrome silent movie at the cinema. Like being suspended on the edge of a cliff, knowing that the sandstone is crumbling under your fingers and there is no-one, anywhere, to hear you fall. I woke up gasping for breath.

Greg's been with me all day. I can't tell Alex; he has enough demons of his own from his past, though he doesn't talk about them. Or hasn't yet, anyway. Besides, it's too awful to voice; talking about it would give it more weight, more solidity even that it already has.

Thank God Alex's eyes are warm; greeny-hazel and smiling, even when he's serious. They're reminding me of something. As I picture them, I think about this and suddenly the image of a Dartmoor stream tumbles into my head, clear as a photo. When I was a child we'd spend most of our summer days on Dartmoor ('If you already live in paradise, why seek it elsewhere?' my father would repeat each time we—my mother, my sister and I—suggested travelling out of the county, out of the country, even.) In my mind's eye it's sunny—remembered childhood holidays usually are, of course. And in the sun the peaty-gold dappled streams glow and twinkle as if they have secrets to divulge if you can just learn to be still long enough. I suppose that they must always have been cold, even in the summer, but I associate them with warmth and peace and a *kind of laughing vibrant energy. They're a different matter in winter, of course, in spate; I have yet to see Alex, or his eyes, 'in spate'.*

I feel overcome, suddenly, by nostalgia; more—a kind of desperate agony of longing for a childhood I haven't thought of for years. A flash-flood of memories. Endless summer holidays; cheese and pickle sandwiches, ginger pop, paddling and lying on hot granite boulders in slow shallows, 'daring' rock-leaps across narrow faster brooks. Dartmeet; the O Brook; Cranmere Pool, bleak and creepy, where so many of Devon's rivers start as an ooze in the peat. Ants in the hamper and wasps around the jam sandwiches. Driftwood fires at the seaside on the rare occasions when my mum could be persuaded firstly to go to the beach at all with the hordes of holiday makers, and secondly to stay past my bedtime. Pony treks (one, anyway; with my best friend Lucy) and letterbox hunting on the moor before many people knew of the letterboxes. No responsibility, no intimation of how it is to be adult. Someone else would pack the picnic, offer you dry clothes, kiss it better if you cut your toe.

I feel guilty about bringing my nightmares, my terrors, with me. These last few days with Alex have been so magical; I couldn't wish to be anywhere else with anyone else.

Tomorrow we'll have arrived and the conference begins the next day; how amazing to share it with someone I can respect as well as love, someone who not only loves me but is as interested in what is ahead of us as I am. I'm so used to not sharing these things that are important to me. And this has been a kind of Garden of Eden time; an unrepeatable few days where we've been almost hermetically sealed up with what is between us, and no-one to interrupt or take it away. It's been timeless; apart from my night-terrors no future, no past, just an ongoing present. I don't know when I last lived like this—

perhaps never. I'm always so tied up in what has happened, what might happen, what should happen, and my agonising over it all.

From Monday we'll be public again; no-one we know unless some others of Betty's students signed up after we did, but no longer this walled orchard we've created for ourselves in our travelling together from England. And then, after, time apart for a while; Alex to fight his environmental battles, me to rest and maybe I'll dare to paint again, once I'm at Susie's place. I'm anxious about that time without Alex, but of course I shan't tell him; shan't tell anyone. There's so much in each of our lives that is unresolved. It's all been such a rush; thank God, because if I'd stopped to think I don't suppose I'd have come. So we've held it all at arm's length: the crises, the guilt, the consequences. I suppose there will come a day of reckoning when we can avoid it no longer, when it will catch up. But not yet; please not yet.

I'm anxious, too, that when I have finally got the space to paint I shan't be able to; I shall lose my inspiration, lose any talent I thought I once had, sit with a blank canvas and a blank future ahead of me. Or worse, lose my nerve and run back to England, spend the rest of my life instructing endless streams of new undergrads in how to deconstruct the American novel, pick clean the bones of the New Generation poets. Oh God.

Why can't I just live for the moment; feel Alex's breath on my cheek, smell the lavender and salt-air, appreciate the colours and the landscape and the wine and the olives and the freedom without deconstructing those, without waiting for them to be taken away, without seeing Greg's eyes—or— just as bad—Kate's imagined eyes—over Alex's shoulder?

I just want to sleep, and sleep, and sleep; really sleep, without any dreams, and wake refreshed beside Alex, with all our loose ends, all our unravelling pasts, neatly knitted up.

* * * * *

As the lapis-blue summer night drops over the land they drive towards Carcassone, rising against the mountainous backdrop with the ochre containing walls of the old city floodlit and spectacular against the night sky. Annie holds her breath; from this distance the new town that she knows has all but engulfed the mediaeval one is below, in the shadows, street-lit but not eclipsing the old city, which rose into the night almost as if floating.

Through the open van windows come the incessant creak of cicadas and the hot fragrance of a Mediterranean July dusk. There is no need to fill the space with more words, for the air between them is already saturated, and no doubt will be again before long. Alex is quietly humming the melody to himself for *Lento;* the words are still to come, but he can feel them incubating. He is in no hurry to force them. He can feel the prickling of a huge creative ferment somewhere inside; the words, when they come, he knows, will be exactly right; soaring words to match the waterfall of the music.

Annie is gazing dreamily out of the window; content, at peace, mindless. Then, without warning and for the briefest second, something strange happens; time splits and she finds herself simultaneously standing on a parapet inside the walls looking out, and sitting beside Alex in the van looking towards the city. She has a disturbing flash of dislocation; out of the corner of her eye she sees herself robed in dark blue cloth from neck to toe, rough and thick against her hand. Her feet are wet and muddy and wrapped in some kind of hide; goatskin, perhaps. There is a noise in her head like a high wind and she feels herself falling. Alex swerves to the verge and slams on the brakes and catches her as she falls sideways, peering at her in alarm. He switches on the interior light and Annie feels a pull in her solar plexus and the moment has passed. She sits up; her face feels clammy and slightly tingly. For an instant strange hieroglyphs seem to be dancing in front of her eyes; triangles, squares, intersecting lines. After a moment the shapes resolve themselves into a distinct symbol; an equal-armed cross, with each end tipped by a small sphere.

'Annie? What the bloody hell happened there? You gave me such a fucking shock, sweetheart! Are you OK?'

She laughs shakily and puts her hands to her face. Alex is looking at her with concern and bewilderment. He reaches up and touches her forehead. She is sweating. He brushes back a strand of damp hair.

'Holy shit, Annie my darling, I thought you'd fainted at the very least; in fact for a dreadful second I'd thought you'd vaporised or something; you almost weren't there! Perhaps you could warn me next time—do you do this often?'

'Sorry Alex; sorry I frightened you. I don't know what happened—I can't explain it, I thought I was falling. I wasn't sure where I was. Perhaps I'm tired.' She turns and gives him a weak smile. He kisses her and puts his arms around her.

'Don't do this to me Annie; I've only just found you. I'm not ready to let you go yet. Are you OK now? Anything you need?'

She shakes her head and holds onto him. 'Just you.' She smiles into his eyes and banishes the symbol.

They had intended to stop at Carcassone and find something to eat, but as they approach the outer buildings of the modern town clustered around the fortified walls Annie feels her heart beginning to thump wildly.

'No, Alex. We can't stop here, not now, not tonight,' she says in her panic. Her throat feels constricted.

Alex glances at her in incredulity. 'What do you mean, we can't stop here? You've talked of nothing else but your attraction to Carcassone all day! I thought it was as much the idea of visiting it at last as the conference itself that appealed to you!'

Annie's knuckles are white, gripping the edge of the seat. She is upright and tense. Her face in the near-darkness looks gaunt and shadowed. Alex feels vaguely annoyed, but more concerned and confused.

'I can't explain it, Alex,' she says again, weakly, apologetically. 'It's not that I don't want to—I'm desperate to visit it, it pulls me like a magnet. I just have this really strong feeling that we mustn't go in tonight, by night. Please. I need to come back by day. It's really important, Alex. Please just try and trust me.'

She looks at him pleadingly. He must think she was crazy; that strange episode, and now this. She knows it is totally irrational; how can she expect Alex to act on her whims, particularly as they were so contradictory? And she has no idea why the idea of going into the town, so hugely attractive to her, makes her feel as if she were suffocating. She can't bear even to look at the looming walls, suddenly. She closes her eyes. She feels utterly, utterly weary, drained, empty.

Beside her Alex sighs, and slows the van resignedly.

'I don't pretend to understand you, lady. I love you; but I'm beginning to think you're an absolute fruitcake. I don't know what the hell's going on in your head, but if it's that important to you, we'll by-pass the town and pick up the road for Foix. OK? We'll come back another day.'

Annie prises her hands off the seat-edge and drops back in her seat. She is still breathing fast and her heart is racing, but now that she knows they're not going into the town she can open her eyes and look at it again. In the blue dusk the new town crouched untidily at the feet of the walled city no longer exists for Annie. In her mind, the ancient walls are transparent and she can see the exact layout of the old town quite clearly; she knows every alley and doorway, the shape and wear of the steps, the texture of the walls. High in the town, in a tiny round top attic, a woman is binding with leaves of some sort the wounds of an older, unconscious, man; his face is hollowed in the flickering light from tapers, and against the roof-angle a nest of swallows is settled for the night. A breeze blows through the unglazed window-slit, and lifts the covering over the woman's dark hair . . . unbearable pain, unbearable . . . *Don't look* . . .

Annie grips her mind hard. She grits her teeth to stop herself calling out. Unable to prevent herself, she puts her hand up to her hair. It feels, as always, thick, cool, glossy. No head-covering. Surreptitiously, she glances down at her clothes, feels the familiar canvas of her jeans, the soft silk of her loose pearl-blue T-shirt, sees her new sandals, bought in Morlaix market on the morning they landed in Roscoff. Twentieth century clothes. Alex is right, she needs her head examining. She turns her face away from the town and puts her hand on Alex's knee, in gratitude, for comfort, for reassurance; and forces herself to smile at him. She can't mention what is going on for her, and she desperately needs distraction. Perhaps this is it; the big crack-up.

She forces her voice and pushes all thoughts of Carcassone out of her head. 'I'm starving. Shall we stop in the next town and find something to eat?'

'If that's what you'd like to do, my darling. Then if we drop down towards Quillan we might be able to find somewhere to park up: I think there was some woodland on the map, and the river must be nearby. Can you have a look?'

'Alex?'

He throws her a questioning glance. His smile is back. She feels something start to uncoil again. Alex has a knack of making her feel totally accepted, totally loved. She had not thought a relationship could feel so much like freedom. She feels her breathing slow and her heart quieten. She lets her limbs relax. *Careful,* says the habitual little cynical voice inside her. *It's early days. You don't really know him. How about when you have to deal with the real world again? How about when the time comes when you want to do one thing and he wants something totally different? How about when he can't run away from his guilt and his family any more? Shut up,* she says to it firmly. *I'm learning how to live in the present.*

'I love you, Alex.'

She switches on the van's interior light and studies the map, curling her limbs under her so that she can lean close enough to feel the warmth from Alex's body. Without taking his eyes from the road, he bends his head to touch hers lightly.

'I love you too, sweetheart.'

And drives on, south into the Languedoc night.

That night they hold each other close and listen to the river from under the trees for a long, long time. When finally Annie falls asleep she has the first dreamless night she can remember since emerging from the coma.

FOURTEEN

There is a huge crash from outside, a clap of thunder, and everyone in the room jumps. Annie, sitting beside the window, looks out. In the distance the great mauve peaks of the Pyrenees rise in wave upon petrified wave towards the sky, which is a strange luminous greenish colour, pale and eerie.

The mountains gather to themselves dramatic electric storms occasionally in summer, Annie remembers someone telling her. Born from a day of intense heat and clarity, without warning around the middle of the day the sky changes colour. Without actually darkening or clouding there is a vast exchange of light and sound chasing each other round the peaks, flashing and rumbling.

Annie shifts, unsticks herself from the wooden chair which had been all the seating left when they reached the conference. Aware that the very precious time they have spent solely in each other's company is about to come to an end for the moment, they have found themselves dawdling on this their last morning in transit. To stop travelling now is paradoxically to move on; to change states, to open their private garden to others. Though looking forward to the conference with anticipation and excitement, neither wants to cross the threshold out of their new world.

The last day in their sanctum, she'd thought to herself as she had lit the gas-stove just after daybreak that morning and pulled the van curtains to let in the sparkling mountainous landscape.

They'd eaten last night's bread with butter and apricot jam, and brie with fat black olives, accompanied by coffee from the new cafetière and the huge green and gold cups they had bought in a Provençale market, along with half a dozen plump amber-green *reines claudes* which Alex had taken down in one hand to wash in the river.

Annie loves Alex's hands. Large, strong hands, they have a delicacy of action in which a surgeon would have taken pride. Like the rest of his frame, they are spare without being bony. He uses his hands a lot when he talks; Annie finds them quite erotic. She'd watched him prowl back up the gentle slope towards her with bare, wet feet, and had felt a powerful rush of desire for him. As he'd held a greengage out towards her mouth, Annie had sidestepped the fruit and slid her arms around him and put her lips to his neck, his eyes, his mouth.

Half an hour later, clothes discarded long ago, the sun's rays were fingering the tops of the nearest peaks. Annie had become conscious that though they were secluded in a remote spot, the black- or navy-clad rural inhabitants would be likely to be on their way to tend sheep or goats or cows or cut armfuls of foliage for fodder. She'd stirred and looked down at their naked bodies, intertwined. How far she had come, she'd thought, in just a year. Lifting herself on an elbow she'd smiled into Alex's eyes. The new light was illuminating the flecks of amber and nut-brown in his greenish irises.

'What's the time?' he'd asked lazily, as she stood up. 'Come here, you gorgeous thing.'

Annie had stepped lightly back, but held out her hand. 'Just time for a quick swim in paradise,' she'd said. 'Coming?'

Subsequently, they arrive too late to install themselves in the more comfortable chairs. The Great Hall of the Manoir is packed full; Annie guesses at 200 people at least, plus the speakers. The latter are seated at the front, on a dais, with microphones. The conference is for the most part to be conducted in French, in which Annie is fluent; Alex less so, but could make out the gist, and as often happens understand a lot more than he could speak. A couple of the speakers, from Britain and America, are speaking in English. All the lectures are to be transcribed into several languages at the end of each day.

Even in this spacious, dim interior, the temperature is enough to make Annie's skin prickle and slide. Her leg is giving her some trouble again today; possibly from the slightly cramped sleeping conditions in the van beside Alex's six-foot frame. Annie stretches her leg in front of her, and thinks that she will endure any amount of physical pain in order to know that she will continue to wake up—or go to sleep—in Alex's arms; though sleep is still difficult for her. Night after night she grapples with demons, with nightmare images and death and chaos. Waking, often with her heart pounding and a cold sweat on her chest, Alex seems like a lifeline, his deep slow breathing and his solid presence diminishing the ferocity and violence of her night-life.

And here they are now at the conference, their overt mutual goal, their rationalised explanation for travelling down together. She looks sideways at him. He is leaning forward and has his forearms resting on his knees. Poked into his shirt pocket he still has the buzzard's feather that Annie found on the riverbank after their swim and handed to him. He'd grinned at her in that full-beam, totally attentive, totally personal way that had so captivated her when she first met him, and which, she had noticed, seemed to melt even the most defensive female armour.

'My darling, with you around, who needs wings?' he'd twinkled, receiving the feather and pretending to lunge for her again.

Now in the lecture hall, he looks transfixed; totally engrossed, presumably, in translating what the speaker, an expert on troubadour imagery, is saying about the elevation of the largely-suppressed feminine principle in the new wave of thought sweeping through thirteenth century France.

Annie is scribbling furiously, translating simultaneously in her head. She had forgotten, if she ever knew, that here in thirteenth century Languedoc women already had a fairly unprecedented equality, recognised as landowners in their own right for example, as well as the elevation being accorded them in the Courts of Love and troubadour poetry. The Roman church of course was still patriarchal, but the Virgin was held in high regard.

There is another clap of thunder from outside. Alex doesn't stir. Like a huge sigh, a sheet of rain suddenly descends from the still-cloudless sky and shakes the leaves of the sweet chestnut trees in the grounds of the Manoir. It seems to Annie that the world is holding its breath—she can almost hear the earth putting out a million parched tongues, easing open in slits and cracks to welcome the wetness.

As suddenly as it started, the rain stops, and once again the day transforms itself into diamond-brightness. At lunchtime she slips her fingers through Alex's and they go off to wander through the edge of the woodlands surrounding the chateau. Everything is steaming; it will be intensely hot again in about an hour, as soon as the atmosphere has dried out. For now, though it is humid, walking under the dripping trees is refreshing.

The woodland, she notices, is mostly deciduous; old oaks and beeches, sycamores, chestnut trees, already in July smothered in plump green prickly fruitcases. The scent of the wet earth, moss and foliage fill their nostrils, make Annie feel suddenly very much alive. From somewhere amongst all these deciduous trees she catches a tang of conifer, cedar perhaps, or pine. Juniper? The sudden sharp fragrance makes her blink; for a moment she's somewhere else, somewhere very emotional, with someone else, also very special to her. She can't for the minute remember where or when.

The land here is so abundant. From now on into the autumn, they've been told, there will be an enormous harvest of mushrooms; and on the edges of the woodland in the foothills are acre after acre of peach, apricot, cherry, many of which have already been stripped. Annie thinks of the fruit exported—small glowing suns to brighten duller colder climates. Because the heat is so intense in the summer, all the fruit-pickers start work at four or five in the morning, and have knocked off by eleven to enjoy the habitual long siesta and drawn-out midday meal. Annie has always thought this must be a great way to live; it would feel like having two days in one, coming alive again in the mid or late afternoon after a long dreamy pause.

Now in these woodlands they come across, too, various ancient rogue apple trees, also laden. Alex has released her hand to go off and examine a fungus, and Annie leans against a knobbly old apple tree trunk, gazing up through its fruit-rich branches towards further layers of trees climbing up the mountainside towards the skyline. Alex suddenly calls her in a low, soft voice, and she turns. At first she can't see him, and for a moment the wooded scenery looks red-tinged and totally alien, despite being similar in species to the Devon woodlands in which Annie has spent her life.

Alex is bent over something on the path, and he motions her to move quietly and gently. Coming close, Annie sees a pattern of sulphur-yellow and black splodges, which resolves itself into a creature, a reptile, small and rounded, like a plump lizard. Suddenly the path seems to be swarming with them, uncompromisingly strong-coloured like a child's painting, and exotic and bizarre like jungle-creatures.

'Salamander!' whispers Alex. 'The rain brings them out. They're equally at home in water or on the earth. They look prehistoric, don't they? And foreign, like we've suddenly arrived in the Galapagos. Did you know that traditionally they're supposed to be able to survive fire?'

Annie looks at him in sudden dreadful horror. Something about his words have jerked a wire in her brain. An icy tug plucks her solar plexus and a scream begins in her head; any moment now it will come out of her mouth, and she is powerless to stop it. She freezes, waiting for what is fast becoming a familiar sensation of falling sideways. The smell of the moist mossy earth and the spicy tang of damp juniper press in on her in waves from every side. Faintly, in the distance, she can hear a crackling.

Alex looks up. Quick as lightning he is on his feet beside her, catches her, holds her carefully, as one might antique glass. He doesn't say a word. He lowers her carefully, sitting back himself onto the damp twiggy undergrowth beneath the trees, holding her against him until her breathing slows. Five minutes later, he pulls her to her feet gently, laces his fingers through hers. He still hasn't spoken. They walk slowly back out through the wood the way they came, and go to find some lunch in the great stone-flagged kitchen.

Today's lectures are in English. The speaker this afternoon, a psychologist as well as cultural historian, is going to be talking about the direct connection between the elevation of woman in the Courts of Love and troubadour philosophy, and the later persecution of women in the witch-hunts of the Middle Ages.

Annie looks at his face. Sensitive, kind, unusual, with an edge of, she supposes permanent, sadness; and when he looks up, she is struck by a profound kind of compassion in his eyes, even from this distance. He is not a tall man, nor particularly remarkable in his physical appearance, but his presence holds everyone in the room. There is an electric hush, even though he has done nothing but walk to the podium.

He starts with a proposition.

'I want to put to you as a hypothesis something that may affect the way we view the Grail and its significance. Indeed, you may already be aware of this.

'The Grail has probably never existed on the physical plane in any tangible way, but only as a symbolic representation of subtle metaphysical truths. What stands behind this symbol—which in itself resonates on so many levels, of which more later—is a vast body of esoteric wisdom teachings, passed initially via the oral transmission—and the troubadours as bards were also entrusted with this—and also via text and image.

'We might today call this body of teachings the perennial philosophy, which has historically so often been transmitted via the myths of a culture, especially in relation to what the great Joseph Campbell called the monomyth. What we now know as the Grail corpus is an essential and significant part of this; and only relatively latterly "christianised".

'I also want to put to you something that needs examination. As you will know, the persecution of the Cathars in this region was also known as the Albigensian Crusade; it was centred on the town of Albi, at the heart of the Cathar religion in Southern France, both topographically and spiritually.

'What you may not know is what the etymology suggests. This may sound fanciful, so bear with me. "Albi" in Occitan, the old language—as this etymology tells us—of the Languedoc, and/or Provencale, actually means "female elf".

There is too the word "white" conveyed by the name Albi (think of the Latin "alba"). In the Celtic languages certainly "white", etymologically, was conflated with "pure" and "holy", as it is symbolically in the West generally. In the Brythonic tongues is also conveyed the sense of the non-material; so, a being from the non-mortal Otherworld.

'Picking up, briefly, on this, I cannot stress too strongly here, by the way, that it is crucial to understand the levels on which these terms are used. We are speaking of "pure", "holy", "white" as qualities of *heart*; a manifestation of what some cultures call the soul, others the spirit, or the light body. They are not terms to be interpreted literally, materially. And of course there is much to say there, in the way the term "white", for instance, has been subverted, politically. If we confuse the levels, view in "the flesh" what has meaning only on a subtle level, atrocities vested in, for instance, the colour of one's skin can and do happen.

'So to continue the thread in relation to the female elf and the town's name: it is hard not to conclude that we may be speaking of the "fairy people" of which most cultures have an equivalent. I hasten to direct you to put out of your minds immediately the childishly naïve picture of centimetres-high winged creatures inhabiting the hedges in the garden, as beloved of folk-tales. The archetype behind this description— elf, I mean—is altogether greater and more profound. Some of you will be acquainted with the Irish/British notion of the Tuatha de Danaan, undoubtedly?—ah yes, a number of you are nodding. In mythology, these are Otherworld dwellers, a race of beings half-god and half-mortal, who live "beyond the sea". You could say that psycho-spiritually they mediate the higher spiritual planes to the human. Think of Elf in this way.

'What has this to do with the Grail, and the Cathars? What this suggests to me is that the Cathar region, as with other places such as the Isle of Iona off Scotland, is a region where "the veils are thin", and the gods speak still—through the landscape, through the higher mind, to those who have ears to listen, mediating a spirituality more ancient, despite its changing outer forms, than orthodoxy would have us believe. This of course may be the true meaning of the idea of the fairy people.'

Annie is rapt, transfixed, and terrified. Her eyes are fixed on this man.

'It is of course also significant that the word speaks of the feminine: *female* elf. The Grail tradition is a matrilinear tradition. Its roots, culturally speaking, may lead back to the Neolithic; or maybe a great deal further than that. Archetypally speaking, its roots are simply in the "Divine Feminine": a role carried by Lilith (and her now-unknown predecessors), Nefertiti, Eve, Bride or Brigit, Bathsheba, Tara, the Magdalene and too all the subsequent bearers of versions of the name Mary. She is the Great Goddess. Of course this role is as consort of the Divine Masculine, in joint sovereignty.

'So let me put to you that one aspect of the quest for the Grail signifies the need for the restoration of the feminine principle, with all its attributes of Heart: love, compassion, conservation of the planet, co-operation, inclusiveness and so forth in order to balance the more individuating, separative and discriminating qualities of the masculine principle. We need both to work in synergy, of course, but the wise have seen for a long time the perils when this balance is not kept. (Perhaps I should add an aside here too: it is a mistake to conflate the feminine principle solely with the female gender, or the masculine with the male. We both contain both, and this is important for what I am about to say.)

'So I suggest, too, that the Grail as a symbol of wholeness also stands in for the "realised man" (I mean "human"): one who has drawn heaven and earth, spirit and matter, masculine and feminine, together in himself, and who knows how to transcend duality. Perhaps this is the matter of the teachings, and the Grail as a chalice is, literally, immaterial.'

There is a profound silence in the room. Annie has an extraordinary desire to weep. Alex seems to feel this; he takes her hand and presses their fingers together. Other than this, the audience seems motionless. In the distance, through the open window, the sound of ruffled leaves suggests a sudden wind.

'So back to the context,' the speaker says. 'The elevation of women—women as symbolic of the feminine principle incarnate, and women too as actual women—in the Courts of Love.

'It is hard to admit that what seemed like a wonderful impulse, the deification of women, actually directly brought about the backlash that led to their wholesale massacre,' he says. 'No-one, of course, could possibly deny that women then, as still now, had too often been victims of patriarchal suppression. The Grail legends seem to address this issue; in them, we see the feminine principle restored to its rightful place in the universe, and the, if you like, "prescription" to achieve this. This is a profound truth; and the Grail Legends, as other people have remarked, are in their way the Tantric Scriptures of the West, offering as they do an insight into the ultimate reconciliation of the opposites, as I said above; of male and female, day and night, light and dark, and so forth.' He pauses to take a sip of water.

He continues: 'Following on from what my colleague this morning was saying, I'd like to just remind you that here, where the Cathar faith was strong in the thirteenth century, women already enjoyed a remarkable degree of equality, both in a secular and political context, and also perhaps especially within the Cathar faith. In the latter they were seen as equally capable of the priesthood, being ordained alongside men as Parfaits (or should I say Parfaites), though not, I believe, ever in quite the same number . . .?' he looks for confirmation to his colleagues and raises dark well-defined eyebrows; someone inclines his head slightly, in courteous agreement.

At the word Parfait during this morning's lecture Annie had experienced a cold frisson; not unpleasant exactly, but compellingly powerful. Before coming here she knew next to nothing about the Cathars, but experiences a profound and private shock of something—fascination? Recognition? Familiarity?—which strikes so deep each time she hears the word that she knows herself incapable of sharing it with anyone. Instead she wants to hug her response to herself, like a child's guarding of a secret and infinitely precious treasure.

Listening to the lecturer now, the word Parfait—despite the morning's priming—again conjures the churning in her stomach; a rush almost of adrenalin. There is something vast pushing at the edges of her mind.

'Quite apart from the religious persecution brought by the Catholic church of the time against the Cathars, by whose exemplary codes of behaviour the Church was threatened, there were also sown the seeds for the later persecution of women.

'With the influence of the Courts of Love, women were elevated to what became, inexorably, eventually an untenable position. The trouble with being on a pedestal is that there's only one way off—downwards. With this kind of adulation, almost divine worship, comes, eventually, fear; our human tendency to test or punish that which we perceive to be different, or better or higher than ourselves out of our own insecurity, our perceived inferiority.

'The final manifestation of this fear showed itself in the witch-hunts of the Middle Ages, where any woman who showed a degree of self-governance, of wisdom, of a willingness to step outside the boundaries of rules laid down by a fiercely patriarchal and hierarchical church, was subjected to humiliation, torture or even death. The supreme ordeal, as I am sure you are aware, was trial by water; if she drowned, you could take it she'd been innocent; if she survived, she must be a witch and would therefore be thrown to the flames. A supremely grim case of heads I win, tails you lose.'

Annie feels herself going blank. For the third time in as many days, she is beginning to dissolve. Sweat trickles into her eyes. She is aware that she must, absolutely must, for Alex's sake and her own, hold on to whatever sanity is left for her. She grips every ounce of willpower she can find to stay upright: forces the speaker's words out of her mind, feels her head full of chaos and jaggedness.

Alex glances at her, and once again grabs her, pulls her to her feet, and not unkindly but with a degree of anxiety that makes him abrupt, marches her out of the room, half-carrying, half-lifting her.

FIFTEEN

Annie wakes, and knows that Alex is elsewhere.

When she opens her eyes and looks at him, from where she is lying on her side in the camper-van against his length, his eyes are open. He's lying on his back with his hands behind his head staring at the ceiling. Always, up until now, she has woken with his arm beneath her neck, or draped over her upper body.

There is a long moment between her waking, and his sensing that she is awake and composing his features into his usual warm delighted-to-see-her expression. He puts out his hand and touches her hair and smiles, but she glimpses a fleeting shadow in his eyes.

Annie feels a cold jolt of fear clutch at her stomach, but before she can say anything he's climbed out from under the thin sheet, all that is bearable in this heat, and goes to put the gas-stove on for tea. He slides the van-door open; it still squeals and groans, despite the thorough oiling they had given it on purchasing the van in England just before leaving.

It is already intensely hot outside. Alex stretches and, still naked and barefoot, steps down outside for a pee. So far they've been lucky, finding beautiful wild sites to park the van not too far from the Manoir, but always fairly remote and mostly woody. They try to park near streams; Annie, to her surprise, finds she has easily shaken off her previous attachment to hygiene and hot showers. She is coming to love being up early, noticing the wildlife and flowers, watching the world shake itself awake. Occasionally they come across the spoor of wild boar; now and then the surprise and delight of a flashing kingfisher adds a new and tiny joy to her day. She finds she enjoys standing in a stream or river that tumbles gushing from the mountains, washing her hair in cool water. She even forgets to worry about water-snakes in her delight at the new and different routines and rituals that are starting to pattern their lives together.

This morning, though, she feels gripped by a slight sense of panic.

'Alex?' she says, as he comes back in and picks up their two coffee-cups from the empty washing-up bowl where they'd piled their clean crockery after washing and drying it outside under the stars last night.

'Mmm?' he responds, pouring water onto teabags and switching the stove off.

Annie doesn't know what to say, suddenly; how can she say *I felt panicky because your arms weren't around me when I woke up?* How pathetic; how childishly insecure and demanding. And how selfish.

'Are you OK, love? I felt you weren't very happy when I woke up this morning.'

Alex leans against the van door and looks out at the morning while the tea brews. Already the pods on the broom bushes outside are popping in the sunshine, and the cicadas creaking. Annie looks at the long curve of his back and his firm buttocks and thinks irrelevantly that she must get up in a moment and wash some underwear; in this heat it will dry spread out on the wild rosemary bushes in less than two hours.

With his back to Annie, Alex says: 'I'm fine. It's the last day of the conference today, isn't it?'

There's a silence. Alex turns round and fishes the teabags out, and drops them into an empty yoghurt pot. He adds powdered milk, stirs and carries both cups back to the bed. He balances them on the narrow shelf below the window running nearly the length of the back of the van on the driver's side, and slides under the sheet beside Annie. She's annoyed with herself for needing his physical presence so much. Just a touch from him comforts her, dispels her fears. He hugs her, then detaches himself and passes her her tea. He reaches out a toe and lightly strokes the top of her foot with it.

'To be honest, I was thinking about Laurel and Sam. I miss them a lot. And what will happen to us? I'm off to the Somport campaign in a few days; we may not see each other for a while. The future's always so unpredictable, isn't it? While we had the conference as our reason for being here together the present was strong enough for the future to have no meaning.' He sips his tea reflectively, his eyes sober.

Annie wrestles with a rush of fear. After a minute she kisses him on the cheek nearest her. 'Do you want to talk about it?'

'I don't think I can talk about the children, Annie; not right now. There's nothing really to say about them, anyway. About you and I—well, we love each other. Time will tell, and all that. We'll be back together in a couple of week's time, won't we? I think I just feel a bit quiet.'

Annie thinks about all this as she washes her underclothes and T-shirts in the river. After their brief conversation in bed, she feels a shadow of her old disabling anxiety; she makes herself move and attend to the business of the day before her emotions immobilise her, pressing her to stay around Alex until things are back to the status quo of the blissful and passionate two weeks they have spent in each other's company. Everything has its own cycle, she reminds herself; I expect it to be all flood-tide, and feel surprised when it ebbs. She sheds her espadrilles and wades into the water, and to distract herself from anxiety about Alex, mulls over the conference and its significance for her.

She feels increasingly drawn by the Cathars. Her original interest in coming to this conference was more literary; it was the rise of the Romance and the poetry of the troubadours that had attracted her. Alex was the one who had been previously interested in the Cathars, partly, he said, because some of their philosophies echoed Buddhism, his own adopted approach to life, and partly because of his fierce interest in minority groups and their persecution. He now is finding himself more and more inspired by the troubadours' world, while Annie feels the stirrings of a fascination bordering on near-obsession with the Cathars, or Albigensians. The more she discovers about their beliefs and attitudes, the more she longs to discover, the more empathy she feels. It is as if they fill a hole in her that has been empty since she had, as a sixteen year old adolescent, chosen to leave the Catholic faith of her upbringing.

Many of the reasons she had isolated in her departure from the Church were addressed, it seemed to her, in the Cathar faith. From the days here she had gleaned a great deal about their worldview. There was evidence that the Cathars believed in reincarnation and/or the transmigration of souls; after death they believed the soul would follow what they called the 'path of the stars' through successive purifications. Their own salvation was less important than being of service to others, and it would seem that the Parfaits at least had highly developed psychic and spiritual healing faculties, including the ability to transcend physical pain. They were vegetarian, and believed that animals had souls. While they did not encourage marriage—they believed that the material world trapped the soul and had no wish to perpetuate it—they believed that both men and women were equally capable of taking holy orders and administering the sacraments. What marked them especially was their utter commitment; massacred village by village, community by community, they went forward one after the other to their death silently and even it seemed at times joyously, rather than betray their faith to save their life.

Standing in the stream, rubbing the square block of olive-oil based savon de Marseille against the cotton garments, Annie remembers the expression of great sadness on the lecturer's face as he recounted the gruesome siege of Béziers, during which the Papal legate, on being asked how the invading army would distinguish Catholic from heretic, had supposedly uttered the famous words: 'Kill them all; God will know his own'. In the silence of the lecture-hall in the Manoir, someone in the row behind them had whispered clearly to his neighbour, in French: 'Man's inhumanity to man; it might be the late twentieth century so the faces will have changed, but the acts go on. Will it never cease?'

Annie, hearing this, had been overwhelmed by a vast desolation that had brought tears to her eyes. In her mind the massacred marched silently, one by one, to their deaths, joined by all those others, in history and the present, who had become scapegoats of human fear and oppression; a huge flood of people connected by their unshaken beliefs, black shadows against an even blacker screen.

And in her mind, superimposed on this, a ripped black canvas, a net, full of holes where all those lives had been stamped out; joined now by the spaces between the holes, the fine filaments of the web connecting person to person, person to all other living things, person to planet, trembling. From somewhere, as she visualised this stark picture, she remembered the Indra's Net of the Hindus; that the tiniest action happening at one point of the web ripples through the whole. Each intersection of the threads of the net contains a jewel; a sparkling faceted jewel, a life, which reflects in its surface all the other beings in the universe.

Sitting there in the conference holding these two pictures in her mind, one so black, and one somehow holding out some small candle of hope, she was suddenly struck by the thought that these ripples in the net might, at some very subtle level, occur forever, trembling through the universe. What did this imply about time? And did it mean that, as T S Eliot said, if all time is eternally present, all time is unredeemable? Or did it in fact mean the opposite; that the endless reverberations of the ripples in their waves and tremors meant in fact that we are given the chance to redeem the moment, every moment? In the lecture-hall, Annie felt she had opened a door onto an abyss; hastily and firmly she shut it again quickly, and reached out for Alex's hand.

Now, standing calf-deep in the river on the morning of the last day of the conference, Annie is certain that whatever else does or doesn't happen, she is going to stay near the Pyrenees until she finds the answers to some of her unformulated questions about those people. On a more prosaic level, she thinks as she wrings out her clothes and piles them one by one into the washing-up bowl, what should she do about work?

On their trip across France, she and Alex had talked at length about the future. Not about their future together, as such; neither felt able to broach that yet, either in their own minds, or to each other. Yet they both know, she thinks, that it is tacitly understood that in sharing their hopes and dreams they are also making space to allow for the possibility that their lives will continue to converge.

Alex, she knows, feels that he can continue over here much as he had in Britain, though without at the moment his courses and residencies. Long-term, he dreams of setting up a studio/workshop in which he might make stringed instruments; a workshop with a recording studio. In the short-term, he will continue to receive royalties—such as they are—on several volumes of poetry and also on a recording contract that he had fulfilled. *Lento* had been commissioned, with part of the advance still outstanding, and when it was finished would be both performed and recorded. Alex has done very little to it for a few weeks, but she senses that he is very excited by it, and she sees how inspired he is at the moment. She knows that like her he too feels vibrant with a creative energy when they are together; there is an almost radioactive charge between them at times. She senses, rather than knows, that he is petrified that if he can't use that energy to produce a masterpiece, it will dissipate and leave him sucked dry and hollow, and forever. At the moment they both know that it is being recycled into the relationship between them and that is just as it should be. Soon, however, it will have to be tested, be put to creative use. That will require a period of solitude; can they trust the current between them to remain free and flowing; will it be a source, a well, to which they can return over and over? Or would Alex's guilt and pain about Kate and the children puncture the vessel so that the precious liquid would drain away unchannelled?

Annie feels that it is now or never for her. To have left England in the way she did, travelling with Alex and simply leaving behind everything, is the most courageous step she has ever taken. Simply to walk out. To return in September to pick up the reins of the job of English lecturer at a provincial university seems unthinkable.

Yet there are big questions. What will she do to earn a living? Even with the insurance from Greg's life, she still needs, for her own self-respect if nothing else, to have a working-life, a professional identity. However, she does at least have for the moment a cushion, so that she can take six months or a year if necessary to see if her old dreams of establishing herself as a painter and textile artist have any substance to them in the immediate future. She has Susie and Jon's farmhouse to go to after the conference; close to Perpignan, it will allow her to pursue her newfound passion for the Cathars. It will also give her a base where she might draw breath and, like a sunflower turning its face to the source of light and heat, realign herself with her natural rhythms and patterns and inclinations. She knows that she is not yet fully recovered from the trauma of the last year; she is also wise enough to know that there will be a time when Alex's guilt, conflict and pain about his decision will require that she has a safe and strong foundation of her own. This might in turn require that she or they have established a physical base here, beyond the van and the hospitality of friends. Suddenly her future is upon her; it is not 'sometime', it is now.

She's pondering all this when she glances up; a shadow in the trees solidifies into a more substantial figure, and Annie's heart misses a beat in shock. Drifting as she has been, for a moment periods in her life seem confused, and she is sure that it is Greg's mother, the Frog, standing watching her. She hears herself let out a noise somewhere between a gasp and a scream.

The old woman stares at Annie, neither friendly nor hostile. Although clearly not Greg's mother, her face is disturbingly familiar. Annie's stomach clenches suddenly. Annie looks back, peeling away the past. The old woman seems at first to be almost a caricature; so much the archetypal folk-tale peasant that Annie almost laughs. She wishes Alex could see her. Looking again, though, Annie realises that she is in fact not that old, and what had looked like a faded black overdress is in fact a battered waxed riding mac of the kind that in England is quite trendy. Her face is creased around the eyes, but her skin surprisingly full and clear. Her eyes are small but not unkind, and regard Annie steadily; 'cannily' is the word that jumps into Annie's mind. There is something rather bear-like about her; perhaps in the gleam of the eyes. The woman shakes her stick disapprovingly at Annie's legs; Annie looks down. She is somewhat skimpily dressed, not having expected to meet anyone. She feels uncomfortable. Belatedly it occurs to her that perhaps the woman is merely gesturing with shocked pity at the scar-tissue on her right leg.

'Allemande?' says the woman abruptly. Annie opens her mouth but nothing comes out. She clears her throat. 'Non; Anglaise,' she replies.

'Ah, Inglaise.' The Southern accent is thick and the vowels distorted. 'Faut courir, y a des tempêtes qui viennent. Faut courir, faut se proteger.' She stares at Annie pointedly. Annie thanks her and looks at the sky. Storms coming? It looks clear and blue as ever to her. She steps out onto the bank and pulls her thigh-length T-shirt down towards her knees. She is acutely aware of the woman's eyes on her as she hooks the heels of her espadrilles up and picks up her washing. She looks up and the woman nods grimly. 'Faut se proteger.'

Annie thanks her again and switches the bowl of washing to her left side, balancing it against her on her hip. She holds out her hand, not quite knowing how else to take her leave. The woman grips it surprisingly firmly and gives Annie a fierce grimace, from between scattered stumps of teeth, that might be a smile, might not be. She turns abruptly and prods her stick into the bank, levering herself up the small incline. Then she gives a slightly lisping whistle, and suddenly the path is alive with goats, fawn and brown goats, each with a bell around its neck. How on earth did I not hear those before? thinks Annie, enchanted. They each glance at her with their unfathomable yellow eyes, then bound after the woman like creatures out of some fairy-story.

It is only as she nears the van that Annie takes in what the woman's words had been—she's dismissed them as pre-senile wanderings. Now they seem menacing, ominous. 'You need to run; there are storms coming. You must run; protect yourself. Protect yourself.' Feeling simultaneously childishly silly and obliquely endangered, Annie does indeed break into a run; thank God, there is the van, there is Alex; he waves, grinning at her.

SIXTEEN

Driving the road from Foix to Perpignan, both Annie and Alex are silent. An ocean of unframed words, unasked questions swell between them; yet both know that they are unnecessary. In England, it had seemed right, urgent even, to have 'plans', individual destinations and reasons for being there to take up the possible emotional and psychological slack after the conference. In a way those had provided the safety net below the highwire of their joint act. Relinquishing the boundaries between them they had sensed, as lovers do—whether from fear or from a deep knowing—that there would come a time when the boundaries, inch by inch, would ease themselves back into their lives.

Annie is thinking how hard it is to live totally wide open, to listen to and live from the heart, to live as a reed lives, rooted, yet surrendering to every breeze. I need to feel I have a handle on the future, she thinks; I can't let go, not totally, not even to Alex. Not to anyone.

Now is the moment to pick up the reins of their separate destinations, their individual lives, and it will be hard to avoid it much longer. Yet both know that it is the last thing they want to do. Without discussing it, both know that the other feels the same; to drive, and rest, and eat, and talk, and make love, and drive and rest again, forever, would be paradise. And both know, too, and know that the other knows, that what is between them is surely strong enough to withstand separation; and in fact needs it, to test, to strengthen, to temper. To give their relationship substance.

Sorting and re-packing the van last night into Annie's gear and Alex's had been difficult, poignant, silent. After it was done they held each other, clutched each other, and their lovemaking in the dark confined space of the van, their joint and temporary home, retreat, was both joyous and painful, explosive, cathartic. Annie had cried; silent racking sobs, and Alex, holding her and stroking her hair, his own cheeks wet, felt raw, turned inside out and lost. When they slid into sleep Annie felt herself falling down a vast echoing tunnel, to emerge into a maze in which she wandered round and round, fingers on the cold metallic-feeling wall, until daybreak.

Looking out at the changing landscape as Alex drives east towards the sea through the foothills, under, unusually, a pewter-purple sky, Annie suddenly sees the faint outlines of a double rainbow. She touches Alex's arm and points.

'That seems auspicious,' he says in a quiet voice, and lapses back into silence. The shrill voices of low-flying swifts filter through the open windows.

'I think I'd like to drive, Alex,' Annie suddenly says. Alex negotiates a tight hairpin bend, and another. He says nothing. They pass in and out of flickering light and shade; glints of sunlight piercing the sombre clouds like metallic snake's-tongues, and caught or released by the dense trees lining the gorges. To their right sits the great stony veil of the Pyrenees proper, dotted with sheep on its lower shoulders, when the summer growth offers valuable if remote and rather thin supplementary grazing to the precious lower winter pasture.

They are climbing, taking the long, slow, steeply-twisting and astonishingly beautiful indirect route, when it would have been far more sensible to keep to the main *route nationale*. Their destination is a hamlet not far from Prades-sur-Tech, southwest of Perpignan into the mountains. Alex will have to retrace his footsteps in a day or two to travel to Somport nearer the Atlantic Pyrenees.

The road dips and swings like a rollercoaster; the van negotiates the hairpins slowly, lumbering. Much of the time the route is single track. Even here in the lowish Pyrenees a great deal of the distance travelled is in first or second gear.

Just as Annie is about to repeat her statement, Alex pulls the van over to a passing-place. To their right is a nearly sheer drop into one of the massive gorges that lacerate the landscape. The trees are different, here; more conifers, a few eucalypts. There has been a recent shower; through the open windows and sunroof stream the intoxicating smell of hot wet pines. Annie thinks that she will now always connect their scent with this moment. The road uncoils ahead of them out of sight into the mountains, shining like a slowworm. In the distance, to the left above the trees, looms the bleak ragged outline of one of the many Cathar strongholds punctuating this area; solitary and stubborn in its broken resistance to the constant ravages, first of siege, then of the elements. Not yet quite absorbed back into the landscape, it still looks one piece with its looming mountain host, pointing stony fingers up beyond the clouds.

Alex just stares at Annie. Annie looks back.

'Annie, my darling, you haven't driven since your accident. Driving a car you know in England is one thing. But this is a van, heavy, very different from your Golf. This is France and we're driving on the right; and this is probably one of the most difficult roads in Europe as it is. To take a kind of maiden voyage in all these conditions is crazy, Annie. I don't mind you giving it a go; obviously it's your choice. But I think you're nuts.'

Annie's jaw is set. She hadn't known she was going to say what she did until she had said it. She also knows that Alex is right; and too that unless she drives the van while Alex is still with her, she will feel trapped, immobile, impossibly dependent, at Jon and Susie's. Alex will be taking the van with him, but it's likely that she can borrow Susie and Jon's vehicle while she is staying with them. However, she'll find it almost impossible to break through her fear barrier for the first time in someone else's, possibly newer and smarter, vehicle without Alex beside her.

'Don't patronise me, Alex.' She swallows. She hadn't meant to sound brittle. Surely they aren't going to fight, now of all times? She knows he is right, and she knows she doesn't want to give way. She also knows she is testing his faith in her; if she drives, a false move on this road, misjudging the weight of the van on a corner or selecting the wrong gear or braking badly on the damp road surface in the face of an oncoming vehicle could be lethal.

Alex is still regarding her. His face is serious. Annie's palms are sweating; there's a hint of distance between them; neither wanting to give way, both protecting themselves against the oncoming separation. I don't want it to be like this, she thinks; why am I insisting on this battle of wills? She also knows that quite possibly she won't be safe, in fact. Am I tempting fate? Is this a deathwish? Why now, when I haven't wanted to drive all the way through France on these long straight open roads?

She looks into his eyes, defiantly and pleading. He looks back, and without changing his expression starts the van up again. He turns his attention back to the vehicle, and, casting a glance over his shoulder at the road behind them, pulls out.

Annie glares at his profile, fuming and in turmoil. He's defied her, made a unilateral decision. She feels speechless with anger and distress.

For five minutes they drive in white-hot silence. Annie is so angry she almost wants to jump out of the van. Alex's profile is wooden. She wants to hit him. She feels herself boil; and suddenly realises how little, in her previous life, she has ever allowed herself to feel angry. But then, she has rarely felt passionately about anything at all, before.

Without a word, Alex takes an unmarked left-hand turn and starts to drop down out of the mountainous area in the direction of the main road they had abandoned much earlier in the day. Annie feels her anger rekindle at his decision to turn off without consulting her; they have a tacit agreement that he will drive and she navigate. Part of her brief is to check ahead on the map for sites, antiquities or promising stopping-places for a break, or to suggest more picturesque routes.

The van seesaws over a narrow ancient stone bridge, and as it drops into the dip on the far side of the bridge they both see a flash of darkly chestnut fur, too late. There is the minutest jolt under the nearside front wheel, and Annie thinks she hears a tiny shrill exhalation, like squeezing a squeaky toy with a rusty valve. She gasps and her hands fly to her mouth in horror and distress. Alex brakes, and the van once again comes to a halt, this time on a grass verge bordering the tree-lined road. Woodland stretches to both sides, and the river is rumbling away behind them. Annie notices the grass glistening with raindrops and the leaves silver-edged in the light slanting from below the clouds. She can't bear to look back behind them; her mind edges away from what has just happened, the animal's pain.

Alex jumps out of the van. The pine marten is unmistakably dead, flattened. He stares. A tiny flower of blood appears at the corner of its mouth, oozes into a slow jewel-red trickle, darkening to a dull crimson. How much damage can happen in one brief careless moment, he thinks.

Annie doesn't turn as he climbs back into the van. He stares at the back of her head. 'Stone-dead,' he says. 'Didn't have a bloody chance.'

Annie doesn't move.

Alex feels empty. The silence stretches out of the van, fills the woods, echoes round the gorge. This morning's silence had been white-gold, kind and loving, if poignant. This silence is grey as the hull of a battleship.

He puts his elbow on the steering-wheel and props his chin in his hand. He stares straight ahead. 'Sorry, Annie, that was a shit thing to do.'

Nothing. 'Annie?' He looks at her stiff unyielding back, and feels suddenly utterly drained and bleak. Impasse. He drops his forehead into his hands. For a second, he has an urge to be elsewhere, preferably in the library working on *Lento*, or out for a burn on his bike on his own, or—and at this his mind jars, and he feels an almost physical stab through his chest— pushing Sam on a swing in the park, with Laurel sitting on a bench close to him, chattering away in her grave grownup way and swinging a sandalled foot. He has a vision of her bent head, absorbed in threading daisies to make a chain. *Fuck,* he thinks, *fuck, fuck, fuck.*

The silence draws on.

Eventually Annie turns her head. A minute or two later Alex lifts his own head to look at her. There are tears in his eyes. Annie is filled with a sudden dread and horror. My God, what is she doing? Her cold anger leaves her in a rush, as if a plug has been pulled. This man with courage, man with heart, who has given up everything to be with her, has apologised to her and she sat on like a lump of rock, closing him out so totally she might as well be a complete stranger on a bus. She stares at him, white, now as limp as she had been rigid. Her hands are clenched in her lap.

'Alex, oh Alex,' she whispers. 'I love you. I'm so sorry. I do want to drive, and you're right, this is a crazy time to ask. I can't bear this distance between us,' and she throws her arms around his neck. She forces herself to face her feelings; to allow herself to feel. 'I don't want you to go; that's what's hurting. And I didn't want to tell you that.' She is weeping now; tears rolling and splashing the front of Alex's white T-shirt.

Alex bends his head into her neck. He feels overwhelmed, out of control. He has a dreadful feeling that he might cry himself.

Several hours later Annie is driving along the main road at the base of the mountains, Van Morrison on the tape player and both of them humming the tune. 'Let go into the mystery, let yourself go,' sings Alex loudly along with the tape, and puts his hand on Annie's knee. Annie smiles to herself and keeps her eyes on the road, glancing from time to time at the speedo. 40mph feels enough for now; and to her surprise she is loving being back at the wheel. The first half-hour was tricky, and she'd felt Alex's nervousness, despite his outwardly cheerful supportive manner. Her own heart had been hammering wildly as she took over at the wheel.

A frank open conversation has allowed both of them to save face and has offered a solution. To come down out of the mountains in any case seemed sensible, as the route was proving so terribly slow that they probably wouldn't have made it to Susie and Jon's house, Les Cerisiers, until late evening at the very earliest. They've telephoned ahead, and are expected for supper at eightish. Annie, swallowing her pride, had suggested that perhaps Alex should continue until the roads had opened out into something more easily negotiable. Alex generously remembered out loud that he hadn't allowed for the fact that of course Annie had driven most of her life on twisting Devon lanes, and he was entirely confident that she would be safe. Back on largely double-track straighter roads, Annie felt that she'd like a short trial run.

Her first attempt was jerky; she crashed the gears and stalled the van twice. It does indeed feel quite different from the car, and it is odd, too, to be perched high and upright, and to see no bonnet. They crawled along at a snail's pace at first, occasionally overtaken by roaring ancient Renault 4 vans and grey battered Citroëns, mud-splattered and thrown at speed around the corners. Either they had no brake-lights, or the drivers just never used the middle pedal, Annie decides, as, in front of her, a geriatric Citroën van, leaning out precariously into the middle of the road, bounces out of sight on a 90-degree bend at more than twice their speed. She starts to ignore the horn-blasting they incur; often it is accompanied by a Gallic gesture or two, but usually softened with a grin as the driver peers into the van on overtaking.

By the time she's been behind the wheel for an hour or so and has successfully negotiated the odd hamlet populated with neurotic dogs and squawking chickens and guinea-fowl as well as the occasional milk-cow, and has driven through a village or two, the *nationale*, when they finally reach it, seems so easy she almost forgets that there has ever been a break from driving. Her spirits are high, and she and Alex seem as close as ever.

Dusk is beginning to streak the sky in front of them as they double back into the mountains, up the steeply-winding road from Ceret through Annecy-les-Bains towards Prades-sur-Tech. During the drive across country from the *nationale* they had swapped seats again, and Annie now has her feet up on the dashboard and is soaking up the landscape and the first promises of sunset. In silent agreement they stop in the centre of the town; there are some thirteenth century cloisters that they both want to look at.

As soon as they step under the arches of the soft yellow-white stone buildings and look across the central courtyard to more arches and red pantiled roofs, Annie feels a profound peace settle on her, like a blanket of feathers. Suddenly nothing else at all matters; not their pasts, nor their futures; not the storminess of their day, nor even whether they will stay together. Just to be here now is enough; and that Alex is here too and is as aware of the atmosphere as she is is like lighting a thousand candles in her heart. She gazes at the flowering bushes filling the courtyard, lifts her face to their scent on the dusk air. All around is silence; a hiatus after the activity of day and before the bustle of the summer evening. The moment feels archetypal; Adam and Eve in the garden. She turns to Alex and touches her lips to his, very gently, before stepping out into the courtyard. The tiny sweet-smelling bush in front of her is an old-fashioned rose, covered in small blossoms. As she looks she realises it is thornless. Carefully she plucks a miniature spray from it and hands it back to Alex, before walking on to wander through the arched cloisters on the other side of the cloistered garden.

SEVENTEEN

A Tuesday. The rectangle of sunlight glossing the flagstones through the open door somehow seems fixed, like a still-life painting. Susie, passing her own kitchen door with the dogs and glancing in on her way out to pick up bread and milk a mile away at La Chapelle Blanche, has the unreal feeling that she is peering in on someone else's house, someone whose past has been captured in a colour photograph.

The kitchen is thick with silence. Annie sits at the table with her chin propped in her hands gazing at Alex, whose own hands are clamped around a mug of distinctly cold coffee—the last small procrastination between now and his departure. He is sitting astride the bench facing the door, half-turned towards Annie, staring abstractedly at the great yew-wood clock on the kitchen wall. Annie has followed his gaze and both pairs of eyes watch the second-hand jerking round. The strident metallic counting of its mechanism scratches at the glassy quiet that hangs between the two of them.

Annie drops her hands and fiddles with the buttery knife balanced on her plate. She stands and fills the kettle, and offers more coffee to Alex, who smiles gratefully and ruefully, knowing that prolonging the moment will only give the illusion of softening the parting.

Susie and Jon have both tactfully disappeared; but in fact Annie and Alex have made their goodbyes already, on the great mattress close to one of the floor-to-ceiling windows of the newly-converted attic room in the farmhouse.

The attic spans the length of the house; from the bed are spectacular views across fields and the cherry-trees after which the house was named towards the wooded skirts of the mountains on one side, and on the other the dramatic sweep of the valley northwest towards the peak of Canigou.

That morning Alex woke first, arms still tightly clasped around Annie. They must hardly have moved all night. He closed his eyes momentarily again and buried his face in her smooth, fresh, rosemary-scented hair. Under the smell of shampoo is her characteristic musky smell, touched with the sharp lingering tang of sex. He suppressed the urge to run his hands over her again, instead letting her sleep—morning had come fast enough, and the longer she slept the longer he could stay in bed and hold her. He sighed deeply.

The room seemed to swim with light. Out of the window over Annie's motionless shoulder Alex watched the geese and goats waddle and bound respectively into the small fenced orchard abutting the house, followed by Susie's leggy figure in camisole top and thin Indian skirt and espadrilles, and he gently hugged Annie close. He knew that the lifestyle of Annie's friends here came close to the perfection of Annie's dreams—and his too, if he is honest—with the animals and vegetables, Susie's painting and Jon making his living as a carpenter (working largely for the incoming English and Germans and Dutch) and furniture-maker. Neither has said anything about this; what point in pre-empting whatever the future might offer them by trying to grab it before its moment has come? And with everything so uncertain there is too much to say, and too little that can be said. So instead of words, they've shared the common language of their bodies, and their love-making over the couple of days they have been here has been exquisitely painful; simultaneously tender and demanding, passionately loving and almost frenzied; sharpened by a kind of poignant desperation. Behind it, they know, is a profound need; their own fears and insecurities, but in addition, too, the urgency of the human soul to both offer everything to, and receive everything from, another human being; to lose and find oneself in one area where mystery still reigns. To lose oneself and find another. So they have yielded their bodies to each other, abandoning separateness, hoping to cement by touch where words can only be clumsy fumblings, approximations.

Alex breathed in Annie's smell and let himself float. He remembered the day of the lavender fields—a few days ago, a lifetime ago. The melody of *Lento* drifted through his head, and with it came, unbidden and unexpectedly, some lyrics: *Beyond words/I offer you the language of the body/Beyond words/I offer you the wisdom of the heart . . .* words started to form into a shape in his mind; he could feel them, a torrent, tumbling like a waterfall from somewhere into his conscious mind. He held his breath, didn't dare move. The first few he dismissed as insufficient, clichéd; and besides, *Lento* was not a love-song; though it might be, he hoped, a celebration of the sacred. He ran the lines that had arrived through his mind again; perhaps, maybe . . . maybe they could be a refrain. He waited. Annie stirred, then lapsed back into stillness. Still he held his breath. Suddenly in his head he heard the chorus, a few voices soaring upwards in a towering wave:

Silence
silence
silence
Silence like the breathing of the sea—(here a couple of baritones too), *silence like the greening of the land . . .* and then the strings, the violins and 'cellos, rising and falling, dying quietly; maybe a woman's soprano, clear and pure, cutting in wordless, used like an instrument, a flute or saxophone, and then again a deeper voice or voices:

Beyond words/an older silence/beyond light, beyond the void/the ebb and flow of laughter, of parting, of return . . . Alex shivered with the adrenalin of the creative impulse. He desperately tried to remember whether he'd packed his dictaphone. All his best ideas happen when he is walking or driving; perhaps now the words would flood in as he drives back across the mountains.

We are clay and we are gold, said his brain. *We are earth and air and water/we are fire/the stuff of stars*—Alex paid attention, re-ran the words to try and fix them . . . *We are carried by great winds/we are shaped by unknown hands— Beyond words, beyond the silence*—and then the notes of a keyboard—an organ?—with an overlay of strings; perhaps reminiscent of the intro to a Handel oratorio, or maybe Taverner or Pärt, but brief. Then the other side of that, the soprano voice again, echoed by a saxophone. Wordless at first, then it could carry the refrain, which could be returned to as a theme linking the orchestral parts. *Beyond words/I offer you the language of the body/Beyond words/I offer you the wisdom of the heart . . .* The whole piece might finish with a half-chant, half-whisper, echoing, along the lines of *I close my eyes/and you are here/open them/and you are everywhere everywhere*
everywhere . . .

Could he bring in some percussion, deep bass notes? Was it all too sentimental? Too much of a love song? Alex felt his heart thumping. He repeated the words over and over until he thought he had fixed them. Yes! They'd need a lot of revision, but this was the start, this was the flood-tide again.

He gently disentangled himself from Annie and reached out for the notebook that he always kept by the bed.

Half an hour later Annie stirred and put out a hand for him.

'Good morning, Muse,' he murmured, and dropped the notebook as she turned her head to kiss him sleepily. 'What a wonderful start to the morning!' he whispered joyfully into her ear. 'I've cracked *Lento,* and my muse is still in bed with me. Who could wish for more?'

And now the moment has come. They sit, and the clock counts, and the third cup of coffee has been drunk, and neither has spoken, or touched each other. From outside, the continued fussing of the geese in the orchard is replaced by the more intrusive whine of a chainsaw, from where Jon is cutting up a couple of apple and beech trees, felled by storms last winter. Through the door floats the sharp smell of tannin from the beech and a fruitier warmer aroma from the apple-tree. Motes of sawdust drift and dance lazily in the doorway. Annie tries to keep her attention on the smells and sounds, on the morning sunlight coming in through the door. She feels obscurely that her undivided attention falling on Alex will make it harder for him to leave than it already is, as if he would have to pick her clinging emotions out of his skin like gorse-prickles or fish-hooks.

Slowly Alex stands and stretches and turns to her. 'Well,' he says, flashing her his full-beam smile, 'well, my darling, time to hit the road, unless I want to be driving all through the night.'

She stands too. He picks up his small rucksack, the one she always associates with hospital and Betty Chadwick, and holds out his free arm to her. They walk out of the door together, pressed close to each other's side, and Annie feels tongue-tied and shy, like a teenager. So much to say. The bantams scatter, clucking indignantly, and Alex lopes over to say goodbye to Jon. Annie waits by the van, and watches Jon switch off the chainsaw. Both men stand awkwardly for a moment; Jon still holding the chainsaw, Alex with one hand in his pocket. Jon says something, and Alex's laugh bursts out across the yard and he claps a hand in a rough hug to Jon's back, then turns and strides back towards her. In one swift movement he gathers her up and kisses her, lets her go again and swings up into the van. He rolls down the window as he starts the engine and leans out and kisses her nose. Still neither has said anything. She opens her mouth, and simultaneously he winks and accelerates out of the yard before she's found any words. Annie stands and watches the van out of sight; the brake-lights flicker at the corner and he hoots, and then he is gone in a swirl of dust.

She stands for a moment, looking at the empty lane, feeling pathetic, feeling abandoned. Tears come. She sniffs irritably and feels in vain for a hankie, then wipes her eyes on her T-shirt. The first day of the rest of my life, she thinks, and then feels further annoyed at herself for the cliché. She resists the impulse to listen for the echo of his van dropping down around the hairpin bends into the valley, and instead forces herself to walk briskly in the other direction towards La Chapelle Blanche, in the hopes of meeting Susie on her way back to Les Cerisiers.

EIGHTEEN

August slides over into September. Day after day continues blue and intense, blazing on into an abundant early autumn. The trees at Les Cerisiers are laden with fruit and the *vendanges* has started; tractors rumble past the yard laden with their cargo of grapes and drowsy wasps and bees. The air is saturated with the smell of crushed fruit and tannins from the local *cave* below in La Chapelle Blanche.

Susie has a simple makeshift studio across the stone-flagged passage from the kitchen. Jon has put an extra window and a Velux into what would have been a single-storey stable for a workhorse or mule. A woodburner keeps the space warm in the winter. Hanging over the ancient worm-eaten door with its enormous wooden latch is a heavy faded brown-gold velvet curtain to keep out draughts from the passageway. Its feel to Annie's fingers, as well as its colour, is comforting, reassuring, like some great benevolent animal guarding the threshold. Through the summer and into the autumn the door and windows stand permanently open. Annie loves this space, loves to be in there in the smells of linseed oil and turps, with Susie's finished or half-finished canvases stacked against the walls, and the ancient rusty nails which protrude all over the cob-lined interior festooned with sketches or notes.

When Annie and Alex first arrived there was a large canvas sitting on the easel, with the foreground, a field of sunflowers, blocked in against the looming indigo-mauve of the mountains. Now this is nearly finished.

Susie has sorted out an old easel of her own for Annie. It is missing its third leg and hinge, so Annie has propped it against the wall near one of the windows of the attic room. They have collected together various hardboards, and Annie has primed them, ready to paint; finding a way back into her old passion. If she can still paint, she figures, she may also find she can still weave; something she has not dared to attempt since she ripped off and destroyed the piece sitting on the loom on which she had been working when Greg died.

So finally, one morning in September, Annie takes out the large old wooden box of tubes of oil-paints and the cloth-wrapped bundle of brushes that she has brought from England, borrows some turps and linseed from Susie and props a sheet of prepared hardboard on her easel. For nearly a half-hour she stares at the board, and its hard white unseeing surface stares back at her, reflecting only her own blankness. Outside a cock pheasant whirrs, and then lifts itself like a clumsy mechanical toy over the low hedge, gliding to a halt in the orchard amongst the bantams. Silence settles again, and the heat outside grows. Annie unscrews a tube and picks up her palette.

She doesn't have a clear idea in her head, only knows that she wants to feel her way back in to colour and form. Her first attempts with the oils after such a very long gap are, predictably, clumsy. In her anxiety to re-acquire her old ease, her facility with image and tone, she finds herself cluttering the canvas with too many starting points and colours.

If she allows this to discourage her, she knows she'll dry up. How to counteract it? Maybe by trying to work in a looser way, without worrying about goals; merely playing, perhaps only allowing herself to work with a certain range, a particular section of the spectrum, at each attempt, knowing that her first few efforts are unlikely to be anything other than 'workouts'. For now she needs to acquaint herself once again with the feel of it, with the way the materials handle and flow, with manipulating the fluid and formless ideas in her head into shapes and qualities that will sit on hardboard and reflect back something that she can recognise.

The hard thing is letting go of her need to organise and structure her ides according to her old methods. Yet not only, she knows, is she too rusty to move straight into her habitual style, but also somehow it will arrest her progress to try to do so. It would be too much an evasion, for that is her past. What is required was a new approach.

She's pondering this as she walks into La Chapelle Blanche with the dogs to collect the bread. An early conversation she'd had with Alex suddenly comes into mind, and his face flashes before her, eyes glowing and big generous smile in place. Annie feels an acute pang of emptiness, a wave of absence, wash over her, and pushes his face out of her mind in order to pay attention to the half-remembered conversation.

Alex had been telling her about his method of working when running a poetry workshop, and about how important, creatively, he felt 'stream-of consciousness' work was as a direct line into the image-rich world of the unconscious. He opened, he said, every session he ran in much the same way. He would start by playing some music, or circulating a collection of postcards of paintings, or photographs, or by reading some carefully-chosen pieces, usually poems, or descriptive prose that was image-based; or he might start with a guided meditation. Then, without giving the students time to think, he would instruct them to write for ten minutes, starting immediately after he had finished his input. They were not allowed to stop, to think or to censor, but purely wrote whatever came into their heads, no matter how apparently irrelevant or ridiculous. Invariably, he said, this exercise produced rich, creative ideas; he compared it to mining a seam of pure gold when you thought you were in tin country.

Suddenly Annie sees that this is the way to take her painting, and, eager to start, quickens her pace on the dusty umber surface of the track to the village. Now that she knows how to move forward, she feels lighter, more joyful. Everything around her seems vibrant, full of life; the thick sturdy growth in the small sloping fields and still-flowering meadows, in the hedges and verges and copses around her, the flash of a butterfly, the darting swallows and swifts, the eager tails of the dogs. She relaxes.

'Hey, Susie,' says Annie over breakfast, 'have you ever used stream-of-consciousness stuff to kickstart a painting?'

Susie looks thoughtful. 'Jon, do you remember when we first moved here, and we felt a bit overwhelmed by it all? We didn't know where to begin, and we were just living in the kitchen, the only bit with a sound roof over it?'

'Do I hell! I thought we'd never survive it. You were sure we'd made a terrible mistake and I was sure every morning when we woke up that one of us would either kill or walk out on the other before the end of the day!' He twinkles at Susie. 'I only think that now on alternate days.'

Susie kicks him in the shin with a bare brown foot in mock anger. 'God. Oh, Annie, it was dreadful. We fought all the time, and each day we'd find something else wrong with the property, or come across another bit of red tape to do with the deeds or rights of way or access that no-one had thought of.' She crumbles a piece of baguette absentmindedly, and sweeps the crumbs into a little pile on the table with the side of her hand. 'It was the first time we'd lived together in one place, too; it's one thing travelling with someone, but it's different when you anchor yourselves to a house.'

'Yeah.' Jon nods agreement. 'Different dynamic altogether. A whole bunch of commitments rear their heads.'

'Travelling is so much more open-ended than living somewhere static, and when we'd actually bought this place it was more of a commitment than either of us had made before.' Susie grins at Jon. 'You see things in each other that you don't notice when you're just travelling.'

'Oh yeah? Such as what?' asks Jon, mock-aggrievedly.

'Oh, I don't know. I can't think of any examples right now. I'm sure I will, though!' She turns back to Annie. 'But it's like when you're moving around all the time, your focus is out there, and you sort of see it side-by-side. And then suddenly you stop and I suppose it kind of thrusts you inwards; you come face-to-face with each other and there's no distraction . . . I think that's what I mean. You can't avoid each other's reality, somehow. Do you know what I mean?' She pauses and looks at Annie and Jon questioningly, then carries on. 'Trying to get this place together gave us a common aim, I suppose, but for a long while, for me, it just seemed to be a kind of mirror of what was going on inside the relationship, you know?— initially all wonderful, charming potential on the surface, but once you dig deeper the cracks show—insecurities and little neurotic habits and doubts start to crawl out—chaos and crumbling walls and leaky roofs and dry rot and how on earth are we ever going to give it a workable inhabitable shape?' She laughs at herself.

Jon looks at her reflectively. 'Didn't know that's what you felt like. I suppose it did feel a bit like that. Miracle, isn't it?' He gestures vaguely with his head at the room around them.

'What was hard, too, you know,' continues Susie, 'was thinking at first you'd been given a bit of paradise; and then starting to see all the faults and flaws and reasons why it wouldn't work. You lose paradise very quickly. The more I saw wrong with the house, the more sure I was that our relationship was really going to fall apart. I was afraid we were beginning to hate each other. Do you mind me telling Annie all this, darling?'

Jon opens his hands, makes a face at Annie, shrugs. 'Feel free! Feels like a lifetime ago now.'

'You'd given up your work, too, hadn't you Susie?' says Annie. 'So that independence wasn't there for you to fall back on, like a safety-net. That must have made you feel a bit insecure as well, surely. None of us ever thought you'd do that, especially for a man. They all missed you in the clinic, apparently—best osteopath in the Westcountry. You seemed to be so committed to it, too. They were all dying to meet the man who'd prised you away.' She glances smilingly at Jon.

'Yes; that was a pretty big trauma. I knew I had to leave, though; I was beginning to go stale; I felt kind of sterile. So it wasn't all down to Jon. In a way, though, it was buying this place together that brought it all home to me; like really burning my boats. I was sure it was the right thing to do, but I felt pretty frightened.'

'*You* were frightened! I was shit-scared. I nearly did a runner to India two days before we were due to leave.' Jon tops up all their coffee-cups and then rolls a cigarette. He goes to sit on the doorstep and stretches his legs out, blowing a cloud of smoke at a wasp exploring the plums in the basket on the flagstones. 'And then we got here and there was so much more work to do on the place than we'd imagined, and we had all that trouble with neighbours and our shared spring—*Jean de Florette* revisited—and you hated not having a bathroom or hot water.'

There is a brief pause. Jon and Susie both look reflective. Annie opens her mouth to ask what all this has to do with her original question about inspiration, but Jon gets there first. He chuckles and picks a strand of tobacco off his tongue. 'D'you remember how all through the beginning of that winter we emptied buckets two or three times a day and even through the night from every room with all the rain? Then after that it froze, and we managed to do about twenty minutes' work at a stretch before our hands seized up and then we huddled around that small pot-bellied stove for another twenty before tackling another bit? We snarled at each other all the time.'

'Yes; and our only milking-goat died, and the ground was too hard to bury her; it was so cold that the birds just seemed to give up and fall out of the sky.' Susie shivers with the memory. 'Part of the reason for being here was to escape from the English winters. But the worst thing was thinking we were beginning to hate each other, when only a couple of month before we'd been so much in love. Oh God, that was a rough time.'

Annie listens with sympathy and interest; and part of her mind is applying their experiences to herself and Alex.

'How did you survive? What made the difference?'

'Bloodymindedness,' replies Jon. 'Pride. I don't like being beaten by something, especially if there's a woman involved.'

Susie smiles wryly at Annie. 'Such a romantic, isn't he? In films they say things like "Oh, I couldn't have done it without this wonderful woman here". But two things, I think, for me. One was realising that perhaps even paradise needs you to work at it. You know, a bit of pruning and weeding and the odd bonfire.'

Annie interjects. 'Yes . . . Alex said once that the key to the Garden of Eden is in making room for the snake. We all try to kick it out or pretend it's not there. It's allowing the bad bits to be there too, isn't it?'

'I suppose so. Not sure. But it's true things changed when I stopped expecting it to be easy and perfect, and stopped expecting Jon to be a god. It was great! I much prefer him as a mortal; it means I don't have to be perfect, either.'

Jon pretends to look aggrieved. 'Actually, not only do I think I do a pretty good job of being perfect, but I'm also one of the most easy and easygoing men I know.'

Susie makes a face at him and rolls her eyes at Annie. 'You reckon?' she says with feeling. 'You wish!—And the other thing was what I was thinking of when we started this conversation. Do you remember that we used to read to each other, Jon?'

'Oh yes, your "Thought For The Day,"' he says sarcastically as he stubs out his roll-up. 'Actually, that's not fair, because it made a hell of a difference. When you're desperate, little things do. It was OK, though; perhaps we ought to re-instate it.' He stands up and stretches and bends over to kiss Susie. 'I must go. Got a couple of window-frames to finish. See you later.'

'So tell me about the "Thought For The Day,"' says Annie after he's gone. They've brewed yet another cup of coffee; some days being there together and talking seems as important as getting on with their solitary work.

Susie takes a sip. 'Damn, that was hot. Burnt my tongue. Oh yes—your question! Kickstarting a creative thing. Well, it was really simple; actually, I feel silly talking about it, it seems so—well, kind of foolish. Anyway. What we would do—first it was me, then Jon started to take turns too—was that I'd go through several of our books. They were stacked in boxes on the floor in here, because it was the only place where they stood a chance of staying dryish, and I'd explore them box by box each week; kind of rationing, you know? So first thing, after throwing the dogs out, I'd get up and make a cup of tea—our bed was in here, too. Then I'd bring back a couple or three of the books from that week's box and go through them in bed until I found a passage or poem or quote that would really inspire me. You know how it is—sometimes you open the book on exactly the right piece, and sometimes you have to hunt it down.' She gets up to shoo out a bantam that was wandering, crooning loudly to itself, in through the open door. 'Sounds stupid but I think it helped keep us sane. So instead of griping at each other all the time, or moaning about the cold, I'd read that bit to Jon while we drank our tea. Kind of setting the tone for the day, and distracting us from the problems.' She looks at Annie a little sheepishly, smiling at herself. 'Sounds a bit pathetic, doesn't it?'

Annie smiles back. 'Not since I know you. It sounds lovely. Was that it?'

'Yep. Very simple. It was just about getting talking to each other, really, instead of dwelling on how hard it all was. Brought up loads of stuff. Supposing I'd read a piece that was about contentment, and I was feeling miserable and irritable, the contrast in a way exaggerated what I was feeling. So I'd try and talk to Jon about it all. He hated the talking about feelings bit but went along with it for my sake. Or he might read a beautiful poem and because I was feeling OK my mood might be heightened, and I'd try and stay aware of that through the day even through the difficult bits and frustrations. Especially. But best of all—that's what I was leading up to!—I sometimes found that the images would stay with me, or the feeling would, and later, just sometimes, a painting would come from it.'

'What kind of pieces did you use?'

'Oh, all sorts. Bob Dylan lyrics. W B Yeats. Song of Solomon. Jon had a book of Surrealist poetry. That was good. Hermann Hesse too, I think. Teachings of the Sufi masters. Tolkien. Tao Te Ching. Rumi. Zen and the Art of Motorcycle Maintenance! Whatever.' She turns her mouth down at the corners self-deprecatingly, then laughs at herself. 'I know it all sounds terribly—New Agey, the way I'm talking about it; but it did make a difference. I felt more—uhhh—creative, somehow. In the way I approached things. Perhaps we should do it again.'

'This fits in exactly with what I was thinking on my walk this morning. What about if we start right now; find a piece and then go off immediately and shut ourselves away to paint? I've been feeling stuck. It wouldn't hurt, would it?'

'That would be wonderful; but I think we might need a different kind of piece for painting. You go and choose a book; one with lots of images. Then after you've read it out we just go off to our separate work places without talking to each other, OK?'

Annie walks into the sitting-room and looks through the bookshelves until Dylan Thomas' *Collected Poems* catches her eye. She opens it at random. Perfect. She wanders back into the kitchen, immersed, and looks up at Susie. Feeling a little self-conscious despite her years of reading texts out loud to students, she says: 'What about this?

". . .My birthday began with the water -
Birds and the birds of the winged trees flying my name
Above the farms and the white horses
And I rose
In rainy autumn
And walked abroad in a shower of all my days . . ."'

They look at each other musingly. Suddenly Annie can see the words leaping off the page in a torrent of shape and colour, and turns and almost runs up the stairs to her easel, now in the loft room, and falls on her paints with the pictures forming behind her eyes to the words singing in her head, and paints with a joy and enthusiasm she hasn't felt for years.

By the time the phone rings at lunchtime, stretches of blue-green and umber broken with thin lines of peat-brown have started to converge and intersect on her canvas and something is starting to take shape. Annie is deeply immersed, fascinated by the images bubbling and forming and translating themselves into colour, line, block and plane. She had expected to be drawn to colours that reflected the southern French landscape, but the ones she'd picked were more sombre and washed out, brooding; more Dylan Thomas, Welsh. There is a simmering going on, a cooking; something is yet to make itself apparent. She is painting almost in a frenzy; inspired and excited. She doesn't hear the phone at first, and Susie has to call twice.

'Annie! Phone! It's for you!—Alex,' she says, holding out the receiver as Annie, looking abstracted, appears through the door. Annie has to make a conscious effort to shake herself out of the painting; she is gripped by it to the extent that she is momentarily disorientated in Susie's kitchen.

'Annie, my darling. How are you?' Alex's voice brings her back, warms and focuses her.

'Oh, sweetheart, it's really good to hear you! Tell me about it all. Where are you?'

Alex, it transpires, is camped out still at the Somport Tunnel site with a group of semi-permanent activists installed in benders, tents and vans. He has no immediate plans for coming back; the atmosphere and shared concerns are exciting and inspiring and the group is possibly on the verge of a breakthrough with the powers-that-be. He is sorry not to have written, or phoned; he's been very involved with the site and the campaign and never gets round to writing somehow, and the phone-box is a few miles away. He loves her and misses her, he adds.

As they ring off Annie feels troubled; something he dropped into the conversation towards the end. He mentioned having spoken to the children on the phone. Annie knows how momentous that would be for him, and her initial reaction was pleasure for him, followed immediately by pain, and she asked him how they were and whether it had been OK to speak to them. There was the tiniest pause before Alex answered, and then he changed the subject.

As she hangs up, Annie feels off-balance. There is, it seemed to her, a slight sense of foreboding in the afternoon light, and her solar plexus feels tight. 'Beware of storms,' says the peasant woman's voice in her head. 'Protect yourself; protect yourself.' She goes back up the stairs rather heavily, and stares at the incoherent shapes on the board on her easel in a rather uncomprehending way, as if they are meaningless splodges put there by a stranger.

That night the nightmares take a different shape, and intensify.

I am over my ankles in thick freezing mud, for there was a torrential downpour last night, flooding part of the courtyard and swirling down through to the cellars. In the middle of the night we raised the healthy to help us move the sick into the centre of the hall away from the staircases where the rains were making rivers.

The snowmelt will, praise be, make the slope once again unassailable for a short while. Our wells and cisterns will be filling; the people were crying with joy this morning, for yesterday we had not enough water to hold out for more than another day, and now we are stronger for a few days at least. Without water we are lost; but Guénon roused me and took me to one side at dawn. 'Isarn,' he said in that voice that chimes through my head, that I would recognise even with closed eyes in a crowd of thousands such as they say gather in the cities in front of the King's men, and yes the Pope's men too, 'it is not just through lack of water that we may suffer, but worse that a greater danger could come from the wells filling at such speed and stirring up the unclean silt.' I see him pause; he looks at me as if to ensure I am listening, or maybe to gauge my strength. He goes on. 'Stronger garrisons than ours have been overcome in the end not by the force of the invading armies but by the sickness of the waters; and indeed we have already lost several to vomiting blood. You know that. Isarn,' he said in his gentle, still voice which reminds me, even now that he is so worn and cadaverous, of a mountain pool, 'Isarn, you must watch with me for the sickness signs. We cannot tell them; it is enough for them to face the assaults without going out of their minds. They need to know there is hope. But we need also to man the wells. I need your help.'

His voice was steady. I could not believe that he did not seem to feel this cold. I pulled my own damp cloak tighter and clenched my fists so that he would not see my shivering. Over the mountains there was more cloud, unsettled cloud the colour of grapeskin. As I watched there was a momentary flicker of sunlight spilling on the mountain peak, gone as fast as a thought. Behind us the day's noises began: the clanking of pails, voices, someone snapping twigs for a fire, a muttering that might be prayer, the stamping of feet from the garrison, a low moaning from somewhere near the outer walls.

I looked up at Guénon, though now he is so stooped my eyes have less far to travel. The look in his eyes was grave with pain. Despite our position—for it is unlikely, we both know, that we shall come out alive—I have never seen fear in his eyes, only an immense desolate pity which is almost unbearable; and I turned away, for now that I, too, am sworn I cannot touch him like that. I grieve still for how it was when we held each other and promised eternal love. But the love is now for greater service, not ours alone. He is limping badly now; the wound festers worse in the damp; it stinks, and there are no clean cloths and precious little fuel or water to spare.

We have burnt most of the juniper bushes that Arnaud and Raimon managed to collect by night after we had repulsed the last assault. The stocks of grain and flour and oil have nearly gone and none of us talks of holding out now. Until two moons ago a few brave sympathisers, unsurpassed in courage and generosity, risked their lives to replenish our stocks or pass us word, slipping through the lines by night, but no more now. We of course do not eat flesh, but there has been none, dried or otherwise, for the garrison who have defended us so loyally and so long, it seems, now—though it is probably only ten moons or so. What healthy livestock we held for the croyants and defenders here with us were long ago slaughtered; the others left to rot where they dropped (what else could we do with the corpses other than fling them over the walls?) after the sickness and starvation took so many. At least with the cold the hosts of swarming meat-flies do not plague us as they did.

The siege and assaults have redoubled, and Guénon doubts now that the reinforcements that we hoped for by the Spring festival time, Béma, that the Papists call Easter, will arrive. Thanks be that Mathieu and Pierre Bonet escaped safely and transferred what is our remaining material wealth to the people of Sabarthes, other than that with which we shall repay our loyal garrison, finally.

Mathieu has returned. It is not time yet for our last treasure, our true wealth and testament, (which some call the Graal, though it does not in actuality resemble that most sacred and dreadful cup of which the scriptures teach and which offers a symbol to those who need a material teaching) to be carried to safety, for we have need of it still for the Spring rites; may God save us and protect us until that time where the forces are evenly balanced, the one against the other in perfect tension, the black and the white, where we may slip through the final gateway beyond the dark and the light.

Since the storming and capture of the tower at the eastern end of the pog we are under siege the last few weeks almost incessantly until last night's downpour, and as the soldiers and lay people who are with us are wounded, we replace them ourselves, men and women.

Mathieu and Pierre talk of a great army of 6000 men-at-arms—more criminals, bandits and mercenary men by far than those Papists who call themselves men of God—how, save by faith and the protection of He who is source of all light and good, can so few of us hope to survive? And yet we have the rocks on our side, for we are of all the hill fortresses one of the most inaccessible, even in good weather, and one of the biggest to ring round with swords and spears. But they have the great mangonel catapults in the eastern tower to challenge our own.

We are now all within the ramparts with the soldiers and under the protection of the Seigneur and his family. We have had to abandon our little dwellings strung out along the feet of the walls facing over those beloved valleys, for there is little—no—protection against so vast a crusading army. This is now our home.

It is as if we are entombed.

NINETEEN

The panic again. Annie lies in bed sweating, holding at bay the fear that glimmers at the edges of her mind. Images from her nightmares tumble and intertwine with phrases from her phone conversation with Alex until she senses herself impossibly entangled, as if she might, as if wrapped in some kind of ferocious deep-sea-weed, be pulled away out of any rescuable depth and drown.

With a struggle she wrenches her mind free, back to her painting, and finds herself out of bed, focusing on dressing, running over in her mind the colours she will work with today, listening to the morning sounds outside her window. She will not follow that other path; she will not give in to this strange madness.

For several hours she paints, semi-tranced, unaware of time or the outer world or issues such as breakfast and her morning walk.

At nine Susie sticks her head around the door. Annie looks quite transfigured, she thinks; she almost glows. She is so completely absorbed in her work that there seems somehow to be virtually no distinction between the painting hand and the painted surface; Susie, observing, finds herself almost expecting to see a tangible connection flowing between the two. The canvas in front of Annie looks alive, pulsing with a strange terrible beauty. Susie finds it hard to keep her eyes on it; it seems intrusive, almost a sacrilege, to do so. She withdraws quietly.

At eleven there's still been no movement from upstairs, no sign of Annie. Susie again tiptoes up and looks around the door, and again she has the sense that she is trespassing. Annie is so completely immersed in a private exclusive world that it's like witnessing someone naked without their permission or knowledge. Susie once more steps back from the door, delighted that her friend seems to have found her way again, but also slightly concerned. The atmosphere in the room seems so obsessive, somehow; and the painting so troubled.

When Annie has still not come down by one, Susie decides to intrude.

She pokes her head around the door again and says in a firm matter-of-fact voice to Annie's back: 'Lunchtime, Annie. It's gone one.'

Very slowly Annie steps back from the canvas, and, in the same smooth slow movement, like a sleepwalker, turns her head to the door. Susie is shaken right through her body at Annie's face; for her eyes look completely blank, disinhabited, as if she has moved elsewhere and left her body behind.

'Annie?' whispers Susie in shock, in fear. And then the moment is gone and the person at the canvas is her old friend, who now sinks down to crouch against the wall and rub her eyes in exhaustion. She hangs her head for a moment, arms on thin black-clad thighs and hands dangling, and looks back up at the canvas, and then at Susie. Her baggy white T-shirt emphasises her slender figure so that she looks frail; the combination of this and her old black jeans give her body a stark angularity that is uncompromisingly harsh somehow, broken only by the two points of flame at her ears, the habitual amber drops. With the light from the window to one side and behind and from the Velux above striking down and across the side of her face at an angle her high cheekbones and the habitual heathery-mauve shadows under her eyes are pronounced. Susie thinks that she looks almost ascetic; both drawn and haggard to the point of looking ill, and yet at the same time lit from within. She remembers the same look on the faces of Buddhist monks in the Thai monastery she and Jon had stayed in, after a longish fast.

'God, Susie, I'm completely wiped out. What time is it? That took me over. It's going to be a powerful painting—can I talk to you about it later on? It's my dreams. Oh God, I completely forgot the dogs and bread. Sorry.'

The two women stand, later that afternoon, in front of Annie's easel. The painting, still unfinished, is indeed quite powerful— 'terrible', Susie nearly says out loud, not quite knowing why, and not meaning it derogatorily. Something in it makes her feel uneasy. She has instinctively crossed her arms over her solar plexus. The choice of colour is strange, for a start. Susie, accomplished technically, nonetheless paints what she sees, and as a representational artist struggles to understand the need for abstraction. If asked she would say that her painting was used to convey the sense of serenity and warmth and natural stability that living here gave her. Yes, she might include hints that nothing is ever quite what it seems; and she would be the first to admit that painting could be used as a defence against insecurity, an attempt to fix what was transient into some sort of permanence. But on the whole her painting is light.

The hint of mystery, that things are not what they seem, is all that her painting and Annie's have in common. Annie's work is raw to the point of being savage, gut-wrenching, painful. And yet Susie cannot at first say why. At an initial glance the main colours in the painting can be read either way. The umbers and ochres and blue-greens would not have been out of place in a romanticised English seascape; a shade lighter and they would be almost washed-out, translucent. Here, though, they have a deeper note, in the way that the Atlantic has, even on a soft day, when you really look at it. The surface calm is deceptive, illusory; it is as likely to dash you against the rocks as lull you to sleep. The whispered threat of darkness, to those who live by such a sea, is always there.

So it is with the painting. Somehow the colours cannot be anything other than threatening, brooding, once you had looked more closely. The effect is exacerbated by the thin peat-brown lines criss-crossing, or rather slashing, the surface in an apparently random way, dense in some places, sparse in others, pooling at the bottom.

Susie stares, and then gasps as suddenly a face appears, and then another and another. As soon as she's spotted them they move, dissolve and reassemble themselves into shadows on the landscape; for indeed, the picture now looks like a landscape. Annie stands without speaking or moving as Susie's eyes pick out rocks, boulders, a crumbling wall at the peak of a mountain? Or merely the junction of clouds and land, shadow and matter? Which is solid and which insubstantial? And there is something about the painting that threatens to pull you in, so that you lose your perspective, your bearings. Susie resists the pull, but finds it hard to turn her eyes away. The more she stares, the more elusive the shapes she thinks she sees become, until, once more, she is looking at an abstract field of overlapping colour, criss-crossed with an angular intersecting overlay. And then just as she turns to Annie, unsure what on earth to say, a last shape jumps out at her from the bottom of the picture; a symbol that she recognises, a cross within a circle.

'Oh, how strange; that's one of the old Occitan symbols. They say that they marked the villages of Cathar believers. Have you seen them cut into the stonework now and then around here?'

Annie feels chilled. She draws breath. 'No,' she says very quietly. 'Not that I remember.'

There is a pause. A fly buzzes around their heads in the afternoon heat and silence. Annie looks out the window north towards the Languedoc lowlands unfolding beyond the foothills, small clusters of whiteish-ochre villages built on the slopes of the higher ground and capped with shallow red pantiled roofs, and further enclosed by smaller purpling mountain ranges and contours beyond them. In the near-distance, at the junction between the Pyrenean foothills and the lowlands and visible only as a subdued terrestrial blazing, darkening now in September as the heads set seed, hectares of sunflowers make minute synchronous adjustments to the turning of the sun. Looming like a stony tumour behind the golden strip is a hunchback shape; one of the many mountain strongholds that, witness to the human atrocities of seven centuries ago, now sit guard, like great wounded animals, brooding and terrible and unforgetting, over the afternoon landscape.

Susie watches Annie, not daring to intrude.

Annie brings herself back to the room, the painting, the symbol. The symbol. She glances at Susie, then away again. 'No. I don't think so. But they're in my dreams all the time.'

The fortress is a stinking mire; the stench of ordure—and sickness, for of the four hundred and more believers and defenders here a quarter nearly are sick and wounded—hangs all the time in the air.

In one of the alcoves an elderly woman with a shorn head is herself shearing the hair of her daughter with slow sawings of a rusty knife. Is the cold better than the parasites? I have noticed how almost no-one now shows the energy even to rid each other of ticks and lice. This troubles me—we must not give up; never give up. Not while there is life and faith and hope. I stare. The young woman whose dark hair litters the stones and will be used in rag pillows for the sick seems far away, her head and thin shoulders resignedly drooped, but the old woman raises her head and her one good eye stares back. Her bone structure is good; she must have been handsome, and I see that she is not so old—perhaps not yet forty. She stretches her lips, which I see are cracked and purple, into a smile. There is love here. I lift my hand and we offer each other the blessing, and I continue.

Soldiers pass me muttering unholy words at a near-run, weapons clanking; from the shouting and turbulence at the eastern end I guess there is trouble from beyond, or even inside, the walls. No-one moves; this is a common occurrence now.

I am proud to be with these people; despite all, there are no screams, only a fairly constant low moan issuing from the hall where the sick and wounded are crowded against what little warmth we can raise. I am so used to the sound now that I forget it is not the sound of a watercourse down a hillside, which it resembles.

The cold again this morning is fearful; the rain has hardened and icy stones drop down Guénon's neck as he crosses the courtyard in front of me to comfort a young girl who has had no will to come in from the elements since her betrothed was killed and hanged from the ramparts in last week's attack. When they die outside the walls we can do nothing now save leave them as carrion, like the sheep. At first we braved finding a gap in the hundreds, perhaps thousands, of soldiers ringing the mountain; some troops are made of local men who can at times be persuaded to look the other way at night, in the cold, but it has become impossible since the sympathisers were routed out and tortured or knifed. After that, we buried them near the walls, though it is almost impossible to dig through the ice and rock. Now it has become certain death to try to find egress from here even to bury the dead.

Word has come of other fortresses where luck has truly deserted them; even, it almost seems, God; the invaders have gouged out eyes and cut off lips and noses to make examples of sympathisers. La Dame Guiraude, chatelaine of Montréal, it is told, after her brother and eighty knights were massacred, was offered to the invading army for their pleasure, and then thrust down a well and buried under a tumble of stones.

I am trained in the ways of death and the flight of the spirit and it is still unbearable to think of these things; how much worse for one such as the young girl whom Guénon comforts, one who has no knowledge of these things. Guénon speaks, while I stand at a distance. I cannot hear his words but I can see the way they caress her. Even in these times my heart swells when I watch him at the work he does so well. The girl stands at the wall like a ghost, unspeaking, ragged and bony now, dark with the wet; when I look at her I see a huge and silent scream, for all of us here. She clings to the wall with purple clawing hands, and will not be drawn, except by Guénon—his goodness is such that he can draw forth an echoing goodness from stones. Even the wild birds attend to him. The girl heeds no-one else; she has lost her speech, and I fear too her mind and spirit. There is an emptiness around her body, a strange dull density, which despite our straits has happened to few of us here yet.

My stomach pains me all the time; whether from hunger or fear and nausea or from the mishandling by soldiers when we fled Carcassone I do not know. I bleed much of the time still. I know in my depths that if I were to live I would be unable to bear a child now from the damage. How fortunate I am sworn to chastity now then! and can love Guénon with all my heart.

I look at him as he limps back towards me, supporting the girl to shelter. As always when he meets me he raises his eyes to mine. As always I strain to suppress my shivering with the cold, so as not to increase his burden with worry about me. I hide my hands. His hands are twisted and knotted with the stiffness and blue with cold, but he does not seem to notice; endlessly blessing, and smiling gravely, and laying-on hands with the power wherever it is called for. He works ceaselessly, and people near him are eased and comforted just to see him. He approaches and I smell the good smell of him, his flesh that once I knew so intimately, beneath the smell of his wound. Again tonight I will offer to dress his wound with rosemary and soucis sauvages; again I know he will refuse.

He asks me for something to let the girl sleep. I look at her, her dulled eyes, in distress and despair. Of course there is always hope, but there has to be some will to live on the part of the sick one, too. Also I have nearly exhausted all my supplies of herbs—I cannot bear now to remember collecting them in my freedom early last summer; the nettles, mountain thyme and rosemary, gentle soothing lavender, the woundwort, comfrey, agrimony, heartsease, the little sun-faces of the soucis sauvages. Instead I give thanks that they have lasted and eased what discomfort they could. I try not to think of before, and the family, all dead now as heretics, and the goats and geese and dogs and another life, where I was simply the stock herd and weaver and called to attend others merely for my knowledge of herbs. So easy.

The other parfaits have already sent their personal wealth, their goods and possessions down to the villages for distribution. I had little.

There is so much love here, even and especially in the midst of this brutality and hardship and cold. No-one has deserted us, not even the lay-people who have no reason to be here

*except choice, for they were offered a truce, a chance to recant
and be spared death. The only ones who have left are those we
sent earlier, badly wounded or mortally sick, to where they
might be safe; but now, of course, we tend those sick, for they
would not be given mercy outside. Each day more of the lay
people ask to be received, to take the Consolamentum and join
us on our final journey. Guénon has tears in his eyes each time
this happens.*

I find there is nothing I can say that is large enough.

*It is bitterly cold and the wind is savage. I cannot feel my
feet, but my robe is only damp today, for I have not been on
the walls like many of them. I tug my own hands out of my
pockets and out of the hand-coverings I made from goat-hair,
and gently pull them over the young girl's fingers. I can tuck
my hands into my sleeves. As I leave to find my herbs one of
the soldiers passes us and whistles a few teasing notes at the
young girl, and pinches her cheek.*

*Sometimes, as now, Guénon sings; a low, haunting chant
like the wind in trees.*

We pray.

Annie pushes out of her mind the shadowy faces crowding and
darkening the attic room, which should be swimming with
light under the September daybreak. She is half-propped
against pillows. Her hands are sweating and her heart thumps;
she makes herself read back what she has scribbled, as if
automatically, in her journal; makes herself look up, familiarise
herself with the room and the surroundings once again, listen
for Susie and Jon's low murmur from the kitchen below her.

Scenes from the night push into her conscious mind still,
jostling for attention, moaning and whispering under her
deliberate thoughts about the room, the views, the sunlight, the
carved wooden figure of the Buddha. Phrases insinuate, insist:

wisdom beyond words, beyond love, beyond death, n'oublie jamais, n'oublie jamais, the wisdom of the heart, love never forgets . . . Annie shakes her head, fixes her eyes on the serenity of the Buddha's face, holds on tight. There is a painful dark-red pulsing behind her eyes and a rising panic and dread in her gorge. Her mind cannot hold these two realities together. One or other must succumb.

She throws herself out of bed, goes to the window to reassure herself that she is indeed in Les Cerisiers, doubting that she will see the wished-for geese, goats, Jon's truck; and thank God, there is Jon, crossing the yard, whistling. Annie focuses minutely on him, his appearance, his twentieth-century working clothes of jeans and T-shirt. She can't stop shaking. As she turns she knocks over the two-legged easel, and snatches up the tumbled canvas, thrusts it face-to-wall. Susie, hearing the crash, calls up the stairs and Annie wipes sweat off her face, goes to the door. *Il y a des tempêtes qui viennent, des tempêtes,* says the voice in her head. Annie thinks wildly there is nowhere to hide.

Susie taps on the door. 'Annie. My God, Annie, what on earth is it? You're white as a sheet.' She puts out her arms, her own heart thumping in sudden panic.

TWENTY

On the Atlantic coast, at the far end of the Pyrenees, Alex is parked up a few steps from a small beach between San Sebastian and Santander.

In the late September morning light he stands with his back to the waves and stares morosely up towards the great chain of mountains squatting between him and the recently-risen sun, simultaneously linking and dividing himself and Annie. With the light behind them they look to him deceptively insubstantial, undifferentiated, almost two-dimensional. The quality of light is filmy; a combination of ray-diffusion around the peaks and salt-spray from the rising tide.

The previous morning he had made two snap decisions, one following fast on the heels of the other, at the time seemingly irrevocably connected, just as the wave crashing behind him merely heralded a succeeding crash, wave following wave to infinity; inexorable, nauseatingly certain. He swings round and stares at the stretch of ocean, notes with a degree of disgust that even here, at this time of the morning, he is not alone, for the waves carry a cargo, a flotsam of little black-clad stick-men, an itinerant population of water-gipsies following the surf along Europe's Atlantic coast. Alex feels land-bound and heavy, suddenly; the grace of the light dancing figure playing with the wave closest to him merely exacerbates his own feelings of immobilisation.

He kicks savagely at the pebbly gritty sand, and walks off parallel to the water, hands thrust into jeans pockets. Yesterday morning, he suddenly knew what he had to do. Now, where by tonight he would be committed to it, he does not.

Yesterday he let himself acknowledge that his gut feeling was that the battle against the Tonnel du Somport construction was lost; lost to commerce, to the demands of big business, consumerism. Lost to ignorance and apathy. No matter how vociferous, how dedicated, a small group of activists drawing attention to the plight of six bears in their wilderness habitat could put up no serious stand against the grinding wheels of industry-based supply-and-demand. In fact, looked at coldly, it was a ludicrous illusion. How could he have believed differently? Of course the six-lane-highway people would win.

He had looked around the makeshift camp in sudden despair. Not a hope in hell. What the fuck were they all doing? What chance did they think dreams stood? Who did they think would listen? And now that he knew the cause was lost, how could he stay? Until an hour previously he had been part of this cause, this campaign; heart and soul in the thick of it. Now he stood at the edge, a cynical bystander, a detached looker-on. And in his blinding plummet into despair and disillusion, he snagged himself on the razor-sharp edges of his desolation at losing his children, and his guilt about Kate. Now, suddenly, there was no choice for him. Anything was better than this impasse, this feeling of being imprisoned by unresolved emotions on every front. There was a boat leaving Santander for England the next night, and he would catch it.

He'd left Somport within the hour, and drove on automatic pilot through the hauntingly beautiful mountain landscape that somehow touched him not at all.

And now here he is, without the conviction or will to head for the boat. Try as he might, he cannot bring himself just to walk away from Annie, and all that she represents.

Maybe if he calls her, hears her voice, he thinks, he will know what to do. Or perhaps he should just get back to the van and drive; drive the other way, drive to Malaga, take a boat for Morocco, lose himself in Africa, take his chances.

He strides towards the van and climbs in, slams the door. He revs the engine savagely, teeth gritted, filling the still morning air with a cloud of exhaust. He notices the fumes, curses his own weakness and pushes the van roaring in bottom gear up the slope onto the road, heads for the next town, the next phone-box.

Dials the number of Les Cerisiers.

'Oh, Alex,' says Susie's voice, 'I'm really glad to hear you. Listen, Annie's not here; Jon gave her a lift into Perpignan first thing; she's gone to the library. They won't be back till dusk. Alex, I'm a bit concerned about Annie—when are you coming back?'

'What do you mean, concerned?' His voice comes out rougher than he intends. There's a brief pause.

'She seems a bit—strange, Alex. Stressed. She's not sleeping well and she just doesn't seem herself. She's kind of obsessed, somehow, a bit faraway. I can't really explain.'

'Fuck, fuck, fuck,' says Alex under his breath; and out loud, 'I'll ring later, Susie.' He bangs the receiver back into its cradle forcefully enough as to elicit curious looks from the couple of elderly men sitting nearby on the iron bench on the edge of the square.

'Fuck,' he says again, out loud. Not quite knowing what else to do, and playing for time, he wanders through the fish-market towards a bar on the opposite side. For a brief moment he loses himself in the colour and the stench and the noise of guttural Basque and Spanish voices; he notices the slant of sunlight glancing off fish-scales of every hue but all tinged with silver. Though vegetarian, he only just resists the impulse to buy half-a-kilo of gleaming whitebait—something which never normally tempts him in the slightest, but which fits, at this moment, with the urge to flee, to become nomadic, untrackable; his eyes, alighting on the tiny silver bodies, have created simultaneously in his mind the image of a flickering beach-fire and a sleeping-bag under the stars. Whitebait grilled on salt driftwood, flaming blue and green, washed down with coarse local brandy, and no-one to answer to, be responsible for; the shush of small shells tumbled in gentle surf, smell of saltspray, rolling murmurous roar of the ocean to drown the incessant mental chatter.

Dreams, dreams.

The bar is dark and rather dingy; utilitarian but furnished with an ancient juke-box that, even at this time in the morning, belts out fifteen-year-old American hits just slightly slow, a semi-tone off-key, as if there were a slipping drive-belt. The décor is unmitigated brown, thick with dripped and wrinkled varnish, which does nothing for his mood save flatten it a little further. The air, too, seems brown; fogged with maxi-strength handrolling tobacco fumes. At least, he thinks, at least the tourists haven't cleansed and sterilised this town yet. That it is still a working fishing-port is obvious from the clientele and the odour that surrounds them. Thank God, too, for their extraverted natures and their loud voices and extravagant gesticulations; today he would drown in Englishness if he were to be surrounded by it, sunk without trace. Here, now, in the dialect thrown back and forth across the room, he catches enough snatches of the Basque language to be sure that it had roots in common with the Celtic tongue: some lilt of the Welsh, harsher notes of the ks and zs of Breton. He could be at home here. But then, in his new nomadic mindset, he could be at home anywhere, or nowhere.

The espresso is exceedingly good; opaque velvet-black, the colour of good Guinness, for which Alex has a momentary twinge of nostalgia. The curl of steam hitting his nostrils cheers him minutely, and he stands to scrabble in his pockets for the few remaining pesetas with which to buy some tobacco to complement his coffee, for today the mood seems right. Seeing the pitiful scatter of coins in his fist—for he had only changed a 100f note at the border—he thinks better of it, and saves what cash he has. You never know.

Outside once more, he stands in the doorway for a moment, looking out. The clear morning is gradually being swallowed by a sea-mist, come in with the tide, and it seems to Alex that the gulls' cries have a new edge to them, which does nothing to ease the sense of desolation which is creeping back in. I need a sign, he thinks; come on universe. What the fuck do I do? I could toss a coin; the answer not being in whether it comes up heads or tails but in my reaction to what it comes up. But there are more than two options, more than two histories, more than two possible futures. A multitude of pasts all leading to now, and a multitude of pathways leading away from here. He wonders idly, distracting himself, whether there was a plethora of selves, too, and whether the path you thought you took, in consciousness, was the only path, or whether other yous in parallel universes took other paths, fulfilling other separate destinies. Whether even a future you is currently taking an utterly different path. What does this do to time?

And meantime, how to reduce Kate and Annie to two separate sides of one coin? He grimaces wryly, and walks around the corner, away from the fishmarket and the sea, facing again the looming mountains.

In front of him now is a smaller market, equally colourful, equally noisy, and more domestic. Stalls of fabric jostling tables bright with pyramids of citrus fruit, with full soft tumbles of late crimson nectarines and peaches, blush-gold apricots and magenta plums; tables of crockery neighboured by cages of flapping fowl, their legs tied; bowls of olives and slabs of cheeses and shirts and shoes and socks. He stops in front of a boot stall; a pair of knee-length pull-on boots in a soft washed-out ochre leather with a hint of darker stitching and a low heel catches his eye. He'd like to buy them for Annie, but actually they are more Kate's style. She'd love them. Spanish boots of Spanish leather . . . *The same thing I want from you today / I would want again tomorrow . . ./ . . . I don't know when I'll be coming back again / It depends on how I'm feeling . . .*

He meanders slowly on, buys some olives and a yellowish round loaf of bread. He breaks off a corner; slightly sweet, slightly sour. The words roll around in his head: *Well if you my love must think that way / I'm sure your mind is roamin' / I'm sure your heart is not with me but with the country where you're going . . .*

So take heed take heed of the western wind / Take heed of the stormy weather / And yes, there's something you can send back to me / Spanish boots of Spanish leather . . .

A bookstall, a welter of languages, Spanish, French, Basque—he stops, chewing. And there it is—his sign. Staring at him from the top of a pile of nearly-new books—*Le Vrai Visage du Catharisme.* He turns the book over. Written by Anne Brenon, director, he makes out, of the Centre national d'etudes cathares René-Nelli, at Villegly, near Carcassone. Near Carcassone! He's stopped chewing, stopped breathing for a moment in his concentration on translating the book's blurb, and in his perpetual delight in the way the universe always throws you the answers, if you knew the questions (and equally often even when you didn't, but simply knew there was a question for the asking). Of course! How could he have doubted? Of course he knows where his path lies; for the moment, anyway. And as for tomorrow—well, he would follow his heart; 'follow your bliss', he remembers, all those months ago. And if in his heart there flickers from time to time the tiny voice of a long-lost nomad, well, perhaps the least he can do is acknowledge its existence.

For now, here is the signpost for the next step. He grins to himself in deep gratitude and hands over the last of his cash to the young woman standing behind the stall. The Basque women really are astonishingly beautiful, he thinks, staring as he smiles at her and she lifts her surprisingly pale eyes to his face, and offers him a paper bag. He shakes his head, still smiling, and on impulse lifts her hand and kisses it, to wolf-whistles from the (male, and astonishingly unremarkable) neighbouring stallholders, along with a torrent of presumably ribald comments. His heart feels several pounds lighter now as he weaves back through the stalls seawards towards the van, to pick up the motorway at Bilbao and travel back towards Bayonne, before heading east again across the stony feet of the mountains once more, to Annie and the Cathars.

TWENTY-ONE

'I think you're avoiding things, Annie.'

Alex stops walking, hands in pockets, and turns to face her. His jaw is set stubbornly, thrust out; even under his beard Annie can see the firm lines of his determination. She has scarcely seen this Alex, but can imagine only too well that once he had taken up an idea he would be totally intractable. His eyes, never cold, are nonetheless grave and unsmiling.

'All of this is an avoidance tactic. Your painting; your obsession with the Cathars; your refusal to talk about your feelings, about Greg, about what you want of your own future. It seems to me that when life gets challenging your response is to escape into your ivory tower.

'Sometimes I think I know what you want of me, of us, and sometimes I haven't any idea whether you even notice whether I'm here or not. It's as if you hold me at arm's length with one hand, but cling to me with the other, and all the time you're locked away in some small remote island home of your own, impenetrable.' Alex hears his monologue and feels guilty at its harshness, but it is time to clear the turbidity between them.

Annie, surprised and wounded, opens her mouth to protest, but Alex holds up a hand. 'Please, Annie, I need to finish this, to get it out in the open.

'Sometimes you're so goddam solitary I feel as if I spend my time knocking on a window between us. Other times I feel as if you're wanting me around simply to stop you having to face being on your own.' He glances at Annie, sees the hurt and surprise in her eyes, followed immediately by the very distance and remoteness that he is talking about. He forces himself to continue, his anger refuelled by her closing off.

'I don't know which frightens me more. You know that clinging to each other can't work, no matter how much we love each other. You know bloody well it won't. You know that another person can never be everything for you; it's only you who can live your life. Isn't it? There are things you need to face, Annie. Have you let go of the past? What do you want of the future? How are you going to make it happen?' His eyes are steady, direct, fixed on hers.

She stares back, unable for the moment to answer. She notices irrelevantly that there is enough of winter in the morning for his breath to hang momentarily in the air between them. Then for the briefest of instants the moment somersaults and Alex's body seems to become transparent, so that she thinks she can see the landscape behind—or rather through—him; familiar, and yet not quite the same. Fleetingly she feels herself start to fall sideways and puts out her hand to brace herself against the low overgrown stone wall bordering the track. Just as suddenly the moment passes and she swallows the bile in her throat and focuses again on Alex. A brief glint of wry humour touches her, self-irony, underneath the nausea and anxiety that accompanies these moments. Alex is right— she does have a tendency to try and escape emotional confrontations, as has just been graphically demonstrated for her. Has he noticed this latest, if subconscious, attempt? She focuses again on him; he is watching her with concern, and some anxiety. Neither has moved, save for Annie's reflexive stretched hand. The dogs, ahead of them, turn their heads towards them. Finn, the older dog, sits down resignedly; Wesley goes to investigate the hedge.

'When I want to talk about these things you clam up. You say how much you love being able to talk about issues, about feelings, with me, but actually it's usually me that does the talking. You listen, but always you have that slightly wary look in your eyes, and nowadays that faraway look, too, as if you're only willing to have part of you in the room with me. Where are you, Annie? What do you really want?'

He stops. Annie's shoulders are hunched, her fists clenched in her pockets. Her eyes glitter; he sees her swallow. 'Am I being unfair? I don't mean to hurt you, sweetheart.'

Annie looks down. Alex notices a smudge of paint still on her cheek and that her glossy black hair is tumbled and uncombed, loose; she is looking uncharacteristically disordered.

When Alex asked her to come too on the morning walk into La Chapelle Blanche Annie remembered guiltily how she had adopted it as 'her' job until a few weeks ago; now when she wakes up all she can think about is immersing herself in another book or more papers on the Cathars, or painting. Unbidden, Alex has picked up the bread-and-dog-walk on her behalf. This time when he asked her to come too something in his voice jolted her back, away from the wet paint on her palette and the torrent of images from her night-dreams. At the back door she had looked at the sky and shrugged on an old wool duffle-coat that had been abandoned by some previous visitor to Les Cerisiers. It was huge on her, and tattered; muddied and slightly torn. Six months ago Annie wouldn't have been seen in the dark in it, let alone in daylight in front of Alex.

Alex had looked at her in it, an anxiously amused half-smile on his lips.

'You know,' he says now, 'it's as if all my adult life I've kind of lived an emotional half-life. When I met you it was all passion and depth of feeling. It was fucking wonderful. I felt so alive. But you seem to have disappeared. I'm so—bloody disappointed, I suppose. Gutted. Where's it gone? I love you. I've been thinking you loved me too.'

After a moment Annie drags her toe in a curve though the dirt and glances at him. She suddenly looks very young, almost childlike, to Alex. In contrast, her voice, replying, is formal; a grownup's voice.

'Yes, Alex, I do think you're being unfair. I'm not looking to you to do any of my living for me; and I wasn't aware I was shutting you out. And how can you talk to me about letting go of my past? You have a past too, and one that you haven't yet resolved either.' She hears her own cool, clipped rational tone with some dismay; maybe he is right, maybe she does retreat when the going gets rough. Partly out of a desire to prove him wrong, and, partly, too, because she knows that it matters that she learns how to trust him with her feelings, she makes herself continue. 'I do want you in my life; and for you, because of who you are, because I'm in love with you—' she stops, hearing the words. 'Because I—it's not just to stop me being lonely. I do try to talk to you about my feelings; I have talked to you about Greg. The reason I don't talk more is because I respect your right not to talk about Kate and your feelings about—about all that. I'm trying to be sensitive towards you and your feelings—not to push you if you don't want to talk.'

Something suddenly pushes itself to the surface in her. It feels hard and cold and sharp, like a steel blade. It takes her a moment to recognise it as anger. Alex is still watching her. She feels her jaw tighten.

'It isn't just me who finds it hard to talk about what's really going on, Alex. I feel as if you're being hypocritical, as well as arrogant. Have you let go? How do you think it feels not to have the slightest idea about what's going on inside you as regards your wife and children? ' She turns her face away from him so that her hair hides her expression.

Alex suddenly has a flash of the bridge, the sullen silence, the dead pine marten on their journey to Les Cerisiers.

Annie's shoulders twitch slightly. 'At least my husband's dead.' There. It was said. Annie carries on staring at the reddish dust in the lane, spattered with darker splashes, like blood, from a chilly November shower. Oh God. The unsayable had been said.

She wipes the back of her hand across her eyes and looks back at Alex. He sees the moisture glitter on her lashes and for a second she looks frightened, vulnerable. Present. Alex feels torn between anger and compassion. For the second time in a few weeks he has the urge just to run, to turn on his heel and escape in the van towards freedom, towards the sunshine and the life of a nomad. Somehow Annie has just evaded him again and all of a sudden he feels he can't be bothered with the complexities of relationship. And, too, she might be right; perhaps he is projecting his own fears and inadequacies onto her. Oh God—round and round in circles, never quite meeting.

He stands still, resisting his impulse to hit back verbally at her words. He will not take the coward's way out, the refuge in flight, in self-justification, in anger—and after a moment he feels himself soften. He steps towards her, his arms open. For a moment she stays where she is, stiff, untouchable, uncompromising; then she lets herself drop towards him and drops her face onto his shoulder. After a minute he pulls back and looks at her with his arms around her waist. She turns her face to his. Her eyes are naked and unreadable, at the same time. There is still a hint of apprehension.

'That was a bit below the belt, Annie. Scorpio tongue,' he says quietly, after a moment.

'It was hard for me to say it. And it's hard to hear you say things like what you just said, Alex. You said something along the same lines that day we went to Carcassone, about my painting, about abstraction being a flight from feelings. Just because I choose to retain some privacy doesn't mean I don't feel my feelings, or that I don't love you. I'm not an extravert like you; I don't have your trusting fiery nature. I take a while before I feel I know someone well enough to show them everything. Give me a chance, Alex; things haven't been easy for me, either, the last year. To put it mildly.' She lifts a hand to run it down the back of his head, over his thick curls. 'Please let's not fight, I don't expect you to tell me all the secrets of your heart; allow me to keep a few, too.' She takes a deep breath, and hesitates a moment, then goes on: 'What I'm doing at the moment is hugely important to me. I feel I'm right on the cusp of something tremendous, something that will make a big difference to how I live. I don't know what it is or where it's leading, I just know that I have to follow it. It *is* my future. Alex; I can't explain it and I feel as if I'm tiptoeing through an endless dark and silent wood . . .' she glances at him to make sure he picks up the allusion to the Persephone card, and catches a slight glimpse of humour, of acknowledgement, flicker in his eyes, and continues: 'It's frightening, and I have to do it alone. The painting and the Cathars are all bound up with it somehow. Do you understand what I'm talking about?'

Alex nods. 'But, Annie my darling, you don't have to be alone to do it.' He picks up her hand and squeezes it, then tilts his head in the direction of La Chapelle Blanche and moves to swing on with her beside him towards the village. Grinning, he turns to her and adds in an exaggerated Irish accent: 'At least, let me walk a bit o' t'way wit' you, me darlin'.'

By the time they arrive at La Chapelle Blanche, any stranger, looking at them, would see a happy laughing couple, obviously in love, as they stroll through the village hand-in-hand, the pair of dogs bouncing around them.

But Annie suddenly has become acutely aware of the chill in the November air, the turning leaves and reddening rosehips, the new absence of the swifts usually swooping and shrilling around the twenty or so stone buildings of which the hamlet is comprised. She is left feeling edgy, somehow, as if she were walking towards an invisible cliff.

And once back home at Les Cerisiers, as she and Alex help Jon stack winter logs against the wall in one of the barns, her mind works Alex's words over and over, the way one's tongue is drawn again and again to probe an aching or chipped tooth. She is aware that she has made no decisions, other than the decisions-by-default that hang around her letter of resignation to the university. Nor has he, retaliates an indignant part of her brain. Shut up, she responds. I'm taking responsibility for my life; that's all I can do. All I have the power to do.

Back at Ide her house lies, with her past, as abandoned and unresolved as the Marie Celeste. Simply to walk out on a life does not, she knows, conclude it; and Annie reluctantly allows herself to acknowledge that at some stage in the future she will have to go back before she can go forwards. She will, she supposes, have to sell the house, and wrap up her life with Greg in the act. All her adulthood. Then what? And where? Despite her better intentions, she feels a flash of anger at Alex and finds herself banging her logs into place, causing both men to look at her in some surprise. All very well for him to talk about her facing her future. Has he mentioned his, or theirs? What does he think will happen about Kate and the children? You can't just walk out on people, on a family, like you can a building. Sooner or later you have to make contact, return to cut the bonds—or renew them.

To her astonishment she feels a constriction in her throat, a pricking in her eyes. How much she would have given when she was sure the time was right (could it really be a decade ago?) and before she had resigned herself to the fact that one or other of them was sterile, to have been able to have a family of her own; how different things would have been to have had children. She knows that Alex would say that the way to happiness is in acceptance of the way things are now, not how your ego would have liked them to be, and that her karma obviously does not include being able to have children. She knows he is right, and today she would strangle him to hear those words, or similar. Easy to be glib when you are not the one who's suffering. And yet, says the other half of her mind, and yet—how must it feel to have children, and adore them, and miss them like crazy, and not able to be with them? To try and imagine a future without them? The future would have to offer some seriously heavyweight compensations.

How difficult it is to be human, she thinks, how hard to take it lightly, dance through life. She suddenly misses Rosa with an intense longing; her sense of fun and laughter, her optimism, the ease and comfort of a friend of the same sex, a friend who knows you inside out and is content, on the whole, with what you choose to give.

She stands up from her stooped position abruptly and, on the pretext of putting on the kettle, crosses the yard towards the house. The sky has cleared, and already, mid-afternoon, there is a soft rosy flush on the Western horizon above the mountains. She kicks her boots off outside the door and goes into the kitchen to find Susie, who is bottling fruit.

'Susie,' she says, stirring the tea a few minutes later, 'did you ever regret not having children? Or is that too personal a question?'

Susie thinks a moment, sealing jars. She carries on wiping them down with a hot damp cloth before answering. Annie is comforted by her presence and the timelessness of a small mundane kitchen ritual. Susie seems so solid, not earthy and lively like Rosa, but in a calmer accepting way. Rosa lives her life and nurtures her family with flair and love and warmth, but only just manages to keep it all together, she declares herself, by the skin of her teeth. Susie is altogether more considered, a natural in the skills of manipulating the material requirements of life.

'I think no, Annie. No regrets. I knew I never really wanted children—there were too many other things I wanted to do. It's not that I don't like them; like most people I enjoy other people's children—for an hour or two at a time.' She piles dirty saucepans and utensils into the washing-up bowl, looking back over her shoulder as she talks.

Annie pours the tea and takes Susie's over to her, then pads over in her stockinged feet to get a tea-towel from the bar at the front of the range.

'I was afraid for a while that Jon might not be as sure as I was; but we talked about it a lot, and we both feel too that adding to the population problem isn't necessarily the best contribution you can make to the world. And honestly I'm as unhappy as anyone else who thinks about these issues about the state of the world and the kind of future children might have in it.' She pauses and turns around, drying her hands, then returns to the kitchen table and writes out half a dozen labels for her jars. The kitchen is silent apart from the clock ticking and a gentle bubbling from the water pipes above the range. 'I had a twinge or two a couple of years ago when I realised I was nearly past it and Jon brought the subject up two or three times—out of fear of losing him as much as anything, I think. Otherwise, no—I've all the animals, instead.' She smiles at Annie. 'Why?'

Annie, stacking the dry crockery back in the dresser which stands, slightly aslant on the uneven floor, against the wall opposite the window, opens her mouth to respond with the fact that she has never really come to terms with her own childlessness and that recently it has been making itself felt again, but before she is able to finish the door opens and the men come in, wiping their hands on their jeans.

'Oh, Annie,' Jon says, washing hands and face in the sink, 'I've just been telling Alex, I forgot to say earlier, there's an old *mas,* a farmhouse, up for sale lower down, the other side of Ceret. You know, the town that Picasso hung out in.' He turns round, face dripping and eyes closed, to grope for a towel, and Annie passes him one from the front of the range. She refills the kettle and finds another couple of cups. Her heart is suddenly thumping.

Jon continues through the fabric of the towel: 'It's cheap, I hear; needs some work on it, but it's weatherproof. I was asking Alex if you two are interested.'

Alex comes awake with a start in the dark attic room. A faint gibbous moon hangs tilted just below the line of the window frame.

Something is wrong. He takes a moment to adjust to the abrupt shift in consciousness from dreaming—unpleasant muddled dreams—to waking. A noise has disturbed him; there it is again. He reaches out to meet space in the bed beside him, and jerks upright into a sitting position as a shadow moves slowly across in front of the moon. Annie, naked, and muttering words that are incomprehensible; not English, but they don't quite sound like French, either. There is something strange about her voice; the accent? He catches one word over and over, a word that sounds like 'gaynon', and something else repeated that might or might not be 'neige' and then 'bless' (or 'blessed'? Or, thinking in French, which it was now resembling, 'blessé'?) Annie's voice is thick and blurred, almost guttural. She sounds distressed. She is obviously talking to herself, but with pauses, as one might on the telephone.

Alex feels the hairs on the nape of his neck prickle. 'Annie?' he says, his voice sharp with fear. 'Annie? Come back to bed, love.'

No response. The muttering continues. Annie is fumbling rather frenziedly at the glass of the window. Alex leaps out of bed and is over beside her in a second.

Annie's eyes are open and she is moaning. She is oblivious to his presence. Alex drops his raised hand without touching her. He shivers; he can feel a sudden shrinking in his solar plexus. He takes a deep breath and watches her run her hand across the windowpane as a blind person might. Sleepwalking, of course. Is it touching or speaking that you aren't supposed to do to a sleepwalker?

'Annie?' he whispers, then gently puts out his hand and very lightly touches her fingers. She moans again and mutters something he can't catch. Her slow deep voice spooks him. He tightens his grip. For a moment she resists him, then raises her free hand and runs it over his face. The whites of her eyes, which as far as he can tell are wide and unfocussed, looking beyond him, raise fresh ripples of disquiet and anxiety in him. He makes himself continue to look at her, then without saying anything gently pulls her hand. She says the word 'gaynon' again, questioningly, and her breathing quickens and quivers. Simultaneously something shifts for Alex; a sense of vertigo, a feeling of something slipping, a tidal wave. He hears Annie say the word again as if from a great distance, underwater even. Annie's voice; yet not. Before he has time to register his own strange state he sees Annie slide sideways, down the wall. Then, in what now seems a too-familiar way, she seems to fold up, crumpled, and Alex catches her and lowers her back onto the bed. He gently eases the duvet out from under her, then tucks her up, and watches her until her breathing reassures him that she is sleeping more-or-less normally.

Beside her, he has a sleepless night, listening to her breathing, punctuated by the odd murmur, and once or twice a moan.

In the morning, leaning over and kissing her when she opens her eyes, he says nothing of the night, though his disquiet continues.

TWENTY-TWO

L'Estang des Sangliers is not far from the little hilltop village of Llauro, which rises in the autumn sunshine like a golden volcanic pimple abruptly out of the flatter landscape immediately surrounding it, the whole cradled in the ring of hills and mountains.

The approach road curves between acres of ochre soil, in places almost desert-like, sparsely planted with vineyards and scattered fruit-trees and scrubby bushes reaching unhedged to the sides of the road, which is bordered with the dry stalks of wormwood and chicory, the seeding heads of fennel and huge leafy mallow bushes. Dotted over the landscape are the darker shapes of pine trees. Annie imagines how it would look in spring or summer with the fruit-trees in blossom, the roadside thick with oregano, and the yellow, mauve and bright blue flowers of the fennel, mallow and chicory, and immediately falls in love with the area.

It is warm enough to have the windows and skylight of the van open. The light easterly breeze seems to smell of the sea. Alex is still wearing a T-shirt; Annie thinks how well the green suits his tan, and notices the way the sun ripples fire through his hair, and with a sigh of pleasure leans her head to touch his shoulder.

The farmhouse is at the end of a stony track that veers off the road to Llauro and doubles back towards the direction of the great distant flank of Mont Canigou. The scenery is abruptly different; hillier, more wooded, greener, and the house itself is on a south-facing slope. Through the trees, not yet quite bare but roots already blanketed with the bright golds and flame and russets of fallen leaves, can be seen another couple of dwellings sketched upon the dark blues, greens and purples of the distant flanks of the foothills. The track curves round in a sweeping arc and debouches into an untended courtyard at the front of the house, roughly cobbled with great round pebbles in soft creamy-white.

'River-pebbles,' comments Alex, bending to run his fingers over the surface of one or two, and crushing the aromatic leaves of the chamomile which straggle, with other small creeping plants, all over the yard.

Annie stands speechless where she has got out of the passenger seat of the van. This is it. She belongs here. This is where she wants to live, without a shadow of doubt.

There are two or three outbuildings, doorless and overgrown with creepers, but, it seems, dry and mostly intact. Tacked to the front door of the house is a bright yellow painted-metal 'A VENDRE' sign, and the name of the agent, José Barrault, with an address in Perpignan. Judging by the flaking paint of the sign and the rust of the retaining nails it has been there for some time. The square house has an abandoned dreaming air, shuttered and yet alive, Annie thinks, perhaps resting, like an old horse. I'm beginning to sound like Rosa, she thinks to herself, and smiles. She takes in the rusty leaves of an old and unpruned vine, still bearing fruit though plundered by birds, around the huge timbered lintel of the heavy wooden front-door, the shallow terracotta roof against the stone walls, which are neither yellow, nor white, nor grey but all three; the stone trough against a wall. To her delight there is a fruiting fig tree beside it. She walks over to the trough and balances on it to peer over the wall. On the other side, towards the west and facing south are the vestiges of an old kitchen garden, walled, presumably to keep out marauding wildlife.

She can hear the distant sound of running water below in the valley. Jon has said that though most of the adjoining farmland has been sold off, an orchard front and back and the meadow that contains the spring-fed pool that gives the house its name are included in the price. Probably the pool is lower down, between the house and the stream.

She breathes deeply. She could be at peace here. 'Mmmm. This is it, this is beautiful, Alex.' She turns to him with her eyes sparkling, her face vibrant with that rare light that suffuses her when she is enthusiastic.

A rush of love for her fills him and he lifts a finger to stroke her face.

She hugs him, hard. 'There's a stream, too. How wonderful. It must be a tributary of the Tech, do you think? Oh, Alex, I could be happy, here, with you.' She moves towards the front door, and Alex pulls her down to sit with him a moment on a crude bench, under what must be the kitchen window, made from a tree-trunk hewn roughly square and balanced on two enormous boulders. Annie leans against him in the warmth of the autumn sun and takes his hand, lacing her fingers with his. With her head on his shoulder she allows herself to dream about how it could be here. Pots of geraniums and marigolds and herbs in the yard, perhaps a dog, some hens? And the two-storey barn opposite the house with an external staircase of stone and two window-openings could house a studio above for her painting and weaving, and a workshop for Alex below.

'Alex? What do you think?' She smiles into his eyes, leans forward to kiss him. He kisses her back, and she opens her mouth, kisses him hungrily, wholeheartedly. Her body softens towards him and he can feel himself stirring, stiffening. She has come back, she is present again, and the doubts that he has been beginning to have recently fly from his mind. This is his woman, the woman he is in love with, the woman he wants. He runs his lips down her white neck and can hear her breathing quicken, her own lips apart. He knows her eyes will be half-closed and her face will have that still, rapt look which manages to be simultaneously both contained and abandoned. That combination in her, presence/absence, is a huge turn-on for him, despite the fact that her absence sometimes drives him crazy. He pulls her to her feet and she presses herself against him, kissing his face. She runs her hands through his hair and down his shoulders, the sides of his body and over his buttocks, then brings them round to the front, slowly, deliberately. He moans and his eyes open. 'Quick! Now!' he whispers into her ear. He grabs her hand and pulls her to the van, and lifts his coat and the picnic blanket out, then runs with her to the orchard they both know will be in front of the outbuildings.

And it is. Watching the November sunlight and the twiggy branches reflected in her eyes where she now lies at the foot of an ancient apple-tree, he feels a specialness about this moment, an eternal quality. Archetypal, almost; as if they are the first couple and this the first time. He knows that she is aware of it, too. All the pain and doubt and uncertainty is worth it for moments like these, moments out of time. Annie points above his head in delight and instantly he expects to see The Apple—the last remaining apple of the autumn and the first apple from the beginning of time. He looks up; no apple, but instead a mass of mistletoe clustered above them. They laugh together. A solstitial rite a month early; mistletoe the symbol of the white semen of the Sky God, fertilising the Earth Goddess at the turning year. Planting seed in the belly of winter, lighting the fires between them once again. A new sun rising.

They catch each other's eyes, reading and communicating in a language older and less corrupt than words; perfectly in tune, perfectly in time. Kneeling over her he replies belatedly, grinning down at her: 'What do I think, my darling? I think this is pretty close to paradise,' as she lifts off his T-shirt and then unbuttons his Levi's, and raises her arms to link them behind his neck and draw him down to her. Very gently he runs his hands over her breasts and down her belly under the waistband of her jeans, and as she lifts her hips he slides the fabric over her buttocks and lowers his body to hers.

They return home via Perpignan, having investigated the pool and stream (quick chilly ablutions) and straightened their clothes and, in Annie's case anyway, brushed their hair in the van. On the journey they discuss the house with some excitement, and the practical issues like their absolute ceiling cost (for they don't yet know the asking price) and whether Annie could afford it immediately from one of Greg's insurance policies without having sold her own house first. There would be, too, Annie remembers from a conversation with Susie, notaire's fees, stamp duty and land registry costs, and any costs incurred in linking up electricity, water or gas if necessary, as well as telephone.

How, Annie asks, feeling her way gently, would he feel about living in it if it were bought with her money? As far as she is concerned, what is hers is also Alex's if that is what he wants, but he needs to feel comfortable about it, too. She knows that of the two of them, it is likely to be Alex who will initially bring in any income, as he has a range of marketable practical skills that she hasn't, so things would balance out. She points this out to him. Neither of them mentions Alex's house or maintenance payments to his family, but both know these hover between them, no less real for being unspoken.

At José Barrault's office Annie is overjoyed by the asking price. Alex has his notebook out—he does some quick calculations and writes the conversions down, passing the paper to Annie. She glances at it, and her heart jumps. Even given the exchange rate she should just be able to do it, though it will take everything left to her except the house in Ide. They know that house prices in France are still significantly lower than in England, but had expected them to be above average in this area as there have been so many non-French immigrants, and the area is not far from the coastal resorts and access to, for instance, Provence. M. Barrault explains that the house is less attractive to foreigners than others nearer the coast or in the Pyrenees proper, and has also been on the market for a long time. Yes, as far as he knows it is still weatherproof, though it has been empty for some years now and really needs gutting inside. Yes, if they are interested he could set things in motion immediately, and it could be theirs perhaps by Christmas.

The next step is to speak to the vendor, a businessman in Toulouse, the son of the original owners, now both dead. Like many of his generation, apparently, he has abandoned the rural lifestyle of his predecessors for the prospects in the city. The keys, however, are held by a family friend in Llauro; M. Barrault's secretary digs out the numbers for the son and the keyholder. The agent looks over his glasses at them as they leave the office. 'You do realise, don't you,' he says in French, 'that the winters can be hard here, and the winds terrible?' They shrug and smile as they open the door.

'These starry-eyed English romantics,' he says to his secretary, shaking his head in slow bemusement. 'New lovers, do you think?'

TWENTY-THREE

Alex and Annie go back the next day to L'Estang des Sangliers, having spoken, not without some difficulty because of her strong regional accent, to Mme Toussin, the keyholder, on the telephone. Her son, Patrice, comes to meet them at L'Estang.

He is a tall, attractive, dark-haired young man in his thirties, a potter who says he has 'done' his time in the city himself and has now come back to his native village to make his living throwing pots out of the local clay which he digs himself, glazed with wood-ash from the local timber with which he fires the kiln.

Annie warms to him immediately, and, with her knack for encouraging people to talk about themselves, asks him what kind of work he produces.

'I am most interested, I think, in making pieces that are not just beautiful, but also—I'm not sure of the word in English— good to use. *Utile.*'

'Functional?'

'Ah yes, functional. I like to make pieces that are similar to the traditional designs of this region, and also *particulier*, unique. I'm not interested in making many that look the same.'

'In English we call them "one-off" pieces. Do you have an equivalent word in French?'

While Alex inspects the external fabric of the building Annie and Patrice wander through the neglected garden, talking about art, about her work as well as his, about the district and its inhabitants, in a mixture of French and English. Unlike his mother Patrice speaks standard French, unaccented.

Annie, already convinced that L'Estang is the right place, takes this meeting with Patrice as further confirmation; here is a new friend, someone involved in the arts, who sounds as if he shares some at least of their ideologies. She promises herself that she and Alex will invite him for supper as soon as they have moved.

After Patrice has gone, leaving them with the keys, Annie turns her attention, with Alex, to the interior of the house, which looks as if it has been untouched for decades.

'The construction's what you might call unsophisticated, but, by God, they built them to last. Look at the width of these walls!' Alex stretches a metal tape across the external wall by the door. 'Two foot six! That's just one block of dressed stone across the width.'

'Any damp, d'you think?'

'Doesn't look like it. The plaster's flaked right off, virtually back to the plain stone, but my guess is that it's just not been touched for years. There'll be a bit of woodwork to replace but there's not too much sign of rot.'

'What about the roof?'

'Hard to tell until it rains. Looks OK at a glance. We'll need to get the timbers looked at but there don't look to be too many gaps from the outside. Couple of tiles, maybe; they'll be the same ones they're still making, the pantiles.'

'I love all those variations and flecks; reds and ochres and rusts and tans and purples and umbers. And the wavy shape. So much more interesting than straight British grey slate. Patrice said he uses the same local clay as they're made from.'

Annie goes to explore the upstairs. The rooms are light and airy, looking over both back and front, with spectacular views down over the trees towards the pool one way, the mountains rising purple-blue in the distance, and the ground sloping gently upwards to the north behind. The shutters are tatty but the beams and floorboards look sound.

'What do you think?' Annie asks Alex animatedly, coming downstairs to find him where he is inspecting a window-frame.

'Mmmm,' murmurs Alex pensively, noting something down. He looks at Annie—her cheeks flushed and eyes glowing. He smiles down at her. 'It's OK, structurally, I think. It needs quite a lot doing to it; I'd quite like Jon to check it over, and maybe we ought to get a proper builder to look at it. There may be building regs we need to know about. We'd need to put a bathroom in—there's only that downstairs sink, and the outdoor bog's primitive even by French public loo standards. And I think we might have to replace the staircase. But thank God nobody's tarted it up. You really want it, don't you?'

'Yes. I haven't felt this sure about anything for a very long time—except about you.' She kisses him on the cheek and slips her arm through his. 'Shall we ring the guy in Toulouse and say yes?'

'Hey, hold on, hold on, Annie! Usually it's me that's impulsive and you that's cautious. Don't you think we'd better get it professionally checked-out first? It there's problems with say, right of access for the farm over there, or if the joists are riddled with woodworm or we're about to lose the bloody roof, I'd prefer to know about it first, hey?'

Annie sobers a little. 'I suppose you're right,' she says in a quieter voice. 'But I'm wondering in any case whether I ought to put the house in Ide on the market; I'm sure now that even if we weren't to buy this house, I don't want to live in Ide again. I'm happy here, Alex; ready to cut my ties. Perhaps I should go back before Christmas and sort it out.'

Alex glances over at her with an eyebrow raised; a little searchingly, it seems to her. 'You've come a long way, my darling. It doesn't feel quite that simple to me, I'm afraid; but some time or other, you're right, we all have to decide where we want to stop.'

Annie's smile fades a little and Alex regrets his words; but it is the truth. The house is indeed special; and he isn't sure yet he has quite managed to cut his ties the way Annie might have hers, though privately he suspects that she too still has a lot of letting go to do. Her nightmares, for instance, have barely eased up; or if they have, it seems they've taken a more disturbing direction even. He himself needs time, still; the events of the last six months have stirred a profound restlessness in him. He cannot tell Annie what turmoil he is in over the family, though he wonders if she suspects.

Annie looks at his profile, and as always is stricken by her rush of love for him. Was loving somebody as much as she loves Alex always accompanied by as much terror as joy? Or is it merely that this is the first time in her life that she has allowed herself to be so known, so vulnerable, with another person? Alex's eyes when he glances at her a second time are as loving as ever and his smile as broad and generous. There is perhaps a faint shadow in his eyes; as likely the knowledge that his words may have hurt her as anything else.

She makes herself face the knowledge that nothing is ever certain. Can she find the courage to plan for her future here, whether or not he is with her? She swallows at this and her mind swerves away from the implications. She steers it back. What other options does she have, right now? How does she want to live the rest of her life?

Alex breaks the silence by suggesting that they could ask Jon if he knows of a surveyor they could consult. Annie puts her hand on his knee gratefully and he picks it up and kisses it and the moment is gone.

TWENTY-FOUR

For Annie's birthday in November, a week after they first found the house near Llauro, Alex has made for her in Jon's workshop a huge but dismantleable Navajo-type frame loom, free-standing. In his mind he has a romantic vision of her planting it outside in some sunny spot at L'Estang des Sangliers where she could translate the inspirational beauty of the landscape into tapestries for the walls and blankets for their bed. For the moment, though, his practical streak has intervened and he has constructed huge wooden feet into which the uprights could be slotted. The whole structure is bolted together for ease of transport, and for the moment it is installed in the attic room. Annie has already applied an experimental warp and made preliminary sketches for a large piece, which she pictures herself weaving in her spare time in the new house; her spring project, she promises herself.

A huge wind has arisen and shakes the panes of the house furiously. On their cushions in the passageway between Susie's studio and the kitchen the dogs huddle at the noise, Wesley occasionally emitting a rather forlorn howl. Annie has abandoned, for the moment, the piece of weaving that has, in the excitement of the new loom, superseded at least temporarily the painting. Despite her absorption and the lit fire in the attic room Annie, distracted by the wind, has descended to join Alex in the greater comfort and security of the farmhouse kitchen. Jon and Susie are both out; Jon to measure up for some work at a town-house in Annecy-les-Bains, Susie to drop off eggs and a small commissioned painting at two different places, and then to shop and swim before picking Jon up. In uncertain weather such as this they tend to combine transport when possible and to keep the amount of time they spend away from home to the bare minimum.

It is early afternoon, and Annie is just about to put two loaves into the oven to bake.

She glances over at Alex reading his book. 'Do you know,' she says, 'I take such an immense pleasure in things like making bread these days. When we were—when I was half of a Young Professional Couple—' she emphasises the words self-deprecatingly—'our friends, or at least our peer-group in our social circle, apart from Rosa, used to look down on such things as either superfluous, or twee and bourgeois, demeaning. Funny how much I've changed.'

She mulls it over. 'Though I thought of us as being country people I suppose we were really part of the urban scene.'

The routine of the simple day-to-day tasks here, which might previously have seemed mundane, have started to create new roots for Annie. By contrast, looking back, she sees now what she has not seen before; that the speed and sophistication of her previous life had not been a measure of its success so much as a cover over its aridity. How strange, she thinks, that healing should be so simple.

Besides, on a more prosaic note, occasionally she feels the absence of good brown bread, and though wholemeal flour is not as readily available here as in England, rye flour mixed with strong white is a reasonable substitute.

Despite the turbulence outside she feels deeply peaceful as she prepares to place the shaped loaves into the greased and floured tins. The act of baking and kneading dough for bread has now become a regular meditative ritual for her, and invariably instils a deep sense of quiet, as if all her mental and physical processes slow to a gentle barely-pulsing rhythm, a warm river of well-being on which she is carried, half-tranced.

Alex, glancing at her from time to time as she works, is moved as always by that still, contained look on her face that accompanies occupations that infuse her whole being.

She happens to look up and catch his eye at that moment. 'What are you smiling at?'

'I'm smiling at you, my darling. Did you know that you have exactly the same expression on your face when you're kneading dough, or for that matter weeding the vegetable-patch or milking the goats, as you do when we're making love?'

Annie, slightly disconcerted, flashes him a startled look and a quick smile.

'Do I? I don't think it does quite the same thing for me!—though I suppose all those things do absorb me. I was just thinking how good it feels to have my hands in this and just to be concentrating on what I'm doing, no more, no less.'

She presses and pats the dough into shape in the tins.

Alex watches her.

She looks up again and smiles. 'I remember you telling me once about that Zen Roshi who said that when you peel an orange, make it your whole life; when you wash the dishes, put all of your being into it. I think I'm finally managing it now and then—how can it have taken me forty years just to learn to Be Here Now?'

Alex chuckles. 'Count yourself lucky! Some people never do.' He returns to his book, ignoring the sudden hails of rain thrown by the bucketful against the window.

Annie opens the oven door to put the tins in and goes to wash her hands.

'Here's a bit you'll like, sweetheart,' Alex says, looking up again. '"We all, as humans, are trapped by our laziness. In the East, it takes the form of doing nothing, an excess of being. In the West, its form is the opposite; eternally moving, addictively busy, an excess of doing. Either way, we avoid the truth of the moment, and its only matter of any importance: which is facing the fact of our living, facing the fact of our dying. And knowing that our choice in each moment is only to be awake to it, or not." Mmm: shit-hot. Spot-on. These Tibetans know what they're about.'

Annie nods. 'Yes, that's exactly how it is. And I'm just beginning to see how it might feel to find the balance of that; the eye of the storm. It's like a kind of stillpoint where you can gather yourself and use the creative tension, rather than it using you. I think I see what I'm trying to do with that weaving like that.'

'Mmmm? Tell me more,' Alex encourages.

Annie leans against the stove wiping her hands, and thinks how much she loves his attentive way of listening to her.

'What I want to try and do is to use just black and white, and have a jumble of incoherent shapes at the bottom of the piece, all chaos and random. Then at the top I'd like to find a way to resolve it into pattern; harmonious, like a dance between black and white. At the bottom it'll be more like a battle. I suppose it's a metaphor. Does that sound pretentious?'

'Well, I dare say to an outsider who had no understanding of art or the creative process it might, possibly. But to me it makes perfect sense—in a way it's what I've been trying to do with *Lento*, I think, though I hadn't really put it into those words . . . But you, the stillpoint; that's it exactly. What did Eliot say about the stillpoint?'

"'. . . After the kingfisher's wing/Has answered light to light, and is silent, the light is still/At the stillpoint of the turning world.'"

Annie replaces the towel and adds more wood to the firebox from the great log-basket. She loves these moments when they are together but separately occupied, and share words or silence, as the mood takes them. Coming home, she thinks; it feels like coming home.

She fills the kettle and stands it on the hotplate of the range, and then, as Wesley raises his voice again in a mournful howl, takes pity on the dogs and goes to let them in. They race in in a frenzy of delight and rush from one to the other of them, whining with pleasure. Gradually the noise and activity subsides and Annie joins Alex at the table and opens her own book and takes up her pen, preparing to push on with her notes from *Le Vrai Visage du Catharisme*. Bored with plodding through the book page by page from the beginning, she opens it at random.

Alex has closed his book and is paying attention to a piece of holly wood he started to carve the previous day. Under the gentle wheedlings and scrapings of his Opinel pocket knife, assiduously sharpened, the graceful lines and alert ears of a wolf's head are beginning to emerge. He is feeling pleased with his attempt; having never tried his hand at carving before, new realms of possibilities unfold before him, from simple sculptures to delicate filigree fretworking on musical instruments. He, too, becomes absorbed in what he is doing; all other concerns suspended.

When Annie gasps, he jumps, the blade slipping dangerously close to his fingers. Annie's gone deathly white, and for a moment he thinks she is going to faint. She opens and closes her mouth; apparently she has lost her voice.

'What the fuck, Annie . . .?'

'God, Alex. God. I—I —' she thrusts the book at him. Her hands are trembling.

He struggles with the French where he thinks she is pointing.

'Christ! Oh, Christ, Alex.'

He frowns and tries to make sense of the words before him. Annie never blasphemes; or at least, he has never heard her say 'Christ' before. Swear, once or twice, yes. He looked back at her face. Here eyes are dark; they burn feverishly.

'Mathieu and Pierre Bonet. Alex!'

He stares at the names in the text, and then back up at her, completely mystified. There is a bead of sweat at her hairline.

She repeats 'Mathieu and Pierre Bonet!'

She looks completely possessed, he thinks, wild-eyed and almost deranged. He feels puzzled, troubled, and now, too, slightly stupid. With this realisation comes irritation.

'OK, Annie, Mathieu and Pierre Bonet. Friends of yours?'

She finds her voice. 'My dream, Alex. Don't you remember? I told you about it when you came back from Somport—I read you what I'd written in my diary the next morning. Mathieu and Pierre Bonet were in my dream.' Her voice is barely audible, but it sounds mechanical almost, forced. She points to the place again with her shaking finger. She is so emotional, so overwhelmed by her discovery and its implications that she can hardly bear to articulate the words. 'It's—they—here it says—they were two of the Cathars who were in the siege at Montségur. You remember—the last Cathar stronghold, where they were all—burnt to death.' Her voice has dropped to a whisper, thin and hesitant. 'I was—I must have been—I was—dreaming about Montségur.'

Alex stares at her in discomfort and then total incomprehension that turns into faintly scornful disbelief. He grabs the book and slams it shut.

'Oh, come on, Annie. For fuck's sake. You're making it up. You can't surely remember names from dreams of weeks ago; and even if you had, these names are probably not uncommon in France. Or maybe you read about it somewhere else. Wake up, darling. I'm beginning to worry about you.' He stands up abruptly to lift the kettle off the heat and quieten its shrieking whistle.

Annie is still sitting immobile, ashen, trembling.

Fucking hysterical women, he broods. I thought I'd left all that behind. He pours water onto the leaves and carries the pot over to the table.

Annie's face as he glances at her is stricken. 'Alex,' she whispers, 'I feel as if you've betrayed me. You of all people should understand what I'm saying.' She swallows and finds her voice again. 'You believe—you know you do—that all is not as it seems . . . that it can't all be explained by—by—reason, logic . . . I'm telling you, Alex, these are the same two people.' She pushes herself up from the table and her unfathomable indigo eyes bore into his, infinitely serious, intense, in pain and shock. She moves unsteadily towards the stairs and mounts them to go and fetch her diary.

Alex, no appetite for tea, puts his head in his hands.

* * * * *

I am in the rough dark blue garb of my faith. Face to face in the darkness, Guénon and myself. The garrison have left us, and Pierre-Roger in disregard for his own safety has enabled the escape of four of us, four Bonshommes, to carry the word still through these dark lands, keeping the flame of wisdom and compassion despite these troubled times. For their safety we do not know for sure which four have gone; but I have not seen dear Mathieu, with his wise eyes and fearless faith, since he came back safe from Sabarthes; nor Pierre Bonet.

We shall not see them again, I think, in these bodies.

There is silence; a deathly chill. Rising in the East is a great Full Moon; it is past the penombre, the twilight time, and the sun has fallen. Soon it will be time. Soon we will tread together the way of the stars. I know this without his telling me.

Guénon hands me an object; small and cold and heavy. I see under the moonlight that it is a half-sphere of white metal, smooth and strange. With his other hand, careful now not to touch my flesh, though I know he loves me well, he hands me the other half-sphere; a perfect match but in reverse, in black metal, or stone perhaps. With one in each of my hands I feel their strange nature begin to enter me; it feels cold beyond life, beyond death. Their inner edges, I note now, are oddly curved and they lock together. A perfect sphere! I have never seen anything as beautiful. I am overcome.

I look up at his beloved face. Guénon does not move his lips but I hear him perfectly. We have moved beyond our separateness, though we touch no longer. I am filled with my love for him; my heart is bursting. His speechless words tell me in the silence that the time is near; the day is coming when the Sons of Light and Darkness and the Daughters of Darkness and Light will join once more, and for us they will never separate again. On that day we will draw breath and it will be the breath of All That Is, for the walls of our holding here will melt like the snows of winter. 'We are part of all that is, Isarn, but this is not our true home,' he reminds me. 'This is not our true home. Il faut que tu n'oublies pas. Jamais. A new sun is rising; on the day of the turning, the stillpoint, we will fly free, Isarn. Do not forget that we are not creatures of clay but creatures of fire, of the stars—we are spirit. We will fly free.'

He is fading in front of me, his hands apart in blessing and I see with a shock of pain to my heart that they are terrible, for they are red with blood. I rush to stretch my hands out to take his, my breath indrawn but he stays me, though without a word. Slowly he steps back; I cannot look at his eyes, for they *are wells of sorrow, nor at his hands; and finally I am alone in the cold night, I and the moon.*

TWENTY-FIVE

It is two days later, and Annie is still unable to open the book, and equally unable to mention to Alex either her dreams or the Cathar heresy, though—or rather because—she is still feeling hurt at his apparently brutal rejection of what she had said. A hole has appeared suddenly in the ground in front of her, and she cannot see a safe way around it. Consequently, though outwardly things remain much the same between them, she has closed away a vulnerable part of herself.

Alex has not mentioned the Montségur incident again; either he is aware that it is swampy ground and is avoiding it, or he has no idea what impact his reaction has had on Annie. Either way, she feels incapable of bringing the subject up herself.

Alex, coming out of the shower that is built into what had been the old dairy off the kitchen, one morning, is arrested mid-whistle by something about Annie's demeanour. He hesitates in the doorway, towelling his hair and eyeing her. She is looking directly at him; rather challengingly, he feels. He takes a pace or two in her direction, slowly.

She looks quite different. He stares, trying to make out what it is. For a start, she is wearing a red jumper that he has not seen before. The poppy-red sets her colouring off perfectly; he is startled at the difference it makes from her usual mushrooms or grey-blues and off-whites and blacks. She also has a determined look on her face, and is sitting upright, rather rigidly, with her legs crossed. All this he takes in intellectually while he is registering emotionally that she is looking both defiant and defensive.

She looks like a woman who has something to say. After Kate's timidity it is refreshing to see spirit; what he has called on the one or two glimpses he has had of this Annie her *Running with the Wolves* face. Nonetheless, he feels somewhat apprehensive under her gaze. He stands and looks at her guardedly, rubbing his hair with an increased vehemence.

He tries for humour. 'Uh-oh. Looks like trouble!'

Annie's face doesn't change. 'Alex. I'm going back to England.'

He blinks. Christ. No beating about the bush. And before breakfast, too. He sits down across from her, the towel around his waist falling open.

Annie is not, as she usually would be, distracted by the sight of his body. 'I just mean for a week or two. I've decided I really want to put the house on the market. It's holding me back. I want to try living without a safety-net. I'll be back before Christmas.'

Alex digests this. He stands up and adjusts the towel and goes to fill the kettle. Nothing like having a cup of tea at moments of stress, he thinks. What a very English displacement activity. Wish I was still a smoker.

'UDI, hey, Annie?'

'What?' she says, not understanding.

'I meant that's a bit of a unilateral decision, isn't it?'

'I didn't intend it like that, Alex.' She tries to keep a defensive shake out of her voice. 'I can hardly ask you to make that decision for me. It's something I've got to do sooner or later; I just feel I want to do it now, before my courage fails me.'

'And then?'

'Well—God, Alex, how can I say? I'm not committing myself—us—to anything irreversible; there was never any question of us going back to live in Ide together, and I know I don't want to go back and live there myself. What is there to lose?'

'When are you thinking about going?'

'Well actually, now. This afternoon. There's a flight out of Toulouse at 4.00 to Gatwick, and with any luck I could pick up a train or coach and be back in Exeter around midnight. Rosa would meet me.'

'Christ. Does that mean you want me to drive you to the airport?'

'Would you? I could go tomorrow or the day after; but now that I've decided I just want to go and do it.'

There is a long silence. Annie resists the impulse to either shut down and become brittle, or try and win back Alex's approval. She sits quietly.

Alex sidesteps. 'You're determined to buy L'Estang des Sangliers, aren't you?'

Annie is caught offguard. 'Well, you know I fell in love with it. Yes; it does feel the right place to me. But—that is, if . . .' she tails off, not quite knowing how to phrase what she wants to say. She is sure that Alex, like herself, had assumed that they would definitely be living together. That is, she had been sure of it. But despite looking at L'Estang and the subsequent interview with José Barrault, they haven't actually articulated this common purpose to each other. How ridiculous to be doubting it. But after the incident with the book she feels wary of making assumptions, and though the distance between them is slight, it is enough to inhibit her asking him outright what his intentions are. She knows him well enough, though, to suspect that, if he feels cornered, he might feel obliged to react with a declaration of independence himself.

'If what?' Two could play this game. He thinks to himself that he is buggered if he is going to make it easy for her if she is intending to steam ahead without consulting him. His pride is at stake.

They eye each other across the table; Alex the puma, Annie the lynx. A bit of Alex is enjoying the combat; Annie sees the hint of a fighting sparkle in his tawny eyes, a flame of stubbornness. Alex sees deep determination in the navy eyes of this woman he loves, this woman who disturbs him, and possibly, just possibly, a hint of pleading. He breaks the gaze and gets up to lift the kettle, whose purr has become a hum, rapidly rising in a crescendo to an ear-splitting shriek. Coffee, he thinks. Strong and black. I'm not an Anglo-Saxon.

He offers truce—hands her a mug. Her wing of hair brushes her cheek and he is suddenly taken back to the university canteen, all those lifetimes ago.

'Well, Annie my darling, it's your house. If you're determined to sell it, there's not a lot I can do. Do you want me to come too, or not?'

Annie lifts her eyes to his once more. Thank God, there it is again, the spark jumping between them. She relaxes a little.

'I'd thought it might be difficult for you, being so close to— Exeter. I don't mind going alone—in fact I ought to really; it's like a rite-of-passage. I'm closing up such a large chunk of my life with the house.' She feels her fists clench with renewed tension; willing him to understand. Part of her desperately wants him to come too; part of her doubts the wisdom of that. And, too, she really does need to do it alone. He regards her without replying for a few minutes. She sips her coffee and tries not to let herself slip into anxiety about the time.

'So when would you have to leave?'

'Does that mean you will drive me?'

'Well, I can't see how else you'd get there. It's a good job the snow's cleared a bit; I wouldn't have fancied getting the bloody van back up these roads a couple of days ago. Did you check with the airport at Montpellier? That's closer.'

'Yes, nothing possible today. Their flight will have gone. Thanks, Alex.' She stretches a hand across the table. He takes hers and squeezes it. She breathes out quietly.

'I suppose you are sure that it's OK for us—me—to carry on staying here a bit?'

'Yes. I checked a few days ago with Susie; I think they're really enjoying our company. And Jon did talk about needing an extra hand with building work, didn't he?'

'I guess it wouldn't hurt for me to make some contacts and check out the area. Any kind of work's better than none, isn't it, at the moment?'

'Do you want me to check with Susie again when she gets back at lunchtime? Though I'm sure it's OK; I think we'd know if it wasn't.'

'I trust your judgement. Where did you get the jumper, by the way? It suits you.'

Annie stands up and makes herself relax her limbs. 'I bought it in the market in Perpignan the other day when I went in with Susie.' She steps around the table and leans against him briefly, bending to kiss the top of his still-damp head. 'I'd better ring Rosa and pack. We ought to leave in a couple of hours; we can always have lunch somewhere if we're early.'

Alex nods. 'I guess. I'd better go and check the oil.'

TWENTY-SIX

Annie's head lolls back against the checked furriness of the Paddington to Penzance train. The rhythmic swaying is lulling her into drowsiness, but she doesn't want to sleep in case she misses her stop. Just past Reading; had it been daylight she would see the beginning of undulations in the landscape, the gentle hints of rolling hills that to her speak of coming towards home ground. She knows that soon despite the darkness her eyes will strain for a glimpse of the white horse cut into the hillside near Westbury; though newer than the other chalk figures on English hillsides, still it never ceases to fill her with a childish sense of excitement and joy, this magical reminder of a long ago time, the Dreamtime.

Darkness eats up the miles. There is a flurry of rain thrown aslant from the west against the train window, and she smiles wryly to herself. Almost all her homecomings have been greeted with rain, though not usually until they touched the Devon border. There, it seems, the heavens open on cue.

December. Touching down at Gatwick the chilly dank night air had descended on her like a sodden cloak, with nothing of the sharp clean cold of the Pyrenees.

Inside the train the heating is full-blast. Annie has the carriage to herself; stretching, she stands and makes her way down the train to see if the buffet car is open, in the hopes of finding a coffee to keep her awake.

Back in her seat, she toes her boots off and draws her legs up, bracing her knees against the seat in front. She opens her book but, unable to concentrate, turns her head back to the wintry darkness filling the window. She stares out unseeing, thinking about winter and the approaching Christmas. Where had she been this time last year? With a slight shock of surprise she remembers: in hospital, of course. It had been coming up to the solstice when she was due home, and she had been filled with both fear and excitement, and, too, a deep sense of desolation at the prospect of an empty house and the demands of an aching still-unmended body. All those winter days still stretching ahead of her, on her own and inactive, recuperating.

So much has happened; so many changes. This time last year she had been lonely and in pain; no idea of what her future would be, and only the visits of Rosa and Alex to break the monotony of the hospital day. It must have been about this time exactly, too, when she had first realised how much she was beginning to depend on Alex's appearances, and aware of a growing emptiness at an unusually long delay between visits. Of course, she remembers now, she wasn't even sure whether they had a friendship at that stage, let alone anything else. After all, he was married and she was still mourning Greg—still raging at Greg—and in some post-traumatic shock. A year! A lifetime.

She closes her book and digs in her shoulder-bag for her diary and flips backwards through the pages. December last year. Her eyes fall on an entry: *For once in my life I really need someone to stand between me and the world for a while, to help me out of this bloody year, to help bring me back from the dead . . .* Ask and ye shall receive, she thinks to herself. How well-loved she had felt, for indeed her friends and family had all stood between her and the world for a while, and most of all Alex. Alex. She has more than come back from the dead; with Alex she has begun to know for the first time how it feels to be really, truly alive, glowing and vibrating in every pore; so alive that it has its own acuteness, its own pain; the agony and the ecstasy of participating fully, actively, in every moment, without subterfuge or hiding.

She turns the page. Another entry: Alex again. *After all, he's only a casual friend, I suppose, no matter how kind he's been; he has his own family and no doubt his own troubles. It was crazy to pour out mine; totally inappropriate. I made myself so vulnerable . . .* Annie glances up and catches her own face reflected back at her in the train window, white, thin, but relaxed and with a glow to it that she knows hadn't been there before this year. I know what I look like, she thinks with a sense of incongruity: I look like someone who's finally and joyfully lost her virginity. Greg once said my face looked 'brittle and self-protective'. Perhaps that has finally gone, dissolved. If I were someone else looking at me, I would say there was a new kind of confidence in my face. The kind of confidence, perhaps, that only happens when you feel secure enough with who and what you are as to give yourself to someone else, someone you trust. Before, I only reluctantly let other people take me, like surrender after a siege, rather than giving freely from an abundance.

That's the secret glow on the face of Mona Lisa, too, she thinks.

She closes her eyes. Her head lolls sideways. How strange to be going back to Ide once again on my own, at the same time of year and in such different circumstances. The same yet not the same. The same yet not the same . . . The rolling rhythm takes her thoughts, makes them circular, until she lapses in her head into silence, gently mesmerised.

The train rolls on, parting the night that peels back to either side of her like a black bow-wave, and finally she dozes, dreaming.

Once again she is driving through the night, uphill alongside the Torridge, away from a party. In the sky ahead of her above the trees stand a sun and a moon, side-by-side. In her dream landscape this seems perfectly normal; as it should be. The darkness is like indigo-blue velvet; comforting, reassuring. She is at the wheel, and there is somebody—a man—beside her. She can't see who it is, but his presence is palpable; a warm, vibrant, generous presence. The atmosphere in the car feels like she imagines it would feel to float in the Dead Sea; warm, weightless, buoyant. The darkness in the car is sweet, like honey. In her dream she is profoundly happy; and when the lorry approaches, looming fast, swerving out around the bend, she drives steadily on past it.

In the darkness the train begins to shudder to a halt. The intercom booms, distorted, and Annie jerks awake, instinctively reaching out for Alex. There is a sudden glare of electric lights and then the train is gathering itself again to judder onwards. Annie's eyes, flicking open, catch sight of two or three disembodied faces like white narcissi under their hoods and hats, hurrying towards the end of the platform, stooped against the night and the weather.

The sense of the dream is still with her; a deep warm comfort that no matter what happens, all will be well. She feels free, somehow, as if she has come through a tremendous ordeal; a rite-of-passage that she hadn't known she was taking. She sits up and collects together her belongings. Eleven-forty; not long now till Exeter St David's and Rosa.

Rosa's small figure is silhouetted against the station buffet as the train pulls in and Annie's heart rises at the sight of her friend. Lugging her rucksack behind her and trailing her shoulder bag, she half-leaps half-stumbles off the train and launches herself towards Rosa, and the two of them hug, laughing and talking all at once. Rain glistens in Rosa's hair and she smells wonderfully familiar; a welcoming mix of dog and wood-fires and damp wool and, faintly, a whiff of warm patchouli.

'Thank you so much, Rosa, for turning out at this time of night, and in this weather!'

Rosa holds Annie's shoulders and stands back to look at her.

'You look—different; looser? More open? Tired, Annie darling; great shadows under your eyes. But you look *well*! You're positively glowing, smouldering!'

Annie smiles. Rosa hugs her again and holds out a hand for a bag. 'OK journey? Hope you're hungry; there are baked potatoes in the Rayburn and a big salad. Oh Annie, I'm so pleased to see you!'

'And me you, Rosa. I've missed you!'

And the Passat swings through the foggy night out of the city over the bridge, Annie watching the swirls and points of reflected street-lights dancing in the river and listening contentedly to Rosa's chatter and fending off the wet-nosed attentions of an overjoyed Troika.

TWENTY-SEVEN

The ten days that Annie spends in Devon are touched with a fierce poignancy.

Unlike Rosa, she doesn't hold sentimental attachments to people or places. Or at least, she doesn't think that she does. Rosa weeps easily and copiously at the merest hint of loss or change; Annie has known her to spend days in mourning at the death of a guinea pig, or the relocation of a friend to another part of the country. Volatile as she is, though, her natural cheerfulness and buoyancy resurrects itself suddenly with renewed vigour after a certain period of time, and she will be as bright now as she was downhearted just hours before. All traces of grief gone and tears dried, she will quickly confront and accept whatever it was that shook her.

Annie, holding herself always slightly aloof, has always felt slightly uncomfortable in the face of Rosa's easy emotionality. However, over the last six months Annie has become aware that the truth is that she does in fact attach herself strongly, with a depth of feeling that threatens to be overwhelming. Perhaps because of this, she realises, she has never been able to acknowledge even to herself, let alone anyone else, how frightened she has always been of allowing herself to become attached to, and therefore dependent on, someone or something.

So walking into her own house in Ide, with all its associations, for one of the last times ever, the next day after Rosa drops her is not easy. There is a sombre silence squatting in the house like death, and Annie finds herself suppressing a gasp. In a matter of moments her energy and will seem to have dissipated, and she finds herself incapable of mobilising her thoughts. Greg's presence still seems to linger; she finds herself expecting to hear him clear his throat, or push a chair back, turn the page of a newspaper. It is as if she's never left, as if the last eighteen months are an illusion, as if France hasn't happened. The house seems to recompose itself in front of her: if she goes upstairs, she's suddenly convinced, the bedrooms will be as they were that last evening, the evening they left for the fatal party near Bideford. Time stops and thickens around her.

Annie forces herself back out into the lane and leans against the wall under the bare branches of the pear-tree and calms her breathing, listening to the sound of distant traffic and the stream, and the alarmist deep-throated clacking of a pheasant beyond the wall.

The house had seemed to grab at her, but she no longer belongs here, nor wants to. Yet it is all the security she currently anchors herself with. Or had done. And however much she might dream of belonging at L'Estang, the facts are that she doesn't, at the moment. Not in actuality, anyway. So where does she belong? And does she have the courage to wait, just wait, in limbo until she knows? She leans against the damp wall and watches a slinky black cat stroll up the street towards her, and wills the hammering of her heart to slow. An ancient Vauxhall crawls past protesting in second gear, splattered with the red mid-Devon soil, and the occupant, ruddied-cheeked and check-capped, turns his head to look curiously at Annie. She pushes herself away from the wall, and turns and makes herself walk purposefully through the front door, slamming it behind her and marching down through the house throwing open doors and windows, despite the cold.

She kicks aside an Everest of mail. In her head she rehearses the list of the things that need doing, until, reaching the kitchen, she finds some chalk to transfer the list onto the blackboard hanging on the wall for just such a purpose. Her heart stammers as she reads the words sitting there still from the summer: 'cancel milk, turn off gas, library, ring SWEB, BT; sun-oil. PASSPORT, notebooks, ?car insurance??, painkillers, sandals, arnica.' 'I LOVE YOU!' shouts Alex's fluid script in yellow chalk and large letters at the very bottom. A life-time ago. She doesn't know whether to laugh or weep. Pensively, hesitantly, she dampens a cloth and wipes off all except Alex's words; then decides to use paper anyway.

She has a mammoth task in front of her; sorting, cleaning and making the house ready to put on the market in ten days, before she leaves, having arranged storage for things that she can't yet ship to France but doesn't want left there on show to prospective viewers.

She pushes out of her head everything that threatens to distract her, working with a focussed ferocity. By early afternoon she has steeled herself and emptied the contents of clothes drawers and sorted them into piles.

She allows herself no sentimentality or lingering as she sorts the outer layers of what is left of her life with Greg into bin bags. She'd expected this to be the bitterest task of all; she manages it without weeping.

Finally Annie stands up and stretches her back, exhausted by the effort of concentrating and banishing her emotional responses. She takes a cup of tea out to wander around the garden. Through the late summer it has started to straggle back to wilderness, lawn uncut, borders unweeded. It has that derelict, inert, abandoned look that well-stocked mature gardens carry in winter; swathes of blackish-brown sodden foliage from tall perennials flopping over beds, broken twigs and massed wet leaves and rotting husks of fruit strewn on the shaggy grass. She makes a mental note to ask Graham, a local man who gardens in the area, to come and do a couple of days' tidying as soon as possible.

Soon, the spikes of snowdrops will be poking heads above the soil at the foot of the wall and in the banks, and already the honeysuckle is budding new leaves; fringes of sugar-pink frills peep from the swollen calyces of the winter almond tree. The witch-hazel is beginning to shake out—surely weeks early— yellow fronds, and its scent hangs in the damp air.

Despite herself tears now prick Annie's eyes. So many years.

She props herself against an apple tree, slowed briefly to the pace of a gardener. Her eyes wander over the sleeping plants and trees; so much history, so much of her and Greg's history, in this half-acre, renewing itself year after year.

She feels herself drifting towards desolation, and pushes herself clear of the tree with her shoulders.

A garden is a kind of palimpsest, she thinks. Someone else's turn to make some history, to add some layers. With any luck, someone else will be watching the Spring bulbs come up, have their eyes dazzled by the effervescence of blossom, receive the abundance of fruit. She hopes they will continue to feed the birds.

Refusing to allow herself to wallow in nostalgia she tips the dregs of her tea under the apple tree and lets herself out of the side-door to go to the phone box, since her own is still disconnected.

She leaves a message on Graham's answerphone and then picks an estate agent at random from Yellow Pages and dials the number. Within a matter of minutes she has arranged for someone to come and look at the house for a valuation in three days' time. Three days to clear and tidy and pack away her past.

So it is done—the first step taken. She looks at her watch and, tipping out the contents of her purse, dials Susie's number, needing badly to hear Alex's voice.

Rosa is to come and pick her up at five. She has left till last on her list for that day sorting through the rest of Greg's papers and her own mail, and catching up with some of the outstanding bills or payments. Methodically she works through several piles, and has cleared a large quantity of paperwork by the time she hears Rosa's car outside. Flipping through the bundle of mail in her hand, still unopened, she stuffs half a dozen envelopes into her shoulderbag. Rosa hoots; Annie, temporarily frozen by a handful of letters with a Bedford postmark, resolutely thrusts them into the bin unopened, her heart hammering, and runs for the door; Rosa will be in a hurry to pick the twins up from football and get back to make tea for them and Dan.

Flopping into the front seat she allows herself, at last, to feel her exhaustion and churning feelings. She passes her hands over her eyes. Dan's warm chubby arms come around her neck from the back seat where he has learnt to escape from his seatbelt and he presses a sticky hand to her cheek.

'Auntie Annie,' he says, in his steady high voice, 'are you crying? Are you a bit fed up? Mummy gets fed up sometimes. I get fed up when Matthew pinches my toys. Did somebody pinch your toy?'

Annie and Rosa laugh, and the moment passes. The car is warm; and as usual cluttered with odd shoes and dog leads and abandoned mini juice cartons and bits of Lego. Rosa has Peter Gabriel on the tape-deck. A wonderful ordinariness. Annie puts her arms back over her head and ruffles Dan's hair.

'I was a bit fed up, Dannie. Your hug made me feel much better, though. Tell me what you're going to have for tea.'

Annie has caught a bus into the town centre to have a break from the house, do some shopping and deposit some clothes at the Oxfam shop. She wants, too, to set in motion the encashment of Greg's insurance policies and to get her hair cut. She's been back a week and is aware how easy it would be merely to stay, to slip into all the old grooves, live with all the old choices. Time to turn around, she thought, before I get caught once again. A mythic image surfaced; Persephone? Psyche? Whoever . . . the heroine, fleeing the Underworld, but making some final mistake, out of carelessness, or inertia, or fear; and her past, embodied, demonised, grabbing her ankle as she flees, holding her back in the Underworld, unconscious, asleep . . . So easy to just stay in Ide, be safe, take the house off the market. So easy, like Persephone—for she'd looked up the myth after Alex's card, all those years ago—simply to eat the pomegranate seeds.

Time to move out of the dream, she thinks. Change scenes, go into town, sort out final details, check trains to go via Shaftesbury to stay overnight with parents, confirm flight, ring Alex.

She drops off the clothes and, early for her other appointments, wanders through the crowds of pigeons and the usual small clusters of Japanese and American tourists, undeterred by the season, flocking around the Cathedral. As usual she makes a detour up the Close to stand outside the archway with its wonderful studded open wooden door that leads into the Bishop of Crediton's quarters. She'd last been here in summer, when wisteria framed the archway with its exotic flowers and opulent scent. Now, in winter, its beauty is different, subtler and clearer, the curves and angles more prominent, the old soft red stone more visible without the foil of flowers and foliage. She loves this doorway; it never fails to lift her spirits. Again for a moment she feels a sense of profound peace, as she had felt in her dream in the train. Sighing with satisfaction, she turns, and cannonballs into Helen, a colleague from the University, who had also attended some of Betty Chadwick's courses.

Helen *swirls*. There is no other way to describe her. Swathed in layers of cerise and royal blue and turquoise, and with her hennaed hair floating around her like Beata Beatrix, she throws herself upon Annie and clasps her tight. Her slightly high-pitched personality and rapid breathless way of talking have in the past often made Annie feel not only exhausted but also somewhat inadequate; a pale imitation of a human being. She recognises though that Helen has a huge heart; too big for her own comfort much of the time. With very little sense of personal boundaries, she is forever being exploited by people who take advantage of her naïvety and natural generosity.

'Annie! What are you doing here? I'm sure Betty Chadwick told me you were in France! Time for a coffee?' Helen sparkles and jangles, and her presence lights up the Cathedral Close.

Annie is pleased to see her. They wander back across the green down to The Café, swapping news, which means in essence that Helen fills Annie in on developments in the personal lives of their university colleagues.

'Do you know,' says Helen, cutting a thick wedge of cheesecake in half and pushing a piece towards Annie, 'I'm so glad to have bumped into you. Synchronicity; I was thinking about you the other day. Do you remember how many afternoons we spent talking about the Grail Quest after Betty's lectures? With that guy, too, what was his name? The poet . . . What happened to him? He went to France, too, didn't he? Do you ever see him? And are you coming back to the faculty, or what?' She rambles on, without pausing for Annie's answers.

Annie remembers how irritating she used to find this habit in Helen. Does she ever listen to anyone else? She pushes the irritation away and concentrates on what Helen is saying. She means well, and after lulling you with her habitual vagueness, just when you are assuming she is a lightweight she takes you by surprise by coming up with an astonishingly acute or incisive comment or insight.

'Well, there's a book you really must read, you'd love it.' She mentions a new book on the psychological aspects of the Grail myths by an academic whose name Annie knows. 'It's right up your street; it talks about the way not only so-called factual history but also 'fictional' history affects us, whether or not we are aware of it, and it examines the links that recur between people across centuries.' She pauses for a split second, waving her fork and swallowing hurriedly. She has that focussed look in her eyes that means, Annie knows, that if she tries to interrupt, Helen will merely raise her voice a fraction and add a firmer edge. The epitome of a teacher in full flow.

'He says that the archetypes in myth have a kind of energy of their own which resonates with different people in different ways.' She forks another dollop of cheesecake into her mouth, and speaks through it, having caught sight of Annie's puzzled expression. 'I know what you're going to say—' she says, as Annie opens her mouth '—what on earth does this have to do with the Grail myths? It may seem like a digression, but actually there is a connection. But in fact it's not just about the Grail myths, but about myth in general.'

Annie subsides into her chair and prepares for a long and possibly somewhat confused listen.

'The idea is that myths carry archetypes, he says they're like psychological blueprints, which recur century after century, each time—each telling—slightly different, a bit more refined, bit more sophisticated. Different people live out different versions—their own version—of each myth, each archetype, and as the myth affects them, so they too affect the myth, and pass their energy on. So there's a kind of psychological gene-bank added to century after century as it is passed on, and anyone who's in tune with that particular archetype might draw on it.' She looks at Annie to see if she is taking it in. Perhaps she sees a wariness or a scepticism in her eyes, because she continues: 'I suppose the way I've explained it makes it sound terribly New Age-y, all crystals and aura-candles, but it's not like that.' She licks her fork. 'Reincarnation, yeah? We've talked about it in the past. Your friend—the one I just mentioned—what's his name—Alec?'

Annie regards her over the top of her coffee-cup. 'Alex.' She has a half-memory of a conversation in the university canteen with Alex about reincarnation. How long ago was that!

'Yes. He talked about it, didn't he? OK, so standard-issue reincarnation: life as a continuous chain—I mean forever, over centuries, the soul never dying but emerging into consciousness periodically, into different lives—where we tend only to see this one life; the part of the link that, like, catches the light, which means that much of the chain is invisible, because to us it looks like a series of, umm, dashes; each of our little unconnected lives, each extinguished. But the other parts of the links are merely submerged, because we look at them with the wrong eyes.' Helen scrabbles in her family-sized loose-weave ethnic basket for a pen, and sketches on the paper-napkin. 'There. This straight unbroken line is how it is, but all we see is, errr, the series of broken dashes -- -- -- -- --. Yeah? OK, OK, you know that. Sorry. —So the broken chain, dashes—' she gesticulates '—is the way we see the individual lives, when all the time they are merely passing in and out of light and shade—dying and being reborn, but actually the energy doesn't ever die, only moves in and out of material manifestation; in other words, in and out of different lives, different bodies. OK, standard reincarnation theory, I guess. I don't know what you think about this?'

'Well, obviously I know the theory of reincarnation. Jury's out for me, I guess,' Annie says guardedly, unwilling to dwell on, let alone share with Helen, the questions that have been beating at her mind since the conference, and her 'nightmare' experiences.

'OK. But this is the interesting bit, and I have a feeling that it may be important for you, though why I haven't the faintest. What he says is that we are each linked across time and space with whoever else has lived out that very particular energy before us.' She pauses and runs her finger around the edge of the plate, collecting up the spare crumbs.

Annie shivers involuntarily, thinking instantly of Isarn. She banishes the thought and wonders instead if Helen is just a very good actress, playing the moment. She isn't looking at Annie, and the pause—for Helen—is uncharacteristically long. Annie knows she hasn't finished. She takes advantage of the silence to ask: 'But aren't we linked across time and space with *everyone*? So are you saying—is he saying—that reincarnation might be explained as a primarily—what, psychological?— phenomenon?'

'No, I think I mean that we reincarnate, if we assume that we do, because the level of archetype needs us to, to bring in particular qualities of energy collectively, as much as we need to, I guess. If I'm not muddling up my theories.

'But get this—might be important, for you. I just have a hunch. Just occasionally, he says, in the right place and if we are receptive enough, we can tune in to one of those others. It's like we catch the right wavelength to pick up their—I suppose you'd call them emanations, which continue to live on in subtle form in the landscape. It's a conjunction of time, space and soul-purpose. That's what he said, close as I remember, anyway.'

Annie stares at Helen. Helen drops the pen back in her bag and scrabbles around again, this time for a lipstick and mirror. She swivels the lipstick up and stretches her lips over her teeth, applying the cerise gloss expertly. She blots her lips together and the dangly earrings she wears catch the light and glitter.

Annie is digesting and sorting through what Helen has just said. Rationally, she still needs to be convinced. And although she's had psychic experiences, usually of prescience, precognition, she doesn't think of herself as either psychic or a msytic; and in fact in the past has preferred not to think about her precognitions at all. Hunches, that's all. But yet certainly to dismiss her recent experiences as mere 'dreaming' is clearly inadequate. She feels a shiver down her spine. And how else, really, to explain Pierre and Mathieu Bonet? She's tried very hard not to seek to explain that, she realises. What was it that the lecturer at the conference said about places where the veil is thin?

She finds her voice. 'OK, so we're all connected. No problem with that at all. But what you're saying is that each of us has the power to affect the energy, or the archetype, is that right? And do we then affect all the lives that have gone before ours, instead of simply our current one? So where does that leave death? And what does it do to time?'

Helen drums on the table with sharp and painted nails and smiles into Annie's eyes, back into her light lively mode. 'You tell me,' she answers. She glances at her watch and pushes her chair back. 'Help! Late again!' and she throws her multi-coloured Indian shawl over her shoulders and stoops to give Annie a quick breathless lipsticky peck on the cheek before rushing out, hair flying.

A second later she flies back in again to say: 'I know what I was leading up to. He thinks that there are more people—proportionately—embodying the errr let's say Grail-Seeker archetype now than at any other time in history apart from the early Middle Ages. Even more than, you know, at the end of last century, and you know how heavily art and literature were drawing on them then. I thought you might be interested in that. See you soon, sweetie,' and with that she is gone again.

Annie sits on over another coffee, abstracted, somewhat stunned, caught in Helen's theory. At the back of her mind something prickles; an edge of tremendous excitement. She'd like to have the chance to follow up the original thesis.

So after coffee and before her hairdressing appointment, Annie wanders down the hill towards the bookshop. As always, she feels completely overwhelmed by the choice once inside the door, but makes for the mythology section.

The book Helen mentioned isn't there. Not in the psychology or sociology sections. Nor philosophy. Unexpectedly disappointed, she turns away. Somehow what Helen said offers a way back to what connected her to Alex, and vice versa; some primary bond that has its roots in the whole Grail/Cathar mystery, and which has become tenuous lately. She is turning to leave, when her eyes are caught by a title: *The Heroic Quest—The Psychology of Myth.* Curious, she lifts it down and opens it at random: *Any journey of significance will leave you changed. This is as true of the inner world as it is of the outer. Even if you come back to the same place, you will not be the same person . . . the same and yet not the same . . .* The nape of her neck prickles at the echo of her own thoughts in the train. She flips through the book. *Sacred Quests . . . Healing the Wasteland & Restoring the Waters . . . The Four Tests of Psyche . . . Persephone and the Underworld.*

Synchronicity again. Good old universe. On impulse, she buys the book. A present for Alex.

Two days later, Annie is ready to leave. Rosa has promised faithfully—a last lifeline—to bring herself and family out for early summer, to christen L'Estang.

The Ide house, cleaned, half-empty and sterile, no longer feels like hers. She supposes, morbidly, that it must be rather like looking at the corpse of someone you once knew, though not well. Familiar, yet not quite; wrinkles ironed-out by leave-taking, disengaged. Spirit flown.

Staying here the last couple of nights had been difficult. It had been time—in fact the only possible time—to scatter Greg's ashes. Rosa had taken her to the woods and then the stone circle out on the moor near Throwleigh that had been one of Greg's favourite places, and stayed with her through the sleepless night afterwards. It was Rosa, too, who had suggested a leave-taking ceremony which involved smashing the empty jar and burying it, and burning the box in which it had been contained. With it, Annie feels finally that her life with Greg is now truly over.

Now, walking down through the village to the phone-box, Annie looks at it all with different eyes; a stranger, coming back to somewhere she once knew. Not hers. Not any more.

No answer from Les Cerisiers. Annie tries again, lets it ring. Damn. She is faintly anxious at the thought of not being met at Toulouse airport. Still, they know she'd been hoping to get back on or before the 21st, in time for Christmas, as well as the solstice bonfire for friends and local people that Susie and Jon had established as a midwinter ritual. She'd ring from the airport in the morning before flying if she couldn't get them earlier; meantime she'd try the village shop for flowers and chocolates and whisky for her parents.

TWENTY-EIGHT

At the same time as Annie is trying to ring Les Cerisiers, Alex is standing outside the Post Office in Perpignan with snowflakes in his hair, hands shaking, cheeks wet.

He'd come into town with Jon to check out a job that had come in which Jon thought he might pass on to Alex, and on sudden impulse had called in at the Post Office, remembering that months ago he'd rung his agent in England to give him the poste restante address here as a contact point.

There are indeed letters; three of them, all addressed in the same spiky black hand. Jonathan, his agent. Alex looks at the postmarks; he's lost track of the days but he supposes there must be about a week to go till Christmas. The date on the earliest envelope is August, the latest mid December, probably only a few days ago. Shit. He opens the most recent. A small slim enclosure fluttered out; he picks it up absently and frowns at the brief note from Jonathan. Curt, you would call it:

Alex.

Your deadline for the first draft of *Lento* is this month. Kindly answer and tell me what the hell's going on. The musicians are lined up; recording due FEBRUARY. Pull your finger out, would you, and give me a ring, for God's sake?

PS: The enclosed envelope arrived yesterday.

Alex turns the envelope over, and feels cold suddenly. Kate's rather childish round handwriting; Alex O'Connell c/o Jonathan Reece. He feels a shit not to have been in touch with the family since Somport.

He rips the envelope open with unnecessary violence. Inside is a single sheet of writing paper with a story-book galloping horse printed along the bottom. Laurel's careful ten-year-old writing fills two-thirds of the page, sloping downwards.

Dear daddy
Please come back I miss you very much.
Mummy cries all the time and Sam is terrible
he keeps smashing everything I cant stand it. I hope
you get this mummy says she dosnt know where you
are but if I rote to you Mister Reece might know. I
love you daddy please come home from Laurel
PS Sam says that he dosnt want anything for
Chrismas except you

Alex leans against the wall in utter desolation and despair. Suddenly nothing else matters; not France, not his freedom, not even Annie. Nothing matters except his children. Swearing, he pushes himself off the wall and thrusts the letter in his jeans pocket, before striding blindly in the direction of the car-park where he is to meet up again with Jon to go and look over the proposed job. He grits his teeth hard and resists a sudden adolescent impulse to put his fist through a shop window, or pull a passing motorcyclist off his mobilette.

Alex has had a tough ten days. Without Annie somehow his reason for being here is gone, and he is finding it difficult to motivate himself to think about L'Estang, or his future here. Unbidden and unwanted, doubts have been pushing their way to the surface: Annie's strange behaviour and obsession with the whole Cathar business. Annie's money, Annie's friends—where was he in all of this? And as for *Lento*—nothing since that burst of creativity when they had first arrived at Les Cerisiers. And while he loves Annie's independence, somehow he feels superfluous, *de trop*. He has no idea whether she needs him or not. Or whether, indeed, he wants to be needed. What he does know is that he feels a blind rage at his sense of impotence.

He also knows that he has not managed to leave behind in England his sense of failure: it lurks, tormenting him every time he thinks about Kate and the family, or his work, or the fact that he can have no part in raising the money to buy a house here. If he could just apply himself to his music and at least get the commissioned piece out of the way his sense of self-respect would be partially restored. But even that seems impossible; he has been far too restless to settle to it.

There is another, almost equally disturbing, reason to leave this place—his sanity. He'd said nothing to Annie, but the morning after their Cathar 'incident', he'd woken up and found on his bedside notepad in his script a poem, titled, even, of which he had absolutely no memory:

Montségur

So they are gone, these Bonshommes
with their healing hands and peaceful ways

gone into the long night's silence, blackened bones
ploughed under Languedoc soil, blood become

sunflowers, grapevines, boar. This
path of the stars. This final transmigration

only to ever more perfect loving.

He has no recollection of writing it; he wasn't aware that he knew what 'bonshommes' meant. He'd forgotten, consciously anyway, until he looked it up, that the doctrine of transmigration was central to Catharism. And 'path of the stars'?—He knows it carries more weight than simply that of a poetic phrase, but he isn't sure he knows, or wants to know, what that weight is. It registers only as a faint prickling, a slight uneasiness.

But it is his poem all right.

Enough. This is Annie's trip. It's all getting a bit entangled, a bit New Age-y.

He isn't sure how much more he can take. The weather, the cold, haven't helped. He hates winter at the best of times. He had marvelled at Annie's equanimity, generally unchanged by external things such as the weather. For him, the winter months each year feel like a mini-death, and even his regular meditation couldn't seem to shift him through it. He feels stagnant, as if his mind were the bottom of an opaque sluggish ooze-filled pond, and this winter is worse than ever. No glimmer of creativity has touched its muddy waters; the churning thoughts that circle like predatory pike move only between anger at himself, a faint and inexplicable resentment at Annie, and a huge and overwhelming sense of guilt and grief about the family. He feels unclean; even his grief isn't clear, to be lived through until it lifts; it too is stagnant, unmoving, because he knows he has not said goodbye or really closed the door. Impasse; unable to move forwards or backwards, he feels as if he is decaying inside.

The letter from Laurel of course merely exacerbates everything; suddenly the pond inside his head is now clogged with enormous boulders. Had Annie been here, perhaps finally he would have to talk about these feelings; perhaps finally things might have started to shift. As it is, he can see nothing other than the oozing mess inside his head.

He thinks back to last winter, and the despair he had felt; the endless Devon rain and the whining children incarcerated by the weather day after day; Kate's demands and her faintly accusing pinched face; the total lack of peace, of creative space. Annie had seemed like a shaft of winter sunlight, her cool uncluttered personality cutting right through the torpid layers, shining healing light into the hidden places. New life dormant for as long as he could remember in the stagnating sludge, had stirred, had started to push shoots up towards the light.

Whenever he had thought of Annie last winter a warmth had stolen over him; the one flicker of hope in what had felt for years like a soul-dead existence. The image that had come to mind continuously for him through the dead months was that of the lotus-flower, pushing its extravagant and incredible face up to the surface, transmitting and transforming all the shit which, surprisingly, offered exactly the rich nutrients it needed to bloom. This thought always made him feel cheerful again; sustained him through last winter until spring, when suddenly, he knew, he had grown his wings back.

And now. And now? Annie's coolness is simply Annie's coolness. It's not always easy. And any relationship, he realises, accumulates clutter.

By the time Jon arrives Alex is scowling and black; nearly incoherent with the tension from the inner conflict. Jon looks at him consideringly and suggests a beer before they discuss the work possibilities, but in the bar Alex is reticent to the point, he knows, of surliness. All he can think about is Laurel's letter, and when they emerge again into the sullen icy air Jon has given up trying to talk about joinery and kitchens.

'What's up, mate?'

Alex remains tight-jawed, and merely grunts.

Jon backs off, carries on strolling towards the pick-up, casting an eye at the burdened sky.

Alex, without a word, slams into a public phone-booth.

Jon stops, leans against the wall. Rolls a cigarette, waits.

The evening is interminable. As Alex stands to clear the supper-dishes Susie glances imploringly at Jon who, unperturbed by Alex's mood, though perfectly aware of it, merely shrugs elaborately and starts talking about preparations for the solstice bonfire. Alex is patently not listening, and eventually he slams the cupboard doors shut on the last dried-up dishes and takes himself upstairs. Susie pauses mid-sentence to listen to his stomping feet and says:

'What on earth's the matter with him? Not a word through all of supper. If I didn't know him I'd feel quite frightened around him right now. Did you see how he shook my hand off his arm? Not like him at all. '

'God knows. Not our problem though,' Jon replies, stretching back in his chair to extract his tobacco from his pocket and roll a cigarette. 'Fancy a cognac?'

Susie's stomach is churning. To calm herself down, she thinks she'll ring a couple of friends and remind them about the bonfire. She makes a list, then picks up the phone. Nothing. Dead—phone lines down probably in the snowstorm they'd had earlier. 'Damn, damn, damn,' she says. 'The phone's dead. You know how it is when you have your mind set to do something and then suddenly you can't do it?'

Jon grunts, not lifting his head from the plans he's spread out around him on the kitchen table.

Susie wanders around the kitchen for a minute, restless. She suddenly feels she should call Annie, who must be due back tomorrow or the day after, and goes over to get her address-book, before remembering that of course she can't ring out.

She'll try her from La Chapelle Blanche tomorrow morning. Should she remind Alex about her imminent return? Or is it presumptuous and interfering? Surely he'll remember anyway, though he has seemed absentminded lately, forgetting small things. Oh God. I'll think about that in the morning, she thinks wearily. Perhaps she'll have a shower, burn some of the incense Annie had brought them. She goes and puts her arms around Jon's neck. 'What about an early night, sweetheart? I'd really like a long hug right now.'

TWENTY-NINE

Annie peers out of the plane window down towards the ground; below thick fog is swirling, and the runway is invisible. As they circle just above the dense bank of cloud that seems to be a ground-fog, she cranes to see if she can see the Mediterranean, but visibility is minimal. The porthole steams up and she rubs her hand over it. It is only midday, but as they circle lower it is dark enough outside to be dusk.

The plane seems to be circling for ages before presumably they get clearance; perhaps other aircraft have been diverted, like this one, because of the freak snowstorm. Here at Montpellier, closer to the coast, snow is rare; as, usually, is thick fog. As they finally descend, a dark shape suddenly looms close by; Annie's heart leaps irrationally into her throat, until she realises it is another plane taxiing past prior to lifting off.

Annie is close to tears. It is as if, away from England, the truth of Greg's death is making itself felt; and, too, the enormity of what she has done is becoming real. Nothing holds her to England now, except the ties to her family.

She can't wait for the plane to come to a standstill, and to see Alex again; it's all she can do to keep her seatbelt buckled and stay in her place. She has missed him more than she could have imagined, and her anticipation is tinged with nervousness, almost dread, her stomach churning. She badly needs a loo. What is the matter with her? She isn't normally this bad. She supposes it is delayed reaction to Greg's ashes, and leaving England; and the fact that she hasn't been able to get hold of Les Cerisiers at all makes her feel somewhat suspended in limbo.

She had resigned herself to a wait at Toulouse until Alex could get to her. She had mentioned before she left France that she was likely to be back on this plane, which of course should have arrived in Toulouse. Now she doesn't know whether to hope he's remembered, which means that he'd have had a long drive to Toulouse and then on to Montpellier, or that he hasn't, so that at least he'll only have to drive to Montpellier—assuming he is at the house. Please God let the phone be working—and let Les Cerisiers not be cut off by snow.

Alex, hunched near the back of his plane, doesn't see the dark shape of the incoming aircraft speeding past them in the fog. As the engines roar he straightens and makes himself breathe deeply as the plane lifts and soars skywards. Normally he would love this moment; the sense of moving high up into the air to be suspended between heaven and earth, between past and future, is exhilarating. He loves flying, and he loves the mechanics of flight, and the engineering minds that made a seemingly impossible process possible.

Now he feels no joy, only a dull ache that seems to permeate every part of him. He'd only just made it to the airport in time, despite leaving Les Cerisiers before daybreak. First he'd had to dig himself out of a drift in the lane, then just the other side of Annecy he'd had a flat. The whole thing was a gamble anyway, because though he'd discovered what time the plane left Montpellier he didn't know if there were any free seats. If there weren't, he didn't quite know what his next move would be. He couldn't have gone back, not now. He'd just have to stay put until the next flight the following day, he'd supposed.

And after that, what? The only thing he could think of that made any sense was to get a small flat or bedsit somewhere, not too far from the kids. The idea of seeing the children regularly offered the only small glimmer of hope in a dark prospect. He couldn't go back and pick up where he'd left off his old life; he knew intuitively that that would be creative and spiritual death. If he could find somewhere, anywhere, immediately, there was a chance he could finish the composition by the deadline. He had to, really, otherwise life would be a mockery, and the last six months nullified somehow in a way he couldn't articulate. All that gain and all that joy needed a vehicle, a channel, and ultimately even a justification.

He feels wretched not having spoken to Susie and Jon. He hopes they hadn't heard the van choking reluctantly into life and slithering its way down the lane. Foolhardy wasn't in it; the lane was an ice-rink, with drifts banked up either side; more than once he'd bounced off a hedge or a wall.

He doesn't know what to want for the future. He can't bear to think of Annie, due back any day now, he supposes. His mind flinches away from any thought of her; to do what he is doing he has to shut her out completely. His mind circles for a moment above the note, the Cathar poem and the spare set of van keys he's left on the pillow in the attic room; he reins it in with an immense effort like curbing a bolting horse and sets it firmly on course for England. Don't look back, he thinks; never look back. This is what I have chosen to do. I'm sorry, Annie my love, I'm sorry. Right people, probably right place, wrong time. But I love you; oh how I love you.

In Les Cerisiers Susie has been trying Annie's number every twenty minutes since about eleven o'clock when the line was restored. Each time she fails to get through she feels a little more anxious, until Jon, home this morning, growls at her to please shut the fuck up and stop pacing, so that he can concentrate on the plans he is perusing.

'Jon, I'm really worried. Where the hell do you think he went? It must have been him I heard at about six; I thought I was still dreaming. It was still dark. What should I say to Annie?'

'Oh, for God's sake. Get through to the woman first and then worry about what you'll say. You're never at a loss for words. I'm sure he'll turn up; probably couldn't sleep, that's all. Now please let me get on with these bloody plans in peace.'

When the phone rings, Susie jumps and runs for it. Annie's voice. Thank God.

'Oh Annie, I've been trying to get you. I was sure you said it'd be today you got back. Where are you? You *are* back? Monpellier? Oh right . . . no, he's not here at the moment. One of us'll come down as fast as we can—it's still treacherous here but the sun's out, sort of, so maybe there'll be a melt . . . No, I'm not sure where he went. Yes, this morning sometime . . .' she tries to keep her anxiety out of her voice. 'Well, he may have gone to Toulouse, of course. No, I will. As fast as I can. Couple of hours?'

Jon looks up at her. 'You're crazy. Have you seen the conditions? I'll go, or we both will.'

Annie turns back into the lounge, crowded with excess passengers. She's piled all her things on and around one of the plastic seats, having spent what felt like an eternity waiting for her two suitcases and rucksack of books—her essentials, the rest is stored in Rosa's garden shed—to appear on the conveyor belt.

She is close to tears again; what a disappointment not to speak to Alex. Still, at least it probably means he's remembered and gone to Toulouse. She buys a strong black coffee and a baguette, despite no appetite. Unable to concentrate she changes seats so she can at least have the distraction of watching the planes landing or taking off, and tries not to count the minutes. Not long, now; not long. God, I've missed you, Alex. He's always telling me I hold back, keep a bit of me shut away. This time I'll tell him how much I love him, how much I need him, how much I've missed him. Tomorrow perhaps we can go and see L'Estang.

When Jon and Susie walk into the airport lounge nearly three hours later Annie virtually throws herself at them with joy and relief, rather to their surprise. Jon, embarrassed, disentangles himself first and bends to collect her luggage.

'Oh, Susie, I'm so glad to see you; thanks for coming all this way. I did try to ring yesterday to warn you but I couldn't get through. Are the roads OK? You didn't pass Alex?'

Susie hugs her warmly. 'Welcome home, love. The house has been empty without you—I swear the dogs are pining. The roads near the foothills are a bit icy; the lane was slippery—sludge on top, frozen underneath. We've got a shovel, some old carpet and a bag of grit in the back of the car, though. No, no Alex yet.' She keeps her uneasiness to herself. 'Give me one of those bags. We're glad to fetch you; I've felt a bit cooped up the last few days, we haven't been out of the house much. We needed to pick up some animal feed anyway.'

Annie shrugs her coat on and shouldering the last of her bags follows Susie through the door. Jon has parked as close to the building as he could get, somewhat illegally. Craning his head to check that the exit is clear so that he can pull straight out without decelerating, he is the only one to spot, dim through what is now quite thick freezing fog, a navy-and-white camper-van parked up against the rear fence, partially screened by a Renault Trafic and the wet black branches of winter trees. He doesn't see a lot of point in saying anything, since he is now suddenly sure Alex hadn't come to pick Annie up. He holds his tongue while his mind works overtime at the implications, and finds himself being extraordinarily gentle with Annie on the way home. She looks frayed to pieces already, poor girl, quite raw and fragile; so different from the brittle aloof academic he remembers from their first meetings in the early days of his relationship with Susie. She is so much more attractive, he thinks, and somehow so much younger-seeming, when she allows herself to be vulnerable, despite the lines of fatigue on her face.

The note on the pillow in the loft-room is scarcely visible, white against white cotton, and absorbed into the cold white glare of reflected snow and winter afternoon light. Written in Alex's fast script, but more jagged than usual, on a piece of the squared paper torn out of a French notebook in which Annie had been working out weaving designs, it is simple.

'Annie. There's no way to say this, and no apologies or excuses. I just simply can't do it; I can't go on without the kids any more. I'm not ready.

'Please don't think I don't love you—I do, probably more than you can imagine. Certainly more than I imagined possible. But I find it's not enough. I know I'm being a shit.

'The van will be at Montpellier airport. It's yours.'

Annie looks up, into the cold afternoon light. There is a moment of extraordinary clarity and stillness, frozen white stillness. Calm, snow-cold stillness; as if nothing matters any more, as if nothing will ever matter again. Almost a relinquishing; like lying down in the snow and letting yourself slip away.

No blood in her veins; only ice, and a creeping cold.

Outside the window between herself and the hard white backbone of the mountains the trees shake knobbly black fingers at the colourless sky; a veil of black lace, a mantilla. A black-and-white landscape inside and out; against the white-washed walls her fragmented half-finished full-size paper sketch of her planned tapestry hangs limp by one corner, mocking, unresolved, dislocated, stark against the blue-grey shadows, a chaos of black and white splinters.

So this is her solstice: this freeze, this blackness, swallowing all light. Chaos winning, after all. No midwinter bonfires, not for her. Falling as if forever into nowhere, she thinks she might burst; a great howl commences and takes over, and she feels herself slide down a tunnel of darkness.

Emergence
France

'…I was still the same,
Knowing myself yet being someone other…'
T S Eliot, *Little Gidding*

THIRTY

Annie is on her knees scrubbing with grim determination; as if she could scrub away the past, the pain, the anger if only she scrubs long and hard enough; if she thinks only of the scrubbing and ignores her frozen hands and the cold seeping through the worn denim knees of her jeans and the shooting pains in her back. In fact, it actually helps to have some physical discomfort to distract her from the boiling raging turbulence inside her.

She stops as she hears Susie's car bounce and rattle up the drive, and kneels upright propping her back with her hands and stretching. Goss, the puppy, sprawled half-sitting half-lying against the door with his back legs and his ludicrously huge feet splayed forwards past his front paws, whines as he hears the car and turns his spotty nose towards Annie. In nervous anticipation of Finn and Wesley—by whom he is both overwhelmed and over-excited—bounding through the door he pees, a little yellow trickle dripping down the uneven still-filthy flagstones towards Annie's bucket. Annie sighs and brushes a strand of hair out of her mouth with the back of her rubber-clad wrist. She extracts a sodden cloth from the muddy water and wipes up the pee, opening the door a crack to let Goss out into the early March chill to meet the visitors.

With a degree of desperation she looks around her. Ten days camping out here since the house officially became hers towards the end of February, most of them spent perched on a rickety chair or on her hands and knees wire-brushing, scraping and scrubbing decades of filth from the walls and latterly the floor, and you could still hardly see the difference. Perhaps she should make a start on the windows before continuing with the floor—with some of the grime gone from the glass and a bit more natural light the place would look less depressing. At least you can now see the old wooden panelling boxing in the staircase between the kitchen and the sitting-room, though exposing it had been a mixed blessing; more woodworm than she had expected, though Jon thought they were old holes, the occupants long since gone.

The truth is that, though she knows she has done the right thing, and that this is where she belongs, she can raise no enthusiasm at all for it, for anything. She goes through the motions, but her heart seems to be missing. When she stops, physically, the great gaping pit of her future opens at her feet, making her stomach lurch and shrink. The only way she can hold the abyss at bay is not to stop, until she knows that if she doesn't, she will faint; at which point she crawls upstairs into the makeshift bed and her layers of sleeping-bags and blankets, to lie awake, blank and restless, often until just before dawn. Then she'll doze fitfully, her sleep peopled with indistinct but disturbing and dysfunctional figures and images until Goss wakes her, whining and scratching at her door, for a dawn pee. She staggers down the stairs, opens the door for Goss, and puts the kettle on the range for herself and, later, Susie if she is there; and the cycle starts again.

At least, she thinks to herself, at least she doesn't have the emotional energy to feel scared or apprehensive about the prospect of living at L'Estang on her own. As long as she can lose herself in the physical demands of getting the place together, she doesn't have the time to worry about it either. Mechanically she makes herself sit down and write out goals for each day, and for each week. She knows that without these notes she will flounder. She hears her mother's voice in her head sometimes: 'Hope for the best, but plan for the worst. If in doubt, make a list; when life takes over, tear it up!' Then she would have a sudden longing for her mother's presence; for her gaiety and optimism, for the safety and security of childhood, for someone else to take over and tell her what to do.

So much to do.

She's had a phone installed as a priority, and the house is served by a spring, so communication and water are not problems, though there is no-one but Susie to whom she talks.

The day she took possession, she'd ordered a trailer-load of logs for the range and the fire, and she, Jon and Susie had stacked all these in one of the outbuildings across from the house. The range has a back boiler so there is hot water, and she is investigating a plumber to install radiators. A bathroom is needed; it feels unnecessarily spartan, with so much else on her plate, to have to use the spidery dilapidated outside loo, full of dead things and rotting leaves, in this cold and her state of mind. Little things like that seem so draining at the moment, more of a problem that they actually are. She doesn't mind washing and brushing her teeth in the kitchen sink, but she feels in dire need of a bath or a shower, despite the fact that she has no energy to take an interest in how she looks, or even smells. Susie hasn't succeeded in persuading her to stay based at Les Cerisiers whilst doing up L'Estang; obscurely Annie feels that the only way she can cope with her new home at all is to be immediately installed, filth and lack of furniture notwithstanding.

Jon has brought her an axe and a chopper as a moving -in present; Susie has brought her a car-full of house-plants which, installed temporarily on the windowsill above the sink and on the broad stone one in the sitting-room, lift the house in a way that nothing else yet has.

'Premature, love, I know; I was looking for something more useful, practical. Something sensible; and then I thought, what would I need most? Something to cheer me and the house up, something living. So here you go,' she'd said, lifting them from their cardboard boxes. Susie has an intuitive knack with presents—they were in fact perfect, filling the house with their living green presence.

She must remember to riddle and top up the range in a minute, and check the other items on her list, make some phone calls. She can't put off registering her presence with the authorities any longer. She must also remind the electricity board that they'd promised to connect her the day before yesterday—candles and the range were all very well, but they make things harder than she needs at the moment. Besides, any day now her furniture will arrive, and she'd love to be able to play music, lift the silence now and then. On the days when Susie doesn't stay, camped out like her on a temporary bed in the other room, the evenings are interminable and unbroken, tasks sliding into each other in exhausting monotony.

Long term, she is determined not to let herself slide back into the despair that had trapped her this time last year, and one way to avoid that, she knows, is to keep in touch with her old friends. She forces herself to picture the future. By the spring, by the time the mimosas are in flower again and the broom blazing in the umber and purple hillsides, she would like to have L'Estang fit to receive visitors. She pictures the vine in leaf and lavender starting its purple haze and swifts back shrilling and swooping round the buildings, scything through the jewel-blue skies. When she imagines how it will look the sleeping countryside springs to life and she can smell the hot dusty resin of the umbrella pines and the rosemary and lavender scented summer air of the Languedoc, and feels comforted. She clings on to the certainty of the cycling seasons, the return of spring with all its promise of renewal, with grim tenacity, as if to let go would be to drown. Adrift as she is, these small securities offer the only reference points.

Meantime, she just focuses on the jobs the house needs, and pushes all thoughts of Alex right out of her head, though a creeping anger persists in making itself felt at unwary moments, followed immediately by the intense pain that lies just beneath it. She's heard nothing from him, and has not attempted to make contact herself. So that's it then, she thinks bitterly to herself; illusion over. Forty now; time to face the prospect of a solitary future. No point in agonising over what has gone wrong; whether she has failed, or him; or simply life. Their time together had been richer, fuller, than any other six months of her life, and she knows there will come a day when she will be grateful for that, and have forgotten the pain, the anger, the sense of betrayal. So she'll have to find another way to live, in time. For now, getting through each day is an achievement.

Susie lurches through the door, arms full of shopping, dogs tailing her and growling at Goss, who shoots towards Annie for security and in his rush nearly sends Susie headlong. The shopping tumbles out of her arms in a sprawl, most of it landing with her on top of it on the table which has been pushed back, along with the two chairs bought second-hand in the market which are the only other furnishings, under the courtyard window. With her usual good humour Susie pushes herself upright and then bends to scratch Goss' ears, and glances at laughingly at Annie. 'Oh, Annie darling, come on, it's not that bad!'

'What's not that bad?'

'I mean it'll all be OK. In the end. You just look so — grim. Serious. All closed-up...' Annie doesn't respond. 'OK then, let's get cracking.'

Annie's face doesn't seem to have changed from its bleak tight expression at all in the last few months since she arrived back in France. Susie can't remember when she last saw her laugh; there is a remoteness about her, and a total lack of humour. In fact, there seems to be a total lack of anything about her, especially emotion, Susie reflects; only this cold dispassion, iron-hard as the wintry ground. Yet she is physically functioning; functioning extraordinarily well.

'Yes, she's coping well; too well,' she'd said to Jon when she went home yesterday.

'Oh, come off it, Susie, how can she be coping too well? Aren't you pleased that she's getting it together?'

Susie had felt a moment's exasperation; any woman would know exactly what she meant. 'I mean it makes me suspicious. It's not right, not genuine, somehow, as if she's forcing it, living on willpower and killing something else in her. It's like she's hollow.'

Jon had looked at her with a hint of a sardonic smile. 'Bullshit, Susie. You're being melodramatic. It'll be willpower that'll pull her through a time like now; thank God she got it together to go ahead with L'Estang regardless of Alex. She could just have totally crumbled.'

'I know; but it's as if she has gone to pieces inside; she's like a shell. She seems so hard, Jon, so angry. And there's just such an enormous amount to do there; you saw the survey. I'm afraid she's going to push herself and push herself until she cracks.'

Jon had shrugged. 'It's not our business, Susie. I've told you I'll do all I can to help her practically, and she's had you for a week and you'll carry on going down there most days for a while, won't you? It's her life though, you can't live it for her.'

Now in the pale light filtering through the dusty windows at L'Estang, Susie looks at her friend. 'Are you sleeping, Annie? You've got great dark circles under your eyes.'

'Dunno. No, not a lot, really.'

'Have you seen yourself lately?'

'No mirror. Don't really care much, anyway.' Nonetheless, she goes to peer at herself in the side of the kettle.

'Oh Annie! That's too blackened to see anything! It'll all be distorted!'

'Mmm. Can see all the extra grey hair, though. God, I look my age, don't I? And a bit.'

'What are you talking about? It's only that wing of hair across your face; the rest is still black. And it's silver, not grey; suits you, anyway. Shall I put the kettle on? Come on—while we wait for it to boil, come and see what I've got for you!'

Annie pulls off her rubber gloves and stands up stiffly. Outside their breath dances for a moment in chill clouds in the air and is dispersed by the breeze cutting across from the coast over the hills.

'Isn't the almond beautiful?'

Annie glances at the swaying tree covered in shell-pink blossom by the gateway. 'Intellectually I know it is; but it just doesn't touch me, Susie. Nothing does. Same with the flowers in the back orchard,' and she gestures through the gate at the lemon-green papery hellebores and the nodding blue scyllas beneath the japonica at the foot of the house walls. 'I feel a bit like a person with numbed feet stretching towards a fire which I can't feel at the moment. One day, perhaps.'

'Can you give me a hand? It's heavy.' Susie touches her arm, then opens one of the back doors of the car, and from the well where the rear seat usually was, now emptied and lined with a piece of old carpet and newspapers, they carefully lift an outsize cat-basket, to the accompaniment of some indignant quackings. 'Ducks!' Annie's face softens for an instant and she looks enquiringly at Susie as they lug the basket out. Between them they carry it over to one of the outbuildings.

'Yep. A Muscovy duck and drake. The duck's one of the lavender ones of ours you always liked. I thought if we barricade the door somehow they'll be OK in the shed for a few days; Jon's making you a run and shelter so you can shut them up at night.'

'Oh, Susie!' Annie throws her a quick look. They lower the basket and Susie goes back to the car for a small sack of straw and a bag of corn. Annie squats engrossed over the basket, peering through a gap in the wicker top. She glances at Susie with gratitude; her face unfrozen momentarily.

'Oh, Susie,' she repeats. 'Perfect. Thank you, Susie; that's perfect. Really kind,' she says with some effort, but meaning it. Annie loves ducks. In happier times she would take delight in introducing them to the pond, feeding them each morning, rearing ducklings.

She straightens and goes into the old piggery, climbing over piles of rubbish—broken hoes, a wheelbarrow minus wheel, a chair with a missing leg, a twiggy pile of kindling, vine-prunings probably years old. She calls back over her shoulder to Susie: 'I'm sure I've seen a frame here somewhere—probably to protect young seedlings from wildlife—yes, here—' she emerges, cobwebs in her hair and powdery ancient dust down her jumper sleeve, dragging a structure of chicken wire and lightweight timber. 'Look, this could be bent into shape to block the doorway temporarily . . .' And the ducks are installed, tumbling over each other in an undignified scramble to escape the confines of the basket, the drake hissing at all and sundry.

Susie takes the boiling kettle off the range and pours it onto coffee-grounds, and the aroma momentarily masks the musty smell of old wet wood and dirt-clogged flagstones. A sudden easterly gust swirls smoke back into the room from the range and Annie coughs and opens the door again. Susie presses the plunger and pours coffee steaming into the two green-and-gold coffee cups from the camper van and hands one to Annie.

'Come on, love,' she says warmly. 'When we've drunk this I'll give you a hand; we could clean the downstairs window frames before lunch. We could sand them down then, couldn't we? You could be on to the painting by next week. There was only one window frame needed replacing, wasn't there? Jon'll be down at the weekend to do that. Just think—when we've finished the house you can start thinking about your real painting again, and your weaving too.'

Annie perches on the edge of the table sipping her coffee gratefully. 'What I'm so frightened of, Susie,' she says on impulse, as if replying to an earlier question, 'is that if I let up at all I shall go under, give up and go back to England. I can't turn back now. If I did that there would be nothing left out of all this for me. I need to know what it all means; I have to make sense of it. I have to make my own way.'

Susie puts her cup down carefully and starts putting away the shopping. 'Go on. I'm listening—'

'You see, I've spent my life drifting into situations because of someone else's wishes, or by default because nothing attracted me more strongly at the time. I've never really determined my own life. Now's my chance, I suppose. I wish it were different, but this is how it is.' She bites her lip and looks at Susie's back, then away out of the window at the wintry trees. 'He's gone; and that's that.'

Minutes pass. Neither of them moves.

'I have to learn how to accept it and not let it dictate my future or my actions. I feel so angry, so betrayed, though. It's awful, but I can't forgive him.'

Susie looks back at her over her shoulder. 'Of course you can't yet, love. You will, though, Annie, you will. I can't tell you how courageous I think you are. And I can see from your face how tough it is. If you can survive this, at this time of the year, you can survive anything.'

'I think the worst of it is that I've lost my faith, my belief— in anything. I can't imagine being anywhere but in this awful bleak black place. I keep thinking of Eliot's *Wasteland* poem. I can't see a way out, you know?'

Susie puts down the packet of pasta in her hand and comes to give Annie a hug. 'You know what they say about the darkest time being just before the dawn. The descent into the underworld and all that. It'll be spring soon; two or three weeks then the equinox; April here below the snowline is usually mild and often hot, if we don't get the winds. It'll be no time at all before they're grazing the summer pastures up above Les Cerisiers again.' She picks up the pasta and carries on sorting through the shopping.

THIRTY-ONE

Annie wakes suddenly in the dark house, her heart thumping..

It is impossibly dark; blacker than black, the house choked with night. She didn't know darkness could be so substantial.

The blackness seems to shiver as a low hum draws near, and on the instant the room is full of people, and a shrill wind is howling somewhere beyond them all, and the hum becomes a chant, a low thrumming chant, over and over, in a strange and archaic tongue, familiar and yet remote, which Annie feels vibrating in her head. Without translating she knows the words, an ancient memory coursing in her blood.

> *'Closing my eyes I see You*
> *When I open them You are here*
> *The Path of the Stars is unfolding*
> *I am surrendered to Your care*
>
> *I offer myself as a vessel*
> *Fill and pour me as You will*
>
> *N'oublie pas, n'oublie jamais . . .'*

Then all around her suddenly the blackness is perforated by flickers and glimmers, points of fire like earthbound stars. In the far distance off to one side the flames are dense, leaping soundlessly. The pyre at the bottom of the hill, she thinks; they've lit it already—and her stomach turns to water and her skin slithers with sweat. Her feet are numb. Pure terror throbs in her skull.

With an immense effort she pulls herself back—no fire, no voices, no hill. A March night on her own in L'Estang, camped out downstairs, for warmth and comfort, by the range; she can hear its gentle crackles and hisses. Goss is whining though, a high-pitched puppy-howl from the floor by her camp-bed, and a wind has got up, rattling the door and the shutters.

Her hands are shaking and her hair is wet with perspiration. She lies rigid in the dark for what seems like an eternity, peering into the blackness, her whole body listening. She forces herself to breathe deeply, leans over to scrabble for the matches to light her candle.

Before she can reach them she becomes aware that Isarn is in the room with her—Isarn's gentle presence, serene though sorrowful. Annie senses rather than sees her hands cupped as if she were holding something precious.

Then Isarn is in her head, speaking to her. Frozen, Annie listens.

When her heart has slowed its thumping she lights a match with trembling fingers, touches it to the candle. Shadows leap around the room. Goss is still whimpering, a low, mournful sound through closed lips.

Isarn's words pour onto the paper, page after page of the squared French notepaper which lies always by Annie's bedside.

We now number more than two hundred, for there are croyants who have joined their hearts to ours and will go forth with us, renouncing all earthly ties, voluntarily . . . none of them will leave, though they had the choice of their freedom when the garrison left at the truce. Surrounding us still are the many thousand besiegers who have been camped and waiting so long; there is a strange silence fallen on them since we agreed the truce.

Not long now. We prepare ourselves for the rites, for Béma, the vernal rising when the dark angels and the light meet in the place of the Grail, when the warring forces all stay their hands and turn to face the neutral angels who for a blink of an eye hold sway on this earthly plane, and the light and the dark in the human soul are in perfect balance before tumbling on again in their eternal tension. We prepare ourselves for safe passage through this doorway between heaven and earth, onwards into the light.

Today Guénon gave the Consolamentum. It was hard to keep from weeping as he touched brow after brow; face after face that is little more than skull now, but each raised to him; each pair of eyes still lit. Amidst the filth and the cold and the hardship and starvation, amidst the stench of sickness and decay and ordure all minds are turned to the place where we are going. We practise Guénon's gentle teachings, lifting ourselves from any holding to these worn sick bodies—for many of our number are now beyond movement and were carried by others. When we finally leave here they must be carried.

Many of us now have embarked on the Endura, the long fast, and some of the newly-initiated accompany us on this journey too, for this way we may let go and pass through more easily . . . Guénon reminds us constantly that the spirit cannot die, that the spark will remain and will return, illuminating wherever light is needed . . . our work is not yet done . . . there are many hearts still to be healed . . . the light will spread through the darkness, sometimes obscured, sometimes flickering, but constant as the sun, unquenchable, for all time . . . our task here is to catch that spark, fan the flame into life, never give up . . . never give up . . . however long the path . . .

Annie pushes down the blanket and sleeping-bag and pulls on her socks from the clothes heaped on a chair next to the camp-bed. The hairs on her neck are still prickling and she feels sick.

The candle gutters in the draught she makes and throws distorted shadows around the room. Her head is full of white noise. She drapes the blanket round her shoulders over her T-shirt and leggings and squats on the flagstones to comfort Goss who is still whining miserably and shivering. Her head feels dull and heavy; she is dislocated, displaced, poised between worlds in an uncomfortable way. Cold sweat sogs her T-shirt. She folds the sheets of paper with shaking hands and slips them inside her diary in an effort to shut away the world of Isarn. Her own is difficult enough at the moment. Terror is mingled with weak light-headedness, as if she hasn't eaten for a while. She has a desperate longing for Rosa, for normality, for the security of her old life, pre-Alex, pre-accident, pre-France. Especially pre whatever it is that is going on at the moment.

She lights as many candles as she can find and dots them around the kitchen, then opens up the dampers on the top and bottom of the stove to draw the fire for tea. Like a kick in the stomach she is winded by the intensity of her bleak loneliness and a sudden fierce longing for Alex; she clamps her jaw and pushes him out of her mind, concentrating instead on breaking and buttering a piece of yesterday's baguette, focussing on her teeth chewing, her tongue manoeuvring, swallowing, the peristaltic action as the bread moves downwards into her gut. She makes herself conscious of every part of her body, naming and feeling from the top of her head down to her toes, focussing, concentrating. *Never give up . . . never give up . . .*

The night seems interminable.

She brings tea back to her camp-bed, allows Goss to climb onto the bottom, on her feet. Looking for further distraction she reaches for a book from the pile on the edge of the table, and her hands find the book she had bought for Alex, all those aeons ago when things had seemed so different. She opens it at random, and finds a momentary flicker of pleasure at the offering of the right words at the right time, the unceasing synchronicity of the universe. 'Healing the Wasteland.' Was it really only yesterday that she had mentioned the wasteland to Susie? She reads: 'An inevitable part of the journey towards consciousness is a wilderness time, the "dark night of the soul" or the "night-sea voyage". At this point in one's life there is a sense of being lost and despairing; it is always 3a.m. and you are always on your own. Our hero spends some years lost in the wilderness, forgetful of the purpose of his quest, wandering rather aimlessly . . .'

Maybe, she thinks, she needs to step out of her own way, out of her own light; let questions and answers become apparent in their own time. Personal happiness suddenly seems the most trivial, the most inconsequential focus for a life. Surely the answer is to do with service, with compassion, with a larger vision . . . she drifts . . . and finally falls asleep with a jumble of words rattling around her head . . . *only the light remains . . . il y a des tempêtes qui viennent . . . never give up . . . never forget . . . never give up.*

The morning breaks clear. Just after five-thirty Annie opens the shutters, and already the sky is lightening towards the hills between her and the coast. The wind has subsided to a light breeze. She steps outside for a moment with Goss, and as if on cue a pair of kites soar out of the shadows and over the house, spiralling upwards, the new light in the streaked dawn sky stroking their dark undersides amber. On the skyline the tips of the snowcapped mountains are already lightly brushed apricot.

Annie breathes deeply, filling herself with daybreak. Her uneasiness is with her still, but more bearable in the light.

Alive. Still alive. She gazes towards the chain of the Pyrenees, below their white peaks purple-shadowed, pooled still with night. *I will lift up mine eyes to the hills . . .* She decides on impulse to take time out, to drive into the hills.

Montségur. Perhaps now is the time.

She shivers in the dawn chill and turns back into the house to make a flask of coffee. Then, having fed the ducks, still in their temporary housing, she winds her old poppy-red scarf around her neck and shrugs on her woollen jacket. She locks the front door with the huge iron key, and is about to slide it under the stone seat beneath the window when she decides to collect her maps, guide-books and Cathar books to take too. As she crosses the yard back to the van, spiralling down on the breeze, unbelievably, floats a primary feather from one of the kites. Annie stretches and just catches it, and carefully she wedges the talisman into the top of the ashtray drawer in the camper before lifting Goss onto the passenger seat and starting the engine.

She heads across country to pick up the road that she and Alex had travelled a lifetime ago. This is a day just for her—time out, healing time; time to forget the bleakness of her days and the disturbances of her nights.

Driving into the sunrise she has a sudden sense that this is, in its way, a quest, a new beginning; that an unseen door in her life has closed and she has yet to walk through the next one. She feels suspended, in and out of time, heavy with her past and simultaneously light with the unknown future.

The journey takes longer than she has anticipated. Driving the lonely winding road amongst the stony wild countryside surrounding her destination, stippled in places with new green and pocked by juniper bushes and small clumps of dark pines, Annie is almost physically winded by her first sight of the stark rocky *pog* shouldering its solitary bleak ruined fortress up towards the sky. Bent forward in the driving seat to peer up at the citadel clinging grimly, pale against the sharp blue of the sky, to its stony host, she is reminded suddenly of a skull and its skeleton. Blank openings, eyeless windows aligned towards the summer solstice sunrise, surveyed bleakly the astounding and beautiful wild lands below. The sheer bony slopes of the almost vertical cliff-face of the summit, haggard and savage above the tree-line, look unapproachable from this eastern side at least, guarded by the impenetrable tangled beard of bushy scrub on the snow-hung lower flanks and punctuated higher up by darker patches; the mouths of caves, perhaps.

No wonder it took so many months to penetrate, Annie thinks, even given the ratio of crusading forces to the besieged Cathars. She dimly remembers reading somewhere that access was finally gained via one of the outlying towers, a barbican on this eastern flank. Gascon mercenaries, wise to mountain moods and routes, had surprised the exhausted, weakened and surely demoralised garrison by night, and were able to install the crushing mangonels, stone-aiming giant catapults, with which to further assail the main fortress.

She has a painfully vivid vision of the physical damage caused to bodies as well as walls by these flying boulders and squeezes her mind tight shut against the images of blood and ripped and mangled flesh, shattered limbs and crushed heads. She's overcome by a wave of anguish and desolation deep in her guts. Something about this place pulls her inexorably at the roots of her being, as if she were a fish on a line. She steers the van to the side of the road and stops.

According to one of the guide-books access is via a path climbing up the south-western flank, approaching the tumbles of boulders and the enduring walls which mark the remains of the ancient terraced Cathar village that had huddled at the feet of the citadel to the north and west. Annie experiences a sudden strong urge to flee; to drive as fast as possible away from this place, which in a matter of seconds has seemed to turn dark; runnels of blackness flooding down in a wild storming dance from the summit. Involuntarily she presses her hand to her mouth, gagging, and without thinking turns the van radio on at full volume. The blast of French jazz which explodes into the interior of the van jerks her back and she starts the engine again, and follows the road around to where she might park.

There are no other vehicles. Despite her desire to be on her own, she is comforted briefly by the sight of the more modern village at the foot of the hill, below her and off to one side, where there will be traffic and people, streets being swept, late twentieth century commodities like rubbish bins and gas and electricity signs. She opens the window to the sunlight; despite the snow on the shoulders of the mountainside high above her the scents are of spring, and faintly on the breeze she thinks she can hear goat-bells. Goss sits upright on the seat, eyes eager and alert, ears pricked, nostrils quivering. From behind the *pog* a bird of prey—an eagle?—soars into view.

Annie picks up the book that Alex had brought her back from the Basque market, *Le Vrai Visage du Catharisme,* and turns to the chapter on Montségur, translating in her head as she goes. A date catches her eye: Wednesday 16th March, 1244.

Today was the 13th. It would appear that the massacre here happened at dawn on the 16th, after two weeks of truce in which they were able either to capitulate, or prepare themselves for death. But surely, she thought, Isarn, whom she was certain was one of the community here, was expecting to celebrate the equinox and the mystery of spiritual renewal and resurrection before giving herself up, with the others, to the flames? How could it be that they died on the 16th? Unexpectedly she finds her eyes filling with tears; somehow the exact day of their death seems terribly important. The rational part of her mind was scornful; to be burnt is to be burnt; whether the 16th of March or the 23rd makes little difference. Not true, she wept, not true; I can't bear for her to have died before they had celebrated the spring rites, the handing over of the dark to the light; the passageway which Isarn knew would be opened at that particular moment through which she might follow her 'path of the stars'.

Through her tears something prickles at the back of her mind from the days when she still practised astrology; something important . . . something relevant . . . the precession of the equinoxes. Is it roughly a day per century by which the equinoxes progress? She struggles to remember. If it were a day a century, what would that mean for 1244? She counts backwards. If in the twentieth century the vernal equinox occurs somewhere between 21st and 23rd March, then in the thirteenth quite possibly the equinox would fall between 14th and 16th March. Her skin prickles. Tomorrow, and then the day after would be their last. In three days' time would be the 750th anniversary of their death . . . She reads further. A quote from the records of one of the Inquisitors:

'The besieged (garrison), without respite by day or night, and unable, these faithless ones, to withstand any longer the assaults of the soldiers of the True Faith . . . abandoned to the besieging forces the castle and its remaining heretics who, men and women together, must have numbered about two hundred . . . Having refused to be converted at our invitation, they were burnt in an enclosure of stakes and fencing in which we had built the fire, and so passed directly to the fires of hell . . . Once again, none capitulated . . .this was the end of the Cathar heresy . . .'

Annie is unable to see with the tears streaming down her face. She shuts the book and opens the door, whistling Goss, then slams it savagely and makes herself walk firmly towards the path. The citadel seems impossibly high, impossibly remote, stretching towards the infinite spaces, symbol simultaneously somehow both of human hope and human despair in the face of threatening darkness.

The mountain is held in a vast silence, untouchable, immovable, a rocky island in a moving sea.

Near the start of the path at the base of the hill is a stone monument, a memorial inscribed and carved with Cathar symbols; three equal-armed crosses, and a five-pointed star, reminder of the meeting of the mortal human with the immortal nature of the divine spirit . . . At its feet is a garland of fresh wild flowers, and heaped all around the base offerings of more flowers, some recent, some much older; of pebbles, of feathers. Annie is deeply moved. *You shall not be forgotten . . . never give up . . . the light remains . . .* She skirts the monument and moves on. Higher up, inside the modern picket fence where the path to the summit steepens towards the ridging of the old terraces from mediaeval dwellings, is a clearing, and Annie is suddenly aware with a raw intensity that this must be where they had erected the palisades and the pyre. The *Prats dels Cramats,* the place, or perhaps meadow, of the burnings, or burnt ones, she guesses. She stands transfixed, unable to move forwards or backwards. The mountain grips her in its silence. There is a stabbing pain in her heart. For a moment she can't breathe and she feels the world sliding, sliding . . . Goss barks at a raven gliding down to rest on a nearby rock, and the sound jerks her back, and then she is fleeing, running as fast as she can back to the solid reality of the van, sobbing, her breath coming in tearing rasps.

THIRTY-TWO

March 16th.

Annie is shaking as she drives up to the foot of the mountain. A twilight hush has fallen on the land and already the shadows have substance. Over the white peaks towards the west the sunset has raked crimson streaks across the sky, sparking fire from the many tiny pooled patches of ice-water dotted around the base of the mountain. The bare shoulders of the higher slopes with the crowning fortress are silhouetted, one-dimensional against the graded layers of mountains receding indigo on indigo into the far distance.

Annie has not slept for two nights and is dizzy with fatigue. Her jaw aches and glands hurt and she feels feverish, but there has been no choice. She doesn't know why she is here, but she knows that her life has been leading her to this. She senses that there is a doorway she needs to go through in order to pick up the reins of her future, her life. The mountain compels her, and like a sleepwalker she can only follow whatever it is that calls her. Her head pounds as she lowers herself carefully from the van, grateful only that she's made it. She is too exhausted to feel fear.

Goss scrambles down beside her, excited at the prospect of an unexpected walk. Annie props herself against the van a moment, getting her balance back, and her bearings. The ruin seems impossibly far away; no chance of arriving there in daylight. Even this easy route up the southwest face is likely to be long and arduous, doubly so by night. She turns back into the van and takes out her walking boots and a fleecy jacket. She sits on the sill of the van to tuck her jeans into socks and lace her boots up, fumbling with tiredness, and zips her jacket.

From the trees off to one side an owl calls, and a small darkish bird with a long waterbird's bill and a rapid flight skims over her head, solitary against the cobalt sky above her. For a second she has a vision of the house at Ide at dusk, the sky full of flapping cawing rooks and tumbling jackdaws before they settle for the night in the tall trees beyond the garden.

A couple of small finches flutter past her twittering and looping, light as thistledown. Swift as an arrow the honed grey form of a peregrine speeds past her at eye-level, and in the time it takes her to release her hair from the collar of her jacket there is a high tiny squeal and a burst of feathers a yard or two the other side of the van. Then the mountain lapses back into silence.

Annie shivers.

She stands up and stamps her feet, wrapping her scarf around her neck. Her breath hangs in the air. She thrusts an apple into her pocket, and a torch, and then reaches back into the map-pocket behind the passenger seat. From her diary she withdraws a photograph, and Alex's parting note. She inserts them carefully into an inner pocket, with a box of matches. Then she lifts out the wreath she's made, twigs of flowering cherry and almond and japonica woven with feathers and foliage. Locking the van, she puts the keys in a pocket and whistles Goss, off after a rabbit. He lollops back, greeting her as if he'd been gone for days, thrusting his wet spotty nose into her palm. She feels a faint comfort at his company.

She quails briefly; taking a deep breath she makes herself look up the stony path, checking the route before night falls. Already dark is washing up the mountainside in front of her.

Pulling her hood up she sets off up the path between bushes.

She has not gone far before she becomes aware that the mountain has come alive. It prickles all over with voices, ancient as the very bones of this land, which seem now to be vibrating with a low deep hum like the roar of sea through a blow-hole. She feels her spine convulse, but makes herself keep walking. Some deep place inside her needs this pilgrimage; for healing, for life. She can feel sorrow bleeding from her like a running wound; too long, she thinks; too long I've spent curled around it while it festers. Time to let go, let it run into the earth at her feet. And the pilgrimage needs her, too; *you are not forgotten . . . we will not forget . . .*she finds herself beating out the words with her steps, *You are not forgotten . . . we will not forget . . . never give up . . . never give up . . . wisdom beyond words . . . beyond words . . . beyond words . . .* someone's missing, someone she loves very much *beyond words I offer you the language . . . n'oublie jamais . . . n'oublie jamais . . .* and then the words take her over and she is swept on a tide of voices, a tide—a flood—of people pouring, stumbling, down the hill towards her and the noise is in her head and outside it and the hum becomes a moan and the moan a chant and they are there, upon her and around her and within her and she is swept up and turned, washed down with them and Goss is whimpering and moaning and then gone and the hill is lit with torches and the human tide, hooded in dark rags of robes, is flooding, singing, a song so pure, so haunting that the stars in the night sky seem to tremble in their sockets and burn brighter, brighter . . . *and we are dragged, though we offer no resistance, bearing or propping our sick and dead amongst us, our wrists strapped and thonged; the soldiers, helpless and frightened at our acceptance of what is happening, mutter and stamp like cattle, prod or club us and Guénon turns and looks into my eyes and his voice swells into the night air, chanting over and over the same words: 'I offer myself as a vessel, fill and pour me as you will . . .' and the chant is taken up and I see these warriors, these hardy mercenaries who jostle and prod*

and drag us unnecessarily down the hill, these who know no better, regard us with fear and dread and then the miracle for which we have trained ourselves happens and I have left my body; we lift as one, a flock of us lighter than feathers wheeling over these dying corpses which we accompany on this their final journey of this lifetime . . . I see them drag my poor bruised bloodied body, skeletal almost already, and my feet are numb, my ankles stumble and twist, and then I see a soldier hit Guénon over the head and his beloved face crumples and a stream of blood bursts from his temple but his voice still pours onto the early morning air as he sends comfort to us all with his chant, and then I see the fires and I see my body cringe and falter, and Guénon stretches a hand and the first Bonshommes are climbing the rough ladders as the soldiers fall back in dread, in bewilderment, in terror, for we are still singing as we throw ourselves into the flames and Guénon turns to me one last time, the light burning in his eyes, and I drink in every detail of this blood-streaked love-filled gaunt face, and he makes the sign of the cross as he chants: 'The new dawn rising promises us the light . . .' and as I see my stumbling body approach the palisade Greg's face is there, his ice-blue eyes are glittering in the garb of a foot-soldier, lance in hand, he is barring the way past into freedom; as if any of us would turn away now. My mouth is open; I can feel the scorching heat blister my face and singe my tonsils and the stench of burning flesh is in my nostrils and now I feel terror; my bowels turn to water and my voice is lost in the crackle and roar of the flames, in the moans and wails and chantings and there is no screaming, only this low haunting hum like the waves on rocks, or the wind through empty caves, moaning and returning forever, and above this faintly in the dark of early dawn a high whistling, like the breeze through eagles' wings
And then the world turns black.

THIRTY-THREE

Under the eaves of his attic room Alex jerks awake, heart pounding in his ears, blood rushing, body rigid. There it is again: a high note over a deep roar. Disorientated, skin crawling with a thin outbreak of sweat, stomach clenching, he strains to hear, holding his breath, peering into the darkness. A wavering note and then closer a roaring crackle; voices, moans, words he can barely make out; something—a phrase, perhaps—that reminds him of *Lento*. A dog's high whine. His mind churns, trying to make sense of the noises.

Somewhere in the building a window bangs; through the open skylight a faint draught wavers, brushing his face. He becomes aware that the muscles at the back of his neck are taut, and then a sharp pain thumps at his temples, behind his eyes, making him groan.

The sounds around him become more pronounced, the roaring approaching fast, until he feels himself shaking. Then the noise is travelling away from him at the same velocity as at its approach, and he realises with sick relief that of course it is one of the late night or early morning express trains heading for Bristol or London.

He lies down again, though his body is still tensed, as if listening. Underneath his intellectual registering is a deep current of unease and nausea, and he senses, rather than hears, a web of sounds still tangling the air. Behind his open eyes colours seem to pulse: black, red, violent shapes intersecting. A strange odour seems to fill his nostrils.

Aware that he won't sleep this way he sits up again and presses the light switch. The room resolves into its familiar shapes: chair, desk, bookcase, tape recorder. Chest of drawers.

Rucksack, walking boots. Photos of Laurel and Sam. He pulls a pad of A4 towards him off the desk and starts to scan a poem cycle he has been working on. Hard to concentrate, though; Annie, whom he's mostly managed to shut out of his mind the last few weeks, is insistently present. Annie, Annie, Annie. And with her, a feeling of profound distress. He supposes it is his guilt and his suppressed feelings for her.

Eventually, in some anger and pain, he gets out of bed, and thrusting his body into jeans, sweater and jacket, he lets himself out of the building and strides towards the canal, as if he might, by walking, free himself of it, all of it; past, present, pain.

THIRTY-FOUR

Renaud counts the goats through the low dark doorway into the stone shelter which has housed goats or sheep through the worst weather of every winter as far back as he can remember, and before that too. The clanging of their bells sets up an echo in the cliff-face that forms the back wall of the shelter. Béli, the brown cattle-dog, watches every movement out of his wall-eyes. Renaud curses. One short again. The same bloody nanny, no doubt, oblivious entirely to the whereabouts of her offspring each year. Swearing, he bends double and squeezes into the shelter, whistling Béli to stand guard at the entrance. He lifts his storm-lantern over the fawn-and-black backs of the milling herd and counts again; yes, a kid missing, and there is the nanny, looking vaguely puzzled perhaps but not especially concerned. Swollen udder, though; could be it had gone missing some hours ago.

Renaud sighs. He backs out, his neck stiff. Calling the dog, he goes into the single storey two-room stone dwelling adjoining the goat-shed to tell Marie he'll be gone for another hour or two yet. She is plucking the partridge he'd snared last night, feathers all over the place. He grumbles; Marie complains that it is far too cold to pluck the bird outside, and indeed it is. A heavy frost is on its way again, and the uneasy reddened sky foretells more hard weather. He has to find the kid before nightfall proper. He collects a handful of the bedding bracken from the store he has cut and packed so laboriously into the little lean-to last autumn, and stuffs it into his heavy wooden clogs, replacing the old straw, virtually all gone now, for extra insulation and to wedge his feet in more firmly; even knowing the mountain as well as he does you don't take risks at nightfall, when the fading light plays strange tricks with the eyes.

Like his ancestors, Renaud is a mountain man; brought up in the lee of this great hill he knows its every voice, its every mood, virtually every stone. He is a man of few words and fewer aspirations, but he has eyes and ears like a hawk's. He listens to the mountain; sometimes it speaks to him, sometimes it shouts, a great bellow which echoes round the circle of enclosing hills. He thinks of the mountain almost as an animal, a great bear, maybe. He lives in harmony with it, and takes notice when it says to. You don't mess with this mountain.

He trudges round behind the house, whose roof grows out of the mountain itself; in the early spring after the paucity and hardship of winter the turfed roof offers a few yards extra grazing, rich with new herbs and spangled with wildflowers.

The light has all but gone. Béli slinks at his heels like a shadow, soundless. They skirt the wide rectangle at the base of the hill; Renaud fancies as always that it glows greener than the rest, even all these centuries later. Here the mountain is folded in upon itself like a sick animal, moaning. Strange how the goats never graze this patch, edging past it as if excluded by an invisible cordon.

At the far side is a dark shape, and Renaud goes to investigate. A van, with foreign number-plates. City-people, no doubt. Early in the year, but Montségur always seems to draw these people on some strange quest. He remembers his grandfather going on pilgrimage when he was a lad; but not to here, not to this mountain. City-people. He supposes that they don't have enough wilderness within—he pictures the inside of their heads, white and shadowless, clean and tidy, everything shelved and labelled, no birdsong, no dung, no apricot sunrises, no time for counting the greening shoots to foretell the summer's harvest; but they don't know you shouldn't mess with this mountain. At night, too. This mountain takes you for its own if you aren't careful; folds you in so that all you can see is the inside of your own head.

He trudges round the van and up the footpath towards the pasture they'd been grazing earlier. His feet disturb some roosting night-bird; there is a whirr and a trickle of stones, falling into the silence. His ears are listening, listening, tuned to animal frequency. He can hear the rabbits nibbling. No bleating though. Béli sniffs the air. They head off eastwards onto a tiny goat-track. Renaud's feet feel the way amongst gorse and broom and thorn and low trees; from time to time there is a tiny burst of scent from the gorse-bushes, despite the cold darkness. He thinks of the peaches budding secretly in the small orchard. Not long now, he supposes, though long enough; winter is tough here, and he is tired of goat-meat, rye-meal and root-vegetables, with only rabbit and the occasional bird to break the monotony.

There is a movement in the bushes some metres ahead, and another. A struggle and then a frightened tiny bleat. God be thanked. Another time he might have been out all night. He puts his lantern down and pushes through the spines of gorse, oblivious to the scratches. The kid is tangled in a thicket of briar and thorn twigs; too young to break free alone. It bleats pathetically, a high thin squeak. Renaud's large calloused hands work patiently, slowly, worming a way through, snapping twigs. The kid struggles in fear and attempts to throw itself out backwards, dropping to the ground in a sprawl of legs and branches. With a word from the man Béli slips around to head it off and it leaps forwards. Renaud catches a leg and curses again as a thorn-tree scratches his cheeks through his beard. Then they are free and he lifts the kid, struggling feebly, and collects his lantern. They head back down towards the main path.

Béli suddenly stops and stiffens, sniffing the air. Renaud stops too, his head cocked. Surely that is a whimper? Not the squeal of a taken rabbit, nor the hoot of an owl, but a high whimper, like a baby. Not one of the mountain's voices either. They listen. Nothing. His imagination. Hard to distinguish between inside and outside.

His belly grumbles with hunger and he makes to stride on again, but Béli still crouches, pointing off to one side.

'Come on, you little fool.' Renaud growls at the dog in his thick accent. 'I want my supper.'

Béli won't move. The kid hangs limp under Renaud's arm. He raises the storm-lantern, frowning. 'Idiot. There's nothing there. Come ON.'

The dog turns his head briefly then looks back. The man sighs and wearily retraces his steps. Then the noise again. Béli growls, low in his throat; from the bushes there is a high-pitched bark. Renaud steps off to one side and follows the noise, which turns back into a whimper, long-drawn-out. A puppy, cringing in the light from the lamp. Beyond that, a dark shape sprawled on the ground. Renaud catches his breath. He has never got used to the flotsam and jetsam the mountain throws up; and now here is a body.

He crouches and puts the lantern on a flat rock, holding the kid still. His own dog is sniffing the puppy all over; the smaller one crouches in supplication and submission.

A woman; beautiful, pale. A dark gash on the side of her head. Eyes half-open and unseeing. Dear God. Renaud tentatively stretches out a hand and withdraws it fast in shock; her face is clammy, sticky with blood, but still warm. What to do? He catches the kid between his knees and reaches for the limp cold wrist—a pulse still. The ground is so cold, but he is afraid to move her. He takes off his old twill jacket and awkwardly stoops to lay it over her, the kid struggling and bleating. Should he leave the puppy behind with her? A moment's indecision, then he picks up the kid and the lantern once again, and calling his own dog in a low husky voice he moves down the mountain in a rapid shuffling stride in his heavy clogs, faster than he ever has before, going for Gaston, his neighbour; further from the spot in the other direction but easier hurrying than on the tortuous narrow stony path back home.

Half-an-hour later the two of them are back on the mountain path, bearing between them a stretcher made from two ash-poles and two old coats, buttoned together.

THIRTY-FIVE

Gaston telephones. Renaud sits with the woman, lowered gently onto Gaston's dark narrow bed and covered with the rough thick brown blankets. She hasn't moved, but she is still breathing. The puppy crouches beside her, whimpering still, as he has all the way back on the makeshift stretcher. Renaud, unsure what else to do, has been through Annie's pockets to try and identify her. A photo of a man—clear laughing eyes in a bearded face, longish curly hair. A note in what looks like English, which neither he nor Gaston speaks. No help. Then crumpled at the bottom of another pocket, with some keys, a tiny scrap of paper with the name Patrice and a Perpignan phone-number. Gaston phones Patrice and the doctor.

Renaud sits in awe of the pale motionless face, in awe of the mountain that delivers such surprises for him to deal with. He's cleaned up the head-wound, gently, his big hands reverent, with some hot water and a clean tea towel of Gaston's. He hasn't liked to examine the body to look for other damage. Now he sits quietly, beside her; patiently waiting.

Patrice drives out immediately, via L'Estang. Though he does not feel that he can call Annie a close friend, he has a great deal of liking and admiration for her, the more so since she appears to be living at L'Estang on her own. Besides, she is in trouble, and Patrice, in common with most people in rural communities, responds when help is needed.

L'Estang is deserted, apart from the ducks. Patrice does not know where Annie keeps the keys; not, by the looks of it, where he or his parents would have hidden them in the days when they were the key-holders. He sits in his car, trying hard to remember the names of Annie's English friends whom he'd met once or twice, and where they lived. Annecy-les-Bains, was it? He frowns. Then, finding a scrap of paper, he scrawls a note in French and sticks it into the latch of the door in the hopes that someone will find it before long, and ring him at the number he's been given. He adds his home number to it.

The doctor's Citroën rattles and swings its way up the rough track to Gaston's. He stoops under the wooden lintel and peers into the shadows. His eyes take a minute to adjust to the darkness. Candles throw distorted shapes over the rough earthen floor. Renaud, still at his vigil, turns his head.

'She's alive, Doctor.'

The doctor nods, and removes his overcoat. Finding nowhere to put it, he lays it on the end of the truckle-bed beside the puppy, who growls, a high thin noise. Renaud picks him up. Whilst the doctor examines Annie, Renaud and Gaston discreetly remove themselves out into the yard. Renaud paces.

The doctor takes his time. At length he joins the men, thoughtful.

'She'll live,' he says in a pensive voice. 'I don't want her moved tonight. I've put a couple of stitches in, all I can do, and bandaged her head. She's semi-conscious, but concussed no doubt and in shock. I'll be back tomorrow morning, first thing. She'll probably need X-rays. Has she been sick?'

Renaud shakes his head.

The doctor thinks for a moment. 'As far as I can tell nothing's broken, but she's badly bruised. All over. As if she's been dragged. No-one else involved, as far as you know?'

Renaud shrugs. 'It was the mountain, Doctor,' he says, simply.

The doctor gazes at him. After a moment, he replies: 'Ah. The mountain. I see. —Keep her warm.'

When Patrice arrives Renaud walks back to Marie, declining a lift, collecting the kid and Béli from the woodshed and the yard respectively.

There is only one bed. Gaston and Patrice spend the night up, huddled round the range, exchanging the odd word, sharing the crude apple-brandy that Gaston distils and keeps for Occasions. From time to time there is a movement from the bed in the corner, causing both men to turn.

At dawn Annie stirs and moans, then vomits. Patrice cleans her up. Gaston pushes from his head the thought that this strange woman might die, here in his bed.

By the time the doctor arrives, not long after daybreak, Annie's eyes are open, if blank. Patrice thinks she recognises him, though she hasn't spoken. The doctor takes her hand, feels her pulse. Speaking slowly, he tells her that she has had a bad fall and that he is going to take her to hospital nearby. Unsure whether she has registered his words, he asks Patrice to tell her the same thing, then between them the three of them lift her gently into the back of his estate car, which doubles as an ambulance. Patrice checks that Goss can stay with Gaston, and then follows them in his own car.

In the clean white hospital bed the young doctor has the stethoscope on her chest and her stomach again. For minutes he is silent. Annie's face, white apart from the purpled bruising showing at the edge of the bandage, is without any expression. She has said nothing at all since waking. The doctor feels down her bruised ribcage and palpates her abdomen. Satisfied, he waits until her eyes met his.

'Good,' he says in his accentless French. 'You'll live. But with the fall you had, you are very lucky not to have lost the baby. Very lucky. We'll keep you in tonight, for observation. Your friend will be back tomorrow to take you home. Is there someone who can look after you?'

Annie's face registers confusion, then shock. She stares at the doctor. She can't think of the words to ask him to repeat what he said. She struggles, then gives up.

'Is there something you need?' he asks, concerned at her expression. 'Are you still in pain?'

'Baby?' Annie manages to whisper. 'Baby?'

Susie and Jon arrive at L'Estang early. The removal men are due to deliver Annie's goods today, and she and Jon have volunteered themselves for the day.

No van. Susie frowns. Perhaps she's gone to buy bread. While they wait, she goes to look at the ducks. No water, and from the agitated quacking, she guesses that they have not been fed yet today. She has just stepped outside to fetch corn from the large barn when Jon calls her, Patrice's note in his hand.

'Oh my God. The 16th—that was two days ago. Quick. I think she keeps the key under the stone there. Oh God. Phone Patrice.'

THIRTY-SIX

*I am in a dark wood, though in the far distance I have the sense
that there is light. I know that where the light is, there is a
doorway, opening onto an unimaginably vast bright landscape.
The doorway has always been there; waiting patiently forever
for my attention.*

*As I focus on the direction where I think I see a point of
light, I see that it is getting bigger, closer, swirls of golden-
green smoke-like light filling the spaces between trees,
enveloping the darkness. I hear music, rippling over the
landscape like water. Then out of the heart of the forest dances
a figure; she is approaching me, arms outstretched, radiant.
She is smiling as she steps towards me; she is blonde, but there
is something familiar in her features. I gasp as I recognise
myself. My twin; my bright sister.*

*'Come!' she says, her eyes full of love. 'I've been waiting a
long time. Welcome home'. . . and then I awake.*

* * * * *

It is late afternoon, intensely hot. Annie is lying on her back
under the old apple-tree, now studded with new small hard
green fruits amongst the silvery lichen. Festooning it still is the
olive-green growth of mistletoe, also starred with the buds of
new fruits, its paired blades of leaves thrust out to the sun. The
sky is criss-crossed with swifts, the air shrill with their cries.
Other than that and the rasping cicadas, the only sound is the
stream below them in the valley, and the occasional blundering
drone of a fat bumble bee.

Rosa is lying on her stomach with her head turned towards
Annie, a stalk of grass in her teeth. Around them is the debris

of a picnic; the bantams have come close to investigate the remains, crooning over the breadcrumbs in the grass. Goss, his feet still puppy-sized but his body taller, sleek, is sprawled with his pricked ears trained on the occasional splash from the pool lower down, where the ducks and ducklings are diving and flapping.

Rosa sighs in contentment, swinging a leg over her back. 'God, Annie, I can't tell you how good this is—just lying here in the sun with you, and knowing that Marcus and the kids will be having a great time on the coast!' She props her chin in her hands. 'And I can't get over how different you look, love,' she remarks. 'It's as if you glow. I've never seen you look like this. After everything that has happened I have to admit I had expected to need to nurse and nurture you and be mopping you up all the time. I was frightened for you.'

Annie watches the thin silver arrow of a plane high above them without speaking for a minute. Her hands are behind her head, resting on a folded blanket; the only position that's comfortable. Her knees are up and the dress has fallen back up her thighs.

'You know you look like a goddess, there, with that belly. And it's the first time ever I've ever seen you with nearly a tan!'

Annie turns her head slowly towards Rosa.

'You know,' says Rosa, 'I quite like that scar on you. It makes you look – I don't know, *wise,* somehow! As if you've lived, really lived. Don't cover it with your hair! And something else I've noticed—you're smiling with your *eyes,* again, at last!'

Annie holds her eyes. 'Yes, I know. I feel so very different, Rosa,' she says at last. 'I can't even begin to tell you. I just feel full of—I don't know; goodwill?—contentment, even . . . ' She smiles privately to herself, thinking how she would have cringed to hear herself speaking like this, like Rosa did, only a year or two ago. 'So much has changed for me.' She looks away again, up at the immense blue sky, and shuts her eyes for a moment. When she opens them again, they are full of tears. She reaches over and takes Rosa's hand. 'I just feel so— complete, Rosa. As if at last I belong in my own skin, but too as if I live beyond it. Is that pathetic? I can't really explain.' She laughs a little shakily. 'I sound like you,' she says, squeezing her friend's hand. 'It's so good to have you here, sharing my life for a week or two.'

Rosa leans over and kisses her on the cheek. 'We've been looking forward to it so much. Marcus and the kids are very fond of you, you know,' she responds, and they are silent for a moment or two. The cicadas, subdued slightly by the noontime sun, are redoubling their efforts now that the day is sliding towards late afternoon, and the air is vibrating with their scraping hum.

'Annie,' Rosa ventures tentatively, 'what about Alex?' She keeps her eyes on her friend's face, half-expecting her to withdraw or refute the question. Annie doesn't flinch, and holds her gaze calmly.

'I don't really know how to answer that, Rosa. I don't feel angry any more, or bitter. I suppose I try not to think about him too much. When I do, though, it's kind of OK. I know he really loved me; and of course he missed his kids. I suppose it was right for him to go back—I hated it, I was devastated; but I respect him for wanting to see them, to sort it out. And there might have been too much guilt for us to survive if he didn't. If nothing else, he needed to make peace with them. With himself.' She looked away and the silence drew out. 'I've got a bit of distance on it. Of course I still love him, of course I wish it could be different. But he has kids. I guess I'm starting to imagine what that must be like.' She sighs. 'I've heard nothing from him, and I haven't contacted him myself. I'm OK. Life is

OK; good, even. ' She pauses again and turns laboriously over onto her side, reaching for a peach.

Rosa waits.

'Those six months were the happiest of my life. Even knowing what would happen, I would still do it again. What he gave me is still with me, always will be. Obviously I don't just mean the baby,' and her hand moves instinctively to her stomach. 'Of course it hurts. Of course I miss him dreadfully. But it's OK, somehow. It's as if he showed me a doorway I didn't even know existed, and I have walked through and the landscape looks so utterly different the other side.' She makes a little face at herself. 'Does that sound pompous? It's the only way I can describe it. I feel—almost reborn. As if I can weather anything. I feel as if I'm really trusting for the first time, trusting myself, trusting life.' She bites into the peach.

'Did you—sorry, hope it's OK to ask – did you ever hear any more from The Blackmailer?'

Annie looks at her blankly.

'That letter?'

'Oh!' Annie's face clouds, then clears. 'Nothing. Guess Marcus must have been right. I'd totally forgotten.' She looks away again.

Together they're silent for a few minutes.

'What about your art, Annie?'

'Well, something's shifting there, too. I'd love to show you. I feel so creative at the moment. Do you remember the black and white tapestry I was telling you about? Well, it's nearly there; the chaos has resolved itself into something I feel very excited by. It's like a dialogue between black and white; it's as if it's mirroring what has happened in my life. It's almost like a dance, an acceptance of how things are, the joy and the pain . . .' She smiles a little self-consciously. 'It's slow, you know, but it's happening. When I've finished this I want to weave a bedcover for Renaud and Marie; you know, the man who found me on the mountain. And then there's Gaston, and Patrice, too. They call in; look out for me. So many people I care about; and so many people I feel cared-for-by.'

'That all sounds great... But, Annie, what about the baby? Aren't you scared? I mean, to have your first at 40, and on your own . . .'

Annie smiles. 'Oh yes, of course I'm scared. So what? I've been scared before.'

'And you had no idea?'

'That I was pregnant, you mean? No, none at all.' She props herself on an elbow, and smiles again, remembering. 'I wasn't myself during those months, and if I'd registered that my periods had stopped I'd just have assumed it was stress or early menopause, I guess. I didn't really notice my body at all. I can still hardly believe it, despite my size.'

In the distance, beyond the outbuildings, the phone in the house starts to ring, its sound just audible through the open door. Rosa makes to stand, but Annie puts her hand on her arm. 'I'll go. Cup of tea?' and she pushes herself off the grass and, barefooted, pads across the orchard towards the phone.

Alex is standing in a phone-box in Roscoff, looking at the water, shaking. He remembers the last time he was here; they were here, also not long off the ferry.

A winter in England without Annie has shown him where his heart really lies, and how little anything else means, or even matters, if what you are doing has no heart in it.

Life is short, he finds himself thinking, over and over; seize the day, live every moment as if it's your last.

Lento has been recorded, received and much applauded; his motor-bike panniers contain a copy of the CD. *Lento* belongs to Annie, who is inexplicably and inextricably linked with his